LOVE'S PURSUIT

Books by
Siri Mitchell

A Constant Heart

Love's Pursuit

She Walks in Beauty

Love's Pursuit

SIRI MITCHELL

BETHANY HOUSE PUBLISHERS
Minneapolis, Minnesota

Published by Bethany House Publishers
11400 Hampshire Avenue South
Bloomington, Minnesota 55438

Bethany House Publishers is a division of
Baker Publishing Group, Grand Rapids, Michigan.

Printed in the United States of America

Library of Congress Cataloging-in-Publication Data

Mitchell, Siri L., 1969–
    Love's Pursuit / Siri Mitchell.
        p.   cm.
    ISBN 978-0-7642-0432-6 (pbk.)
    1. Puritans—Fiction.   2. Massachusetts—History—Colonial period, ca. 1600–1775—Fiction . I. Title.

    PS3613.I866L68   2009
    813'.6—dc22

                                                          2009005411

To Tony,
for giving me the courage to believe.

SIRI MITCHELL has written six novels, two of which (*Chateau of Echoes* and *The Cubicle Next Door*) were named Christy Award finalists. A graduate from the University of Washington with a business degree, she has worked in many levels of government and lived on three continents. Siri and her family currently reside in the Washington, D.C., metro area.

Others were given in exchange for you.
I traded their lives for yours because you are precious to me.
You are honored, and I love you.

Isaiah 43:4 NLT

STONEYBROOKE TOWNE

Massachusetts Bay Colony ~ 1640s

1

"DO YOU NEVER TIRE of being good, Susannah? Do you never think any rebellious thoughts?"

I turned my eyes from my sister and back to my work in the blueberry canes. "Aye. I do."

Mary gasped, though I detected laughter in the sound. " 'Tis not possible."

" 'Tis not only possible. 'Tis probable. Like this one I think right now, about you." I threw a blueberry in her direction.

She dodged it. "I shall report this harassment to the selectmen. At once!"

I looked up at her tone, for Mary was unpredictable and she might have done it just for spite. But her eyes were dancing despite her labors and the unseasonable heat. Warmth rose in my cheeks as well. But it was not the sun that scorched my flesh. It was my own conscience.

My sister's question had found a mark too close to the condition of my soul. To those in Stoneybrooke Towne, Susannah Phillips was indeed a fair and obedient girl. But I knew myself to be vastly different than the person they imagined me to be.

Aye, I did tire of being good. And I did think rebellious thoughts. Often. Especially on days like this one. I wanted nothing more than to abandon my task and plunge into the nearby brook. I longed for the luxury of one hour, one minute, that needed nothing done.

And more than anything, I wished John Prescotte would finally ask for my hand in marriage.

I was truly wretched. And I knew it. But the problem lay in my past. I had been such a meek, dutiful, obedient child that people had grown to expect nothing less from me. The weight of my unblemished past bore down upon my conscience unmercifully. What if today were the day when my secret thoughts became known? What if today were the day when the town found out how wicked I truly was?

Would that I were like Mary, who had been a hellion and constant thorn in my parents' flesh. Anything might be expected from her. And the least bit of goodness was cause for praise. I, however, was freely cited as an example of the godly woman every young girl wished to be. Except that sometimes, I did not want to be that woman at all.

If only I could tell one person what darkness lurked inside . . . then at least I might be able to contain it. And who but Mary would better understand?

Grandfather.

My grandfather would have understood. I could tell him anything . . . could have told him anything. For a minister he was uncommonly understanding. But we had left him behind when we moved from Boston.

A droplet of sweat slid beneath the collar of my shift, and then continued between my breasts on its journey to dampen the waistband of my skirt. I might have removed my hat, leaving only the linen coif covering my hairs to shelter me from the sun, but it would not have been modest. Yet perhaps I could admit to just one thing. "I would give anything to remove my hat for a moment."

Mary paused in her picking to look at me. "Anything? Even taking on the week's ironing? Twice in succession?"

I shrugged. I should never have admitted such a thing.

Quietly, softly, she began to hum a hymn.

My eyes lifted from the berry canes as I looked at my companions laboring. Like me, they were bent over blueberry canes, their felted hats marking their places. The clothes on all of our backs had been dyed sad colors, shades dark or dull made duller still by the constant toil required to wrest a township from the savageries of this new world.

Please, God, let no one hear! I reached out and grabbed hold of Mary's arm.

Touching the felted brim of her hat, her lips curled into a sly smile. And then she began to hum even louder.

Beside her, our brother, Nathaniel, paused in his task. "Mary? Why do you—"

Our sister hushed him and then poked him in the ribs with a finger. "Sing."

"But—"

"Do it."

He sighed as if it were beneath him, a great lad of ten years, to understand the thoughts of a sun-dazed girl. But then he emptied a fistful of berries into his pail, stood, and, taking off his hat in deference to the holy words of the hymn, he opened his mouth and began to sing.

Immediately, the berry patch sprouted heads, male and female, all of which were swiftly bared as the tune was taken up and the words were sung.

> O Lord our God in all the earth
> how's thy name wondrous great.
> Who has thy glorious majesty
> above the heavens set.

And it *was* wondrous to hear God praised under the canopy of His own sky in the midst of His own creation . . . and more wondrous still to feel the breeze ruffle through the linen of my head's covering. Beside me, hat clasped in her hand, Mary had closed her eyes in an imitation of pious worship. For a brief moment, I forgot myself and did it as well. And I stored up the memory of the coolness to last me through the rest of the day.

As the last word of the hymn forsook us and withered away in the sun, the heads of our townspeople, hidden beneath hats once more, bent toward their work.

All but that of the minister.

He looked at Nathaniel for one long moment, then finally scratched his beard, shook his head, and returned his attentions to the berries.

Mary tossed a blueberry into my pail. "Fail not to tend to the ironing. This week and the next."

I could have pretended I had not heard her, but I had sinned enough for one day. Oh, what my rebellious thought had wrought! Had I not thought of picking berries uncovered, I would never have mentioned it to my sister. Had she never heard it, she would never have begun humming the hymn. Had she never begun, she would never have pulled Nathaniel into her schemes. My own foolish thought had enticed two others into sinning. Two weeks of ironing was not punishment enough.

A babe cried farther down the patch, and my eyes lifted toward the sound. I saw my friend Abigail plant her bottom on top of her pail and take her son up to her breast.

Abigail and I had been friends since before our move to Stoney-brooke, since Boston. A year older than I, she had been an example, in our youth, of everything I ever wished to be. First in womanhood, first in church membership, first in marriage. And now, in mother-hood as well.

I had not talked with her in . . . weeks. I had seen her, of course, on the Sabbath at meeting, but her attention was devoted to her babe, to her husband, and to her home. In fact, there seemed a dearth of maids in town. All of my friends were now married. Several of them were with child. The others with a babe in their arms.

I wanted nothing more than to join their ranks.

That I was not of their station was not a thing of my own choosing. I waited on John Prescotte, and he waited on the blessing of his father. But his father had been ill. And John, as the sole son, had to care for his family before he could turn his thoughts to me.

But perhaps next year at this time it would be me in Abigail's place. I hoped and prayed for it with all that was within me.

For certain the year after.

Soon I would be married. Soon I, too, would be called Goodwife.

Goody Prescotte.

Soon.

❧

I bent to my task, plucking berries across the tangle of canes from the Phillips sisters. From Susannah and Mary, and their brother Nathaniel. They thought they were so clever, those two sisters, scheming to spend a few moments hatless in the broad of the day. I hope they enjoyed it. They would find out soon enough that stolen pleasures must eventually be paid for. But far be it from me to judge. *Rejoice, O young man, in thy youth; and let thy heart cheer thee in the days of thy youth, and walk in the ways of thine heart, and in the sight of thine eyes: but know thou, that for all these things God will bring thee into judgment.*

I tore my eyes from the spectacle of them and pulled my hat down tighter around my ears. So tight that I could no longer see them. So tight that I could not see my husband's approach.

"Small-hope."

I jumped as he said my name.

He took a deliberate step back as one might do from a half-tamed beast. "I wanted only to know if you needed water." He held out a dipper toward me.

"Aye." I took it from him and drank of it. And then I bent to take up my work once more. "Thank you."

I do not know if he heard me.

❧

Mary sniffed. "She will bite his head off one day, and then what will she do?"

I looked over toward my sister. "Of whom do you speak?"

"Goody Smyth. *Small-hope.*" She said the words with something near derision. "I cannot understand the care that Thomas takes of her. Nor why he dragged her here from . . . wherever it was from which she came."

"Newham. She came from Newham." I glanced up from my pail at Thomas. He was a familiar sight. As familiar as anyone else in the town and more so, perhaps, since we were nearly the same age. He, the elder, by several months. Not so handsome as some. Certainly not so handsome as John. But the worst that could be said of him was that his eyes looked in danger of popping out from his head and his cheekbones were so sharp Mary once swore she could skin a rabbit on them.

Swore! She had sworn on a thought as foolish and ill-spirited as that. Only, it was true. She probably could. And that was the maddening thing about Mary. Though two years separated us, looking at her face was like looking into a glass. We both were fair, though her eyes tended toward chestnut, while mine had the look of moss-eaten bark. We may have looked like doubles, yet she could say nearly anything she wanted and always she was forgiven it. Woe unto me whenever I tried the same. I had learned, quite well, to keep such thoughts inside my head.

If any could hear my thoughts, they would think them pernicious indeed.

Thomas was the town's only blacksmith. He was needed, he was important, he was valuable. Whatsoever things are true, whatsoever things are of good report; if there be any virtue, any praise, then I must think upon those things. 'Tis what the Holy Scriptures instructed. I *must* try to fix upon those things. I did try to fix upon those things. But why could I not do it?

One thing was certain. Thomas's . . . appearance . . . would not have stopped any girl from marrying him, and he could not have felt a need to look for a wife beyond our township. No one knew why he had done so. He had gone into Newham one day for a certain smithing tool and returned with a wife instead.

Mary gave voice to my own thoughts. "It must have been that no one else would have her! Though why poor Thomas should feel so burdened . . . 'tis not as if she birthed a babe too soon after their marriage."

She had not. And had yet to, for all that they had been married for three years.

I cast a glance at the woman from beneath my lashes and then at Thomas. Though I did not want to, I could not help but agree with Mary. Our friend had taken to wife poorly. If I had any sympathies for the couple, they lay with him. But one thing was true: We had gossiped enough for the day. Both of us. " 'Tis the wounded that seek most to wound."

"It would not hurt her to be pleasant."

"Nor would it hurt you."

Mary glared at me before pushing to her feet. She stood there for a moment, looking round the patch, and then she walked over to Thomas. She spoke to him a moment before taking the bucket from him. And then she picked her way through the canes to where Simeon Wright stood. He was watching his mother, and all the rest of us, pick berries.

What was the girl about? And why did she seem so brazen?

Simeon Wright with his flaxen hair, pleasing manner, and cool blue eyes, was the object of many girls' ardor. Girls of Mary's age. That he had not yet chosen to marry only seemed to increase their devotion.

At Mary's approach, Simeon looked toward her, but then his eyes moved past my sister to fix upon me. Even across the stretch of barren between us, I could feel the weight of his gaze.

2

I RESOLVED NOT TO give Mary's flirtations another thought and turned my meditation instead to my task. How perfect God's plan that the blueberry should ripen in June. That the picking of them could be done absent the sting of black flies and that it could be accomplished before the planting of cabbages and the mowing of hay. That there should be one summer's day absent the pulling of weeds or the making of biscuits . . . was that not God's just and perfect rest from labor?

I heard myself sigh.

It was not helping. True, virtuous, and praise-worthy thoughts did not work when they were not what one was truly thinking.

A cough alerted me to another's presence.

I looked up and, recognizing John Prescotte, scrambled to my feet.

He reached out a hand in aid.

"Thank you, John."

"Susannah." He dropped my hand and came to stand beside me. Shifting his feet, he crossed his arms, shot a glance toward his shoes.

I smiled at him.

He began to smile at me, then tugged the corners of his lips back into place. Squinting, he surveyed the barren around us. "Looks to be the start of a fair summer."

"Aye."

"If the wheat crop does well . . . if God allows it . . . I am of a mind to start building a house of my own. My father's health improves daily. And he has deeded me a portion of his land."

My heart thrilled with the news. If he meant to build a house, then he also meant to fill it with a family. "And why should you not?"

He did smile then. And his eyes twinkled as well. "Why indeed." As he looked at me, I felt my face color. Perhaps I had spoken out of turn. Perhaps I had been too eager. But it was time. It was time for him to build and time for us to wed. And why should there be any shame in that?

"I was thinking of building on the end of Father's land. That is . . . my land. He should be well enough this fall that I could start to work my land instead of his. I was thinking . . . near that stand of trees . . ."

"By the brook?"

He nodded.

" 'Tis a lovely spot." And it would be just far enough away from his parents' that I would feel as if the house were my own. But close enough to my own mother's that I would not feel too far gone. It was perfect.

" 'Twas my thought as well." His eyes held mine a moment longer before he drew in a deep breath and inclined his head toward where his mother and his sisters worked at picking. "I should return to the picking."

"Your father does better?"

"He gains strength. And more of it every day."

" 'Tis good news."

"Aye. The very best. Good day, Susannah Phillips."

As John walked away, my father came to stand beside me.

"Good man, that John." My father said the words as if he had spent some time thinking about them.

"Aye."

"And Simeon Wright as well." He left the words for me in parting.

Simeon Wright? What did Simeon Wright have to do with aught? Besides the fact that it was him upon which my father depended to practice his trade.

I returned to my berries, unsettled in my thoughts. The expectation of happiness that John had brought with him had somehow been pushed aside. My hands worked of their own volition. My thoughts refused to be gathered.

Simeon Wright.

He could have no interest in me. No more than in the other girls in town. Why should he? And, furthermore, he was not one of us. He had not been part of our congregation in Boston, though he had been welcomed quickly enough once he made it known he intended to build a sawmill. And, further, once the move had been made and the town lots established, he had volunteered that his house be the garrison to which half the town would retreat in the event savages attacked. He had even brought brick from Boston for the building of it. Simeon Wright was a town selectman, indeed the town's premier citizen. But unlike most of the other girls my age, I had never given one thought to marrying him.

I had John.

Of course, marriage to one like Simeon Wright might be advantageous, and unions were arranged for lesser reasons, but I did not know the man. It was said he had two and thirty years. And he was handsome. He stood shoulders above the rest of the men in town and his fair hair seemed to shoot sparks at the sun. Though I had noticed, more than once, that his ready smile and his eyes seemed at odds.

But there was no reason for me to think of him. And even less reason for worry.

I had John.

❧

I am my name. I have small hopes. But the largest of my small wishes is that I be overlooked. In my experience, the less one is noticed, the less trouble one encounters. There are those by whom I have no wish to be seen. Simeon Wright is one of them. I have no wish for trouble from that man. Nor from any like him.

I have had trouble enough already.

I recognize Simeon Wright for what he is. I doubt the Phillips sisters do; I doubt they can. The younger chases after him, yapping like a puppy at his heels. The elder is puzzled by his glance. She does well to question. He is a riddle. Will she solve him in time?

How can she? She possesses no clues. I know the answer, but then I have seen such riddles before.

They cannot read the signs, those sisters. They have been petted and worshiped and adored. They have been raised by a father who loves them and provides for them. Why should they have knowledge of any other kind of man? Of any other kind of life?

They do not know what it is like to wish you had never been born.

Yea, better is he . . . which hath not yet been, who hath not seen the evil work that is done under the sun.

❧

Mary returned from Simeon Wright and soon picked her way out into the barren in front of me. Nathaniel picked toward me to close the gap she had created.

"Susannah, I have been thinking . . ."

I dipped my head to hide my smile. Nathaniel was always thinking. "Of what were you thinking?"

"These blueberry canes grow along the ground."

"They do."

"They grow in the dirt, and at times they plunge their heads back beneath the soil, but always they resurface."

21

"Aye."

"And though it might seem like a new plant, every time it raises its head again, you have only to pull at it to bring to light the whole. 'Tis all one cane."

"It is."

"Is that not an example of grace?"

"How so?"

"The canes are like people. We all live in a state of sin. And sometimes we plunge ourselves into it and hide from the love of God. But if we do, have we not only to raise our heads once more toward heaven to be rescued from our filth?"

" 'Tis one way of looking at things."

"We try so hard to bury our sin. But if we look back on what we have done, we realize that God can create something from the whole of us. And that we cannot hide ourselves from Him."

"Aye. 'Tis true."

"Can this not be my conversion experience?"

I sighed. I had conversations like this with Nathaniel by the dozens. " 'Tis not internal, your example, Nathaniel. 'Tis external and wrought from your own knowledge. 'Tis God that must do His work in your heart to convince you of His love. What is wanted is an experience of the inward work of grace. There must be some sign, some change. Otherwise any who wanted could call themselves Christian, and who could doubt them? If we are truly part of the elect, then God will show us."

"But I want to be a member of the church. I want to have an experience so I can tell everyone about it. I want so much to be saved. Why does God not want me? Why can He not speak to my heart? Why can I not know?"

"It is not given to us to know God's mind."

"But how then shall I be saved? How then shall I know? Does God not want me?"

Did God not want him? Who could say? How could any of us know what God wanted? How could any of us know who God intended to save? The best we could hope for was a sign. An experience. A sort of indication from God that might signal that He had indeed chosen us. And then one could be permitted to join the church and receive communion. But, even still, one could not know for certain. The only hope was to keep working, keep hoping, keep praying. Keep proving oneself worthy of God's grace. "I do not know who God wants, Nathaniel. How can any of us know? We can only do. And hope."

"But—"

"Keep hoping." I only told him what I was telling myself. I had not had a conversion experience either. Though I heard the Holy Scriptures read each night, though I had attended meeting on the Sabbath since I had been born, though I had knowledge aplenty, and though it had always been my hope that I might become a member of the church before my marriage, I had no conversion experience to declare. No inward change that would signal any faith. Keep hoping: It was all that I could do. That . . . and discover how to become the good person that everyone thought me to be.

A babe's cry sliced through the drowsiness of the afternoon. It was ours. I looked round for Mother.

She saw me and inclined her head toward the tree where the town's infants had been drowsing in the heat.

I pushed my bucket toward Nathaniel and then went to see to the child.

This one always woke angry and just now he was sitting, legs splayed in the dirt, rocking back and forth, face red as a beet. I picked up his cap from the ground and set it back on his head, tying off the strings beneath his chin. Then I bounced him to my hip.

Little legs circled my waist and tiny hands clasped the collar of my shift.

"Hush-a, hush-a." I kissed his tear-streaked cheek. "Nightingales sing in time of spring! Time cuts down all both great and small! An eagle's flight is out of sight! A dog will bite a thief at night!" As I jostled it, the babe shushed and finally smiled. I took it as a sign to disengage its fingers from my collar.

When little heels began to kick at my hip, I set him down on the ground and took up the leading strings that trailed from his dress so that he would not fall as he toddled.

How many times had I done this? Looked after a babe of our mother's? My earliest memories included the cries of a babe. There was always one to be had, to be held. And this one . . . this one looked to be healthy. And strong. He might yet live to the age of seven, when he would be breeched and take his place among the boys of the village. He might yet live to pass down my father's name to his own children.

There had been another John Phillips, named after my father. A boy older than I. The firstborn. And he had lived until just after Nathaniel's birth, when he had died of a lung sickness. After that, after Nathaniel, there had been two others with that name, but they had died in quick succession. I stooped and embraced the mite. There was joy to be had in a babe, and until Mother birthed another, Babe is who this boy would be.

I chased him round the tree first this way and then that, enjoying the cool of the shade. But the berries waited and soon I gathered the child into my arms to take him back with me to the barren.

But as I did, I noted a crackling in the wood behind us. And then something snapped.

A savage? Were they upon us already, just as Simeon Wright had warned?

Nay. A savage could go like a spirit through the woods, leaving no sounds to mark his presence. Least that is what the men said. This thing then could be no savage. It must be a bear. One which would not be pleased to have its access to berries denied.

I moved to warn the guard, but he had already come to the alert. He put fingers to his lips and whistled.

Behind us, the work ceased of a sudden in the barren. And then the field exploded with movement. Mothers leapt through the canes to gather up their children. Men came at a run with their muskets. Quickly, shoulder to shoulder, they walled off the women and children from the danger. And even as the men moved into position and the women and children shrunk back from them, Simeon Wright was barking orders.

The noisome rustling grew louder and closer and then, finally, it broke out of the wood into our clearing.

In the time it took Simeon to tell the men to stand down, a sigh of relief rippled through the women and laughter broke out among the boys.

It was not a bear.

It was a man.

3

THE MAN MIGHT AS well have been a bear. His black hair fell in shaggy waves long past his shoulders. The wide brim of his hat had been pinned up on one side with a drooping feather, and his great boots flopped open at his knees. It looked as if he had been at battle with the forest. And if he had, I must say that the forest had won.

"My horse slipped a shoe, and I find myself to be quite lost. Is this, by any chance, Stoneybrooke Towne?"

Simeon Wright held up a hand to stay the laughter. "It is."

The stranger pulled his hat from his head and swept it toward the ground as he bowed. "Captain Daniel Holcombe. From the king's army. At your service."

A great murmur arose at his words.

With one look from Simeon Wright, however, the wordless noise ceased. "And what has His Majesty to do with us?"

The man smiled. It was an easy smile, a smile that ignored the dozens of muskets that were still trained fast upon him. "His Majesty? Not one thing. But the governor heard you have fear of savages. And he sent me to train up a militia."

"We have a militia."

He replaced the hat upon his head and passed a finger along the feather to prop it up. "Do you, now? All the better. It will make the task that much easier."

There was a tightness to Simeon's mouth that I did not understand. "And how did the governor learn of our . . . threat?"

My friend Abigail's father cleared his throat. "I mentioned it when I went to Boston for the vote. Asked if we could be sent some help."

Simeon Wright stepped toward Goodman Baxter. "We do not need the help. We can contend with the savages." He turned his head, as if to address those of us who stood behind him. "As long as everyone stays close and does not wander far, no one will be harmed."

The captain had been glancing back and forth between the two men. "Seems to me that if there is fear of savages, then there must be some doubt as to your ability to repel them. And, besides, the governor asked me as a personal favor. Cousin to cousin."

To give shelter to a captain of King Charles's army—a king who held himself above the law, who had no ear for his people, a king who tortured the pious and dredged up ancient and devious schemes to tax his citizens—was one thing, but to give shelter to a cousin of the governor was another matter entirely. The governor's loyalty to a higher law, to God's law, could not be questioned.

And neither, then, was the captain's.

In a matter of minutes it was settled. My father was a carpenter and his profession had allowed him to build us a comfortable house. Unlike most houses in Stoneybrooke Towne, it had both a kitchen and a parlor as well as a loft upstairs for storing goods. Last year, he had added a lean-to for use as a dairy house. After Simeon Wright's, it was the largest house in town.

The captain would board with us.

Thomas Smyth would shod his limping horse.

The town would train up a militia.

And then, the captain would leave.

The care of the stranger arranged, we retrieved our pails and returned to our labor. The sun was fast slipping toward the horizon. Our work was nearly finished.

❧

"Are we done?" Thomas asked me the question as he pushed to his feet. He pulled his hat from his head and wiped his brow before replacing it. I had forgotten how fair he was. It was a rare day that his face was not darkened by the soot of his fires, his knuckles not blackened by the ashes of his hearth. But the touch of the midday sun had pinked his cheeks.

I peered into the iron kettle that rested on the ground between us. It had been the recipient of at least twenty pails of berries. "Aye. We are done."

He reached down a hand toward me, and after a moment's consideration, I placed my own within it so that he could pull me up. And then I tugged it from his grasp as quick as I was able.

Thomas bent and lifted the kettle with an ease that belied his wiry frame, reminding me, improbable though it was, that he was indeed a blacksmith. We walked home together, the kettle swinging from his palm in the space between us.

I heard a bird laughing and looked over to see one skittering down a tree trunk at the edge of the clearing. It ran heedless of its destination, looking as if it would plunge headfirst into the ground.

Crickets moaned around us, unseen within the grasses that hid our feet from us.

" 'Tis difficult, women's work."

"No more difficult than a man's."

He remarked upon my words with raised brows. It was not often that I spoke to him without his having asked a question.

I rebuked myself for the mistake.

"Strange, the king's man showing up like that . . . but I suppose God knew we needed him?" He looked at me with expectation, as if he wanted me to speak once more.

I would not do it.

After a long moment, he turned his eyes from me and fell silent.

The silence gave me room to think. Space to consider. There was sure to be trouble now. The king's man had a look about him in spite of his ready smile. A look that told me he knew, as surely as I did, what sort of man Simeon Wright was. It would not do for him to stay here long.

If he did, he might never have the chance to leave.

I had just finished setting out a dinner of biscuits and cheese when I heard someone hail the house. I only had time to hurry back behind the table when a shape appeared in the doorway. Its identity was veiled in a shadow thrown by the last golden flare of the sun's setting.

I gripped the table and tried to remind myself that there was no man here who would harm me. Least not a man so short. But still I could not keep myself from looking toward my shelves to see what tool might be taken to hand.

Then the form stepped through the door, and I perceived it to be Goodman Phillips. Relief flushed my face.

"Is the smith in?"

I nodded. "At the smithery."

He cocked his head. "The smithery, you say?"

I nodded once more.

He turned and left.

But the stranger was there too, and he paused in the door, his form, that floppy hat, and those great boots silhouetted against the sky. And then, finally, he left.

Trembling, I put a hand to the table and eased myself onto the bench.

༄

Once Father and the captain returned from the smithery, we situated ourselves at the table for supper. Father sat first, at the top of the bench, of course. Our guest was seated on the bench across from him, our mother on the bench next to Father. I next to the captain and Mary next to Mother. Nathaniel slid into his usual place at the foot of the table. In several months the babe would take up his place, standing at the end, but for now he sat in our mother's lap.

Father withdrew his hat as he prepared to pray, and a moment later, the captain followed Father's example.

Mother extinguished the taper, for why would it be of use when our heads were bowed, our eyes closed?

Hands folded, Father began to speak. "We give you thanks, O gracious God, for all of the mercies you have shown us. We know that the Christ never ate but that He blessed His food and gave thanks to you for providing it. Like the beasts, we eat and drink to stave off our weakness. And in doing so, we cast ourselves once more upon your great mercies."

How long would the captain be with us? Where would he sleep?

"Without the creatures you first created and then tended, we would have no meat with which to strengthen ourselves. Without the plants that you first planted and then tended, we would have no bread, no drink with which to fortify ourselves. May we be ever mindful that you have given us to eat so that we might live. That you had never intended that we live so that we might eat. . . ."

When would the savages come? And when they did, would we be able to withstand their attack?

"We thank you with humble hearts for the creatures that have given their lives for ours. We thank you that their sacrifice might end in our sustenance. That their gift might remind us of the gift of your son. We know that our bodies, which we so carefully feed, shall, though we know not when, become food for the worms. And for this, we thank you as well. We remember those among our Christian brethren who do not live as we do in this Zion. We remember those who live oppressed, downcast, and imprisoned for their faith *in our own native land*. We ask that you would save them. Quickly come, Lord Jesus, quickly save.

Put down those who commit such atrocities in your name. Defend your church from enemies both without and within."

No one at the table, save the babe, could doubt that it was of the king and his oppression that Father spoke. I pitied the king's poor captain who sat in our midst, until I gave into temptation and turned my head enough to look at him . . . only to see him watching me. He gave one solemn wink before lowering his head . . . and I was the one left trapped in my father's glare when his eyes opened upon the final amen.

I endured Father's wrath by pretending that I had not noticed it. And by rising to take the taper to the fire to relight it.

As I returned with it, the captain had begun to laugh. "I hardly know whether to eat or to forsake such things as meat and biscuits and drink in order to spare some creature's poor life."

Father frowned. "Why so?"

"I had not known there to be such complexity—nay, such morality—to do with eating. Pray, do all simple tasks require such onerous dealings?"

"Pray? . . . Aye, we do it all the time. How can we live without God's breath within us? How can we exist without His grace? And how can we go about our doings each day without being mindful of the creatures that nourish us?"

"It seems, then, that you have gratitude to spare."

Father stared at him for a moment and frowned. He reached for his knife and dipped it into the salt cellar, and then the rest of us dipped in our own knives, each by turn.

Father took up his spoon and cleared his throat. "You have come to our shores of late?"

The captain nodded.

"And how is England?"

"Ill. Dying. Torn at the seams by those who wish to see a king . . . I know not what. Do they want him deposed? Or merely muzzled? 'Tis difficult to know."

31

It sounded as if he supported the king. But how could that be if he were a cousin to the governor?

"Watch your words. Your sympathies might be misconstrued."

The captain blinked at Father's words. "Might they? But are we not all citizens of England here? Are we not all subjects of His Majesty?"

"We are subjects of none but God!" At Father's extraordinary pronouncement, all grew still. The rest of dinner was eaten in silence. And after dinner, when Father opened the Bible to read, the captain took himself out into the night. Upon his return, Father climbed the ladder to the loft. After much shoving of this and that, he called a warning and then slid a frame out over the edge. The captain reached up and took it from him.

It was a sort of bed, framed low to the ground, but strung tight with rope.

The captain seemed to regard it with much appreciation. "My thanks."

Father grunted in return and stalked into the parlor to take his sleep with Mother. The captain spread his blanket upon the frame and then took himself out-of-doors.

Mary and I hurried to change into our nightclothes before he returned. We needn't have worried. The sweet odor of tobacco soon wafted through the door, and we were long hidden in bed before the captain returned.

"Stop pushing, Susannah! Would you have me flatten the babe against the wall?" Mary was always complaining.

"Nay. I only wish to make room for Nathaniel, the great lug. You know how he tosses about."

She reached out an arm and pulled me closer. "There now. He can have his room to move and we can have our sleep."

Our brother soon came to join us, and we heard a rustle as Mother and Father climbed into their bed in the parlor.

Sometime later, I heard the door push open. Through a gap in the curtains, I saw a sliver of dark blue sky. I watched over the top of Nathaniel's head as the captain shut the door. He stepped over to his bed, checked his musket, placed it on the floor beside him, and then rolled himself up into his blanket.

But he did not go to sleep. I could see an ember's light reflecting from his eyes.

We both stayed awake, he watching the fire and I watching him until the rhythmic rustlings from my parents' room became too loud to ignore. I blushed to hear them that night, though I never had before.

I closed my eyes against the sound.

I do not know what he did.

⟋⟍

Thomas had finished the Bible reading.

The hour was late. I took the book from him and placed it back into its box.

He banked the fires while I slipped from my clothes, hung them on a peg, and then pulled a night-shift over my head. Quickly, before he had finished his task, I creased the bed linens and slid beneath them, all the way to the wall. The cracks in the logs sometimes let in a breeze that freshened the close summer air. But the reason I placed my back to it was so that I might not sleep defenseless.

I closed my eyes as Thomas changed. Opened them as he got into bed.

But he did not look at me. He never did. He entered with his back to me and would not turn over for the entire night.

I am certain he hoped nothing more than to set my mind at ease with his habits. It was the kind of man he was. But still I lay there awake until I knew he had fallen into sleep. Deep sleep. 'Twas a habit formed long ago, and nothing I did, nothing I thought, nothing I reminded myself of allowed me to break it. Even the mice had ceased their scrabblings by the time I closed my eyes.

4

THE NEXT DAY THE captain was up with us at dawn's first light. He left the house with Nathaniel and Father, the three of them like ducks in a row.

Mary and I took turns washing our face and hands, then brushing off our clothes and helping each other into them. While Mother sat and put the child to her breast, we found a coal to start the fires and added more water to the porridge.

Mary poured out a drinking cup of cider and put it in front of Mother.

I started the preparation of the day's biscuits. Taking a crock from the shelf, I measured out a portion of mother dough, added flour and water, kneaded it smooth, and set it aside to rise. My sins ever before me, I filled the smoothing iron's heater with coals and set the iron within it to heat.

Some time later the men returned. Nathaniel might have been fetching water and Father might have been milking cows, but it was quite clear that the captain had not joined them in their labors. As we ate of Indian meal porridge, he gave a succinct report on our town.

"How am I to guard you? Were there a stockade, it would be

much easier. Were there even just one road to watch, 'twould not be difficult. But there are three roads, with marshes and meadows and streams running betwixt them. And hills and valleys and the wood. The savages could approach from twenty different directions and slaughter you all before I could even put my musket to my shoulder."

Father had not bothered to look up at the captain's tirade. But when the captain paused, he spoke. " 'Tis why there are garrison houses."

"And where are they?"

"There's the meetinghouse midway along this road here. There's Collier's on the road to Newham. And there's Simeon Wright's at the mill. When we are attacked, we're to retreat to the garrisons. With walls built three feet thick, they're meant to withstand any onslaught."

" 'Tis a good plan once one determines there is an attack. But tell me this: How does one know? What will be the signal?"

Father looked up once more from his trencher and inclined his head toward my brother. " 'Tis Nathaniel will tell us."

"Nathaniel? By what sort of magic?"

"Get the drum, son."

Nathaniel rose from the table and pulled his drum from under the bed. He came to stand beside Father.

"Tell him how it will be done."

"If there is an attack, then I am to go to the meetinghouse as I do on the Sabbath, and I am to beat a warning."

The captain stared at our brother for a long moment. "And how are you to get there? Nay! How are you to know that the town has even been attacked?"

Father signaled for Nathaniel to return the drum to its place. And then he turned his attentions to the captain. "Do you not know the Holy Scriptures? 'Let him which is on the housetop not come down to take any thing out of his house: Neither let him which is in the field return back to take his clothes.' "

"I have no doubt that such an attack would be brutal . . . savage. But what I ask you is this: How shall you know?"

"Do you not think that if the savages come, then 'tis the Lord's judgment fallen upon us? And who can stay the Lord's judgment? Who can withstand God's wrath?"

"So you say that if the savages do come, 'tis some . . . divine judgment?"

"Aye."

"Then why am I here? I can train you to fight. I can post a watch, but this town is indefensible. If they come, then many will die."

"Aye. 'Tis the way of living."

" 'Tis foolishness! There is danger and it is known. If you would allow yourselves to be gathered into a stockade . . ."

" 'Tis God who holds our times in his hands. 'Tis God who decides when each person should die."

"So then you do nothing?"

"We watch. And we pray. 'Some trust in chariots, and some in horses: but we will remember the name of the Lord our God.' "

" 'Tis well and good for you to watch and pray, but 'tis I tasked with the problem of how to make you ready. And how would I defend my actions before God if I fail at my duty?"

"There are things that do not fall within our control. The time of dying is one of them. You seem, like your king, to have a lamentable lack of knowledge of the Holy Scriptures."

"Perhaps. But I know much of the baseness of men. I was the king's man once, 'tis true. But more than that, I was a man of wrath bent on destruction. 'Tis one thing to follow an order and 'tis another to find pleasure and delight in it. To kill because I was . . . skilled. 'Tis why I left England. There is a madness brewing there that I want no part of." He stood from the bench, nodded to Mother. And then he moved to leave the house. But not before one last word. "And perhaps there is a sort of madness here as well."

" 'Tis God alone who saves!"

The captain's reply was a salute.

It only served to enrage Father the more. "He is a heathen."

The babe fussed on Mother's lap. "Then perhaps God has brought him here for the saving of his soul."

Father glared at her.

Perhaps not.

The captain kept himself from our presence during the next few days, coming back only for meals and to retire in the evenings. He did nothing to interrupt our routines and gladly gave himself over to Mother's hand during the week's nitpicking, and so we ignored his presence when we could. But during meals it was impossible. He assailed Father with questions.

"There is an area far to the east of the town that looks to have some industry at work upon it."

"Across the river?"

"Aye."

" 'Tis the common."

The captain ate in silence for a while, examining our faces as he did so. Finally, after Nathaniel looked at him with blank face, he laughed as if he were at the receiving end of some familial joke. Then he turned back to Father. "The common what?"

"The common wood."

"But it must belong to some man in particular. There were signs of recent work done there."

"Nay. 'Tis no one man's, but the town's. There might have been some work done there this spring past, but it has been made quite clear that no one is to venture so far as that. Not with the threat of savages."

"But what if someone did wander that far? And cut that wood?"

Father shrugged. " 'Tis for the cutting, but 'tis also for the paying." He shook his head. "And one would have to pay dearly for those old oaks. . . ."

"I saw no oaks."

Father looked at him sharply.

"What would happen if someone did cut them? Without paying?"

"You saw no oaks?" Father pierced him with his gaze for a moment, but then his mien relaxed. "Then you must not have known on what you looked. There are oaks aplenty there, and I will have to pay to cut some of them myself this winter . . . or would have before the savages made themselves known. 'Tis Simeon Wright who supplies me now."

"Have you no woods of your own? I would think a carpenter—"

"I did have. They were destroyed by fire in the spring."

"Just your own woods?"

"Mostly. The wind blew the flames into the neighboring plot. But mine was the only one completely destroyed."

"Before or after the Indians were seen?"

Father thought about it for a moment. "Before, it was . . . I might have petitioned then to cut wood from the common, but 'twas March and then April, the busiest of the year's months. And by then it was too late. The savages had come."

"Must you get your wood from Simeon Wright?"

"From where else would I get it? Boston is too far, and we have been banned from our own wood."

"Yet he has wood enough to spare?"

" 'Tis his profession, though he charges a—" Father broke off speaking.

"He charges . . . ?" The captain seemed as interested as the rest of us in what Father had meant to say.

"Aye. He does."

"A miserable piece of work that you are left with none."

" 'Tis the way of it. Once the threat of savages is lifted, I will trade what's left of my woods for someone else's land. 'Tis certain one of these farmers will be glad to get it."

"Tell me about that threat."

Father's lips pressed into a thin straight line. "If you have questions about the savages, then ask Simeon Wright. 'Tis he who saw them and he who put us all on watch. With double the men."

"Is he the tall one? With eyes that could freeze a sea?"

"Aye."

"Was there no one else with him when he saw them?"

"Nay."

"So he saw them . . . one time? And that was it? And then a report was made in Boston?"

"Aye. And you were sent."

"Pardon me for asking, but why should the governor—"

"Why should the governor respond to a cry for help from such as us?"

The captain nodded.

"If he does not, then 'tis only a matter of time before the savages that wander through our wood wander right into his mansion. 'Tis *that* the reason why. If we do not stop them here, then what is to prevent them from going there? We are the first and last defense for Boston. But building a Zion was never meant to be easy. We must press on to fulfill our high calling. God prepared the way for us. Now 'tis our duty to take it. Both the land and its people."

❧

Following his business with Thomas, I had seen the captain often about the township. He was always peering about, looking around. And once, when I had been on the ridge walking the hay meadows, he had looked right at me.

It had surprised me. Astonished me. Usually no one saw me. And never unless I was with Thomas, when they were required to greet me for reasons of civility.

I relied upon my invisibility. It was my protection. My refuge.

But though he had seen me, the captain simply nodded. Smiled. Walked by without speaking.

I turned to watch him after he had passed by.

He had a remarkable way of being. Of walking. A confidence

that appeared unshakable. A self-assurance that bordered on the extraordinary. And he seemed completely unafraid of the savages. One could feel safe in his presence.

I felt safe in his presence.

In fact, the temptation was strong to follow him and revel in that feeling.

Nay. Some things were better conquered alone. Fear was one of them. Just two years ago I would not have even left the house by myself, never mind climb the ridge entirely and utterly alone. But my convictions did not stop me from watching him until he disappeared from my view.

There was a man to stand up to Simeon Wright.

The essence of him was good. And honest. While Simeon's was pretense and deceit. The captain would never surrender to one such as Simeon Wright, but if the two clashed . . . when they clashed . . . I did not know who would triumph. Nor what would be the outcome.

5

I DECIDED TO VISIT Abigail one forenoon after having tended the garden. Before she had been wed, Abigail had lived just two houses down from ours and been my dearest confidante. Now she was at the opposite end of the road, a good two dozen houses away. It was not often I could afford the time to visit her.

Mary begged to accompany me, and since she had finished scouring the pots, Mother allowed it. I toted the child on my hip while Mary walked beside me.

As we passed the first house, Goody Ames's, she stepped out of her door to greet us. "I saw that captain of yours today."

Mary answered before I could. "He is not Susannah's captain."

"Nor should he be! He was up to Mister Wright's, pacing atop that hill where their house sets. He had his musket up to his shoulder. What do you think he was doing? Drawing sights on something?"

I shrugged. How would I know?

We passed on by Goody Baxter's but were stopped at Goody Turner's, three houses down. "Do you know where I saw the king's captain yesterday?"

I jounced the babe to keep him from complaining.

"He was down to the river, climbing all over the bridge. His breeches were wet. Do you think he fell in?"

"If he did, it was his own fault."

"Mary!" Though propriety made me scold her, she had only said what I had been thinking. And good thing, for if she had not said it, the words might have slipped right off my tongue. And then I would have been known for what I truly was.

Mary turned from Goody Turner to me. "If it was not his fault, then whose was it?"

The child began to squawk and so we turned away and continued on. But not long, for we were slowed once more as we reached Goody Hillbrook's.

"That captain sure gets around. I sent my girl to the pond for scouring plants after her lessons and she said the man was there, ducking behind trees and then wading right into the water. What do you suppose he was doing?"

This time we had not truly stopped, and so, walking backward, we both pled ignorance.

Once Goody Hillbrook had gone back inside, we set our faces toward Abigail's and picked up our pace. But the questions galled me. "If this is the thanks we get for boarding that man . . . ! Now everyone will know our business."

A frown set a crease between Mary's eyes. "And what will have changed? They have always known our business."

Perhaps I should have kept my sentiments to myself.

As we approached the next house, Goody Blake stepped out.

Mary linked an arm through mine. "Quick! Turn your head. Pretend you do not see her."

But it was too late. I lowered the child to the ground, keeping tight hold of its leading strings. Since Goody Blake was a gentle soul, we paused. But we were soon joined by Goody Ellys and her daughter Goody Metcalf, who were walking toward us down the road.

"That captain has been skulking through the wood. Nearly frightened Goodman Ellys to death."

"My boy told me he saw him down to blueberry barren where he first appeared."

"And I heard he was down to the brook."

I smiled, nodded, and tried to disentangle ourselves from their conversation. "If we're to see Goody Clarke before our mother needs us, we should be about the doing of it."

"Abigail? She has a pale look to her."

"That babe of hers might be teething. He's gone red in the face and drippy in the nose."

" 'Tis about the time for it." Goody Blake turned to me and reached out to pat our babe. She reached wide and I turned so that her hand could fall on its head. "Still and all, don't let your little one linger there too long."

"Tell her to spread some ale on the babe's gums."

"Or press her thumb up to the top of the child's mouth at night."

A none-too-gentle tug on my arm from Mary led to us taking our leave.

"If one more person asks me what the captain might be doing, I might just tell them he's getting ready to kill them all. And I know it because I watch him clean his musket every night while Father reads the Bible!"

I could not save myself from laughing at Mary's words.

The rest of the length of road we received reports on the captain's whereabouts. He had been to the brook and down to the pond. He had visited the minister's way down at the end of the south road and had been seen at the top of Newham Road. It was evident that in all his wanderings, he had walked the extreme limits of the township. From the swamp in the north, to the brook in the south; the river and the blueberry barren to the west and the sawmill to the east.

And then, finally, there was only one house left to pass: Smallhope Smyth's. We slowed our step, expecting at any moment to be stopped, though I don't know why. She was rarely seen. She never went anywhere, never spoke to anybody. 'Twas Thomas who drew their water and went to the grist mill for meal.

Past Small-hope's house stood Abigail's. My friend's door, like all the others in town, was open in an attempt to entrap a breeze. I stepped in the door. "Greetings, Abigail! We have come to—"

She came at me with the hiss of a serpent, pushing me right back out the door. "Hush!"

"We wanted—"

"I just got the child to sleep. He's been crying and shrieking and wailing and . . ." She paused, an ear cocked toward the door, then sighed. "And now all my work is for naught." She turned on a heel and went back through the door.

I glanced at Mary.

She pulled a face.

I shrugged. How was I to have known? I followed Abigail back inside. As my eyes adjusted to the dim light, I could see her in the corner by the bed, holding the babe to her chest, turning first this way and then that with him. The little mite was crying so hard, he choked on his own tears.

"Abigail, do you want me to—"

She spoke without stopping, without turning. "Go."

"But we could—"

She did turn then and walked toward me. "What? Do you think you can stop him from crying?"

Surprised by the harshness in her tone, I found I did not know what to say. And if I was not mistaken, Abigail herself was on the verge of tears just as hot and heavy as her babe's.

"Just go."

"But—"

"Please."

As I looked around I saw much that I could have done. Put dishes away, tended to the cooking, done the mending. Stoked a fire that had almost extinguished itself. If she had asked, I would have stayed. And Mary and I together could have worked wonders.

44

Abigail's hands, gripped around the bundle of the child, were trembling.

I extended my arms toward the babe.

She only clutched it tighter, shaking her head. "Go."

Why should I fight her when she was in such pitiful a state? But then, how could I not? I stood there, undecided, until Abigail turned her back on me and began singing to the babe.

I gave up. Turned on my heel and nearly walked right into Mary on my way out.

She picked up our own mother's child and hurried to catch up with me. "What is it? Is the babe sick?"

"I do not know."

"Is Abigail sick?"

"I do not know."

"Is—"

"I do not know!" It seemed I knew nothing about my friend anymore.

"And so now what are we to do?"

"About what?"

"About going home. I have no wish to be questioned once more like some prisoner before the king's bench about the goings-on of the captain."

Neither did I. The road that unfurled before us seemed more like a gauntlet than a simple path leading toward home. "We could go by the hay meadows."

Behind the road we had just walked, the earth rose steadily up to a ridge. On the other side of the ridge lay a vast meadow that the town had divided into hay lots. If we kept to the meadows and fashioned a path through the hay, then we would, God willing, meet no man or woman intent upon asking unanswerable questions about the captain.

And 'tis that which we did.

With the child straddling my waist, it took some work climbing the hill and clomping through the grasses, but at least we did it at our own speed, without being stopped every twenty paces. Wresting our skirts from the clutches of the grasses behind us, we held them up before us as we walked.

Crickets jumped now and then through the hay, pursued by sparrows. But aside from that activity, it was a lonely, desolate place. It came to me of a sudden, that though the hay lots were not forbidden us, no one knew we were there. The hairs on my arms stood on end as I realized that a shout given up from the ridge might not reach the houses down below. And a spider began to creep up my spine. A sure sign of being watched.

By a malignant eye.

Perhaps my lack of moral fortitude and laziness in wanting to avoid the townspeople had resulted in bad judgment. I knew a sudden, desperate urgency to descend the ridge for the relative safety of the road below. Even spurious questions were preferable to being discovered defenseless in the hay lots by a savage. Especially when charged with the safety of the babe.

I lowered my head to kiss the sweat-dampened curls at his neck beneath his cap, and he squealed in response and reached up with both hands to grab the rim of my hat.

"Mary?" No need to alarm her; I simply wanted to be freed of the child to find the quickest route toward home.

"Aye." The sound of her voice came from behind me and to my left.

I held out the child toward where I supposed my sister to be. "Could you take him?"

When I felt her take him up, I worked at his tiny fingers to pry them from my hat. Cries of protest came as I was finally released.

"Hush-a, hush-a." Mary held the child out in front of her and pulled a gruesome face to make him laugh.

I turned forward and began to walk at an angle that would intersect with the ridge, intent on finding a path down to the house. After several minutes, I realized that my unburdened strides had taken me far ahead of Mary's encumbered ones. I paused for a moment on the ridge, looking down at the houses below, and then I pivoted, intending to rejoin my sister. Instead of striking earth when I set my foot down, I encountered a stone. With my balance thrown off, my weight fell onto my other foot, the one anchoring me to the incline. But it collapsed, causing a sudden burning pain, and pitched me down the slope.

I landed hard on my shoulder. The suddenness of the fall cast my legs over my head, and I rolled several times before I came up against something hard and stopped.

That something wobbled.

Looking up, squinting against the brightness of the sun, I saw a form waver for an instant above me, and then it bellowed and threw up its arms.

A savage!

They had finally come.

6

I TRIED TO SHOUT, to send up some warning, but my breath was expelled by the force of the savage as it pounced atop me.

I squeezed my eyes shut. Waited for death.

To my amazement, instead of words spoken in a heathen tongue, I heard laughter. "And here I was, waiting for savages!"

I opened my eyes and found myself looking straight into the captain's.

"Are you all right?" he asked.

I gasped for air, then finally succeeded in pushing the words from my throat. "I would be better if you would remove yourself from me."

"I am certain you probably would." With amusement flashing in his eyes, he rocked forward, off my stomach. Then he dropped a knee to the ground and extended a hand to me.

I ignored it and tried my best instead to sit. Successful, I took a careful deep breath. It caught. I coughed. Tried again. My chest trembled as it expanded.

The captain leaned close and began to pluck grasses from my sleeves. "Did all savages look like you, I would quit my worries and welcome them here without another thought."

"You did not have to dive down upon me."

"Neither did you have to roll yourself into me. Although I must say, it was completely unexpected and therefore tactically sound. Perhaps I should have the men at watch post themselves right there," he gestured toward the ridge, "in preparation for launching themselves in a roll at the enemy. 'Tis as good a strategy as I have ever devised."

I pushed his hand away from my sleeve.

His gaze left my eyes and came to rest at some point beyond my shoulder. "Tsk." He leaned closer.

My breath caught once more.

He reached out behind me but then almost immediately straightened, putting distance between us. "Such a bad end to such a dreadful hat." He handed it to me.

Streaks of dirt were smeared across the crown. The brim had been battered. "You do not like my hat?" Why did he not like it? It was just like everyone else's.

"I could never look without prejudice upon anything that would hide your lovely locks from view." He reached out a hand to capture a curl that spun in the breeze below my shoulder. It was then that I realized that my coif had disappeared as well.

I gathered up my hairs, spun them around my hand into a bundle and slapped my hat atop them. Then I pushed from the ground, intending to start a search for the coif. As I gained my feet, however, my ankle buckled once more. I cried out in pain as I stumbled.

The captain, still on one knee, caught me as I fell. "I place my humble person at your service."

I could only protest his falsehood. "You are not humble!"

He chortled as he gathered me to his chest and came to his feet. "Nay. I have been graced with many things, but that particular quality does not number itself among them."

Had he no shame? No remorse? To clutch my person to his broad chest in the plain light of day? Such things were not done. And why was I so fixed upon his chest and his eyes . . . those eyes

49

that were as varied as the ocean, shifting from light blue to indigo with every glance.

With great effort, I brought my fascination with his person to a halt and concentrated upon his words instead. Had he not just recognized within himself a sin? But though recognized and identified, he appeared to suffer no guilt from it! What kind of man was he?

A shout from the ridge above us made the captain turn. As he did so, he faltered for an instant as if trying to keep his footing.

I threw my arms up around his neck.

"I wish I always had my arms filled with such a grasping woman! 'Twould be Paradise indeed."

He made as if to drop me and when I screamed, he tossed me above his head instead. And then he caught me up close against his chest again. He smelt of tobacco and leather and . . . the wind.

"You must let me go!"

"Must I?" We both watched Mary as she appeared at the ridge. He called at her to come join us.

"Truly, you must."

"But then how would you get home?"

"You cannot carry me," I protested.

"I cannot? I think I can. I am." He glanced at me. "Ah, I see. You mean I *should* not. Are you certain?"

" 'Tis not . . . seemly."

I felt his shoulders shrug beneath my arms. "As you like. I suppose there are other ways of going about it." He shifted me within his arms and then threw me over his shoulder. Gripping me at his chest about the knees with his arm, he let my own arms and head flop loose at his back.

Beating upon him with my fists did nothing but make him laugh. I doubted a hammer could knock a dent in that rigid back of his.

Mary was smiling long before she reached us.

"A new manner of transport, Susannah?"

I might have glared at her, could I have lifted my head high enough to see her.

"I would think walking more comfortable, if not more prudent," she continued.

"She has turned an ankle."

"And so you turned her over your shoulder?" There was a sauciness in Mary's retort that ought to have shamed her. Indeed, it ought to have shamed me. But the thing of it was, she had me wishing that I were walking beside the captain, talking with him, looking into those changeable eyes instead of being flung over his shoulder like a sack of meal.

"What else was I to do when she eschewed my, arms?"

"I did not—"

My words were jolted from of me, as the captain began the descent toward home. Mary walked beside him, keeping him in conversation as I tried to keep my hat on my head and clutch at the captain's waist for security at the same time.

☙

I walked up to the hay meadow after the Phillips sisters had left Goody Clarke's house. My path had nothing to do with following them. As I had on the day when I saw the captain, I often walked the meadow of a forenoon, after weeding in the garden or sewing and before beginning preparations for supper. Despite the grime of his profession, Thomas was a simple and tidy man who left little in the way of a mess behind him. Our home was small. There were but two of us living within it. On a day like this one, the air heavy with humidity, I liked to walk the ridge to catch the breeze that skipped off the crest of the hill and continued on without descending into the valley. It was a good thing to build beneath a ridge for shelter from winter's cruel gales. But in the summer, it was insufferable. And in this one thing, I chose not to. Suffer.

I treaded lightly, carefully, not willing to step through a sparrow's nest from sheer carelessness. The sisters' trail was easy enough to spot. It bored straight through the meadow grasses, oblivious to beast or fowl. My eyes scanned the field, looked through the bowed grasses to see movement. Over there, where they rustled first this way and that, might be a fox. And over there, where they shook in clumps forming a jagged line, might be a hare.

I wandered over to the edge of the ridge and looked down upon the houses, so orderly, so precisely placed upon the meandering road. I liked knowing that none of them, none of those goodwives in those houses, imagined that I was up here. None of them knew that I was looking down upon them. After feeling, so often, for so long, that they and those like them were looking down upon me, it gave me great satisfaction to do the same to them.

The string of my thoughts was severed by a motion down the hill and to my left.

I turned in that direction, shifting my hat to shade my eyes from the sun.

It was Susannah Phillips.

And that captain.

I took a step closer. They were . . . she was . . . he had lifted her into his arms. But now he was throwing her over his shoulder.

I felt myself smile, so I tucked my chin into the collar of my shift. But that did not stop me from watching.

Susannah's sister had joined them and now they were walking down the hill toward their house, all three of them. Four of them. Mary carried the child.

That they would cavort so openly. And laugh so freely. Did they not know they tempted God? I knew how quickly laughter could turn to tears. I knew how swiftly madness could follow mirth. Better not to laugh. Better to keep one's head down, keep one's hands busy, and keep one's self in hiding. As much as possible.

Susannah's hands reached up to clamp her hat onto her head.

The captain spun round, causing her to fly out from his back.

I could not hear the sisters from where I was, but I could see them. Quite clearly.

What would those goodwives say? With any luck, they would

never see, never know. Surely on this day, at this hour, I was certain to be the only one watching.

I turned my eyes from them and kept to my course, but again, my attention was drawn by a motion. I looked up across the valley to the other side of the ridge. The side where it curved around by the sawmill. And it was there I saw him.

Simeon Wright was standing on the crest of the hill, fists at his hips, watching the goings on beneath us both.

I let myself sink down into the grasses and then sat there for a long while, rubbing my arms against a sudden chill.

❧

Mary went before us into the house.

I could hear Mother long before I could see her. " 'Tis the last time I will give you leave for visiting of a forenoon! What have you to say to account for yourselves?" I heard her step closer. "And why do you carry my daughter across your shoulder like a sack of flour?"

"Because she turned an ankle and did not think it seemly for me to carry her in my arms."

As he dumped me onto a bench beside the table, it seemed to me that there was a smile lurking in my mother's eyes. She knelt before me, lifted my skirts, and untied my garter.

And then she paused for a moment and lifted her head to look at the captain.

He sighed, threw up his hands, and left the house.

Then she slid the stocking from my injured foot and poked and prodded until I was near to writhing at her examination.

"There is no break, but there is a swelling. And you won't be much use to me for a week." She shook her head as she drew my stocking back on and settled my skirts around my legs. "I had thought you had a sound head upon those shoulders. 'Tis Mary with her candor and high spirits that I have worried over all this time, and now I see that it should have been you."

She pushed to her feet and took the child from Mary, sending her out to the garden for field balm.

"What am I to do with you?"

"I am sorry."

Her face softened and she came close to pat my arm. "I know you are, child. What were you about?"

"We were coming back from Abigail's. By the hay meadow."

"The hay meadow? And why?"

"Because we were stopped along the way, going, at every house by every goodwife wanting to know about the captain."

"Ah. Well, then you have paid for your folly."

I supposed I had.

For the remainder of the week, I was relegated to the menial duties of knitting and scouring pots, entertaining the babe, and churning milk into butter as Mary took over my tasks of biscuit making and fire tending and cooking.

But worse, I was subjected to the captain's amused glances whenever I happened to meet his eyes.

At least my humiliation was limited in its scope. None but the family, and the captain, knew of it. It would have shamed me to think of John having seen us. But it shamed me even more that though I could recall with vivid clarity the captain's scent, and though I could remember the many variations in the color of his eyes, I could not do the same with John. Had he gray eyes or green? Blue or brown? And why was it that I did not know?

7

IF I THOUGHT MY humiliation at the hands of the captain had been accomplished in secret, I was disabused of that notion at meeting on the Sabbath.

"Why was the captain carrying you in his arms in broad daylight down the ridge?"

"I thought you had your hopes pinned to that John Prescotte."

If my ankle and my courage had allowed it, I would have turned on my heel and marched right out of the meetinghouse. But good girls did not do things like that, and folly had to be atoned for.

"I had turned my ankle, and he was trying to help me. As for John, I do not know of what you speak." The less said, the better, the faster the talk would cease. At least that is what I hoped.

"Is he not joining us today?"

I looked in the direction Goody Ellys pointed and saw the captain, musket at his shoulder, marching round the meetinghouse.

I shrugged. If he did not, then he was liable to be fined for refusing to attend meeting.

Goody Ellys clucked. And then she continued with her questioning. "So . . . you fell off the ridge?"

I nodded.

"And what were you doing up there?"

I sighed and heaved a prayer toward heaven. God answered: Nathaniel began drumming the rest of the congregation into the meetinghouse.

As soon as I was seated, I could not know which was worse: to be accosted by questions or to be rendered light-headed from the heat. As the minister took his place and led us in a confession of sins, sweat trickled down my brow. Babes fussed in their mothers' laps, and now and then a clucking or a shushing could be heard above the minister's voice.

Throughout the prayers and singing, the prayers and readings, the prayers and the sermon, I alternately wiped wet palms against my skirt and then set them against the smooth wood of the bench beneath me. And all the while I watched from the far edge of my vision as the captain paced round the building, up one side and down the other.

And I wondered what he thought of us. Though I do not know why. And as soon as I caught my thoughts wandering in his direction, I yanked them back toward the minister and his sermon.

❧

The Sabbath meeting was one of the torments of my existence. No matter that I walked with Thomas to the meetinghouse, the moment we stepped inside we were separated, man from woman. He to the one side, I to the other.

Of course, I knew how to be still. And quiet. I could sit for hours with a stillness of soul that rendered the space around me void of my presence. I knew how to breathe so softly that I stirred not even the air in front of my face. And I knew how to sing so that none could discern my voice from the chorus of all the others. But still, in the meetinghouse I became a woman, joined to the other women in the town, even though I did not know how to be one.

How did one leave aside their memories to sit without shame in the house of God? How did one accept the look of another not as a challenge, not as a warning of danger, but as a simple passing glance . . . as nothing at all? How did one become an unquestioned part of something so great, so wonderful, as this community of souls?

The questions were not ones that I could answer. They were the product of my overabundant curiosity, for I did not aspire to something so grand. I was unworthy. More than any of them knew. But I wondered just the same. And I observed.

So much could be learned by watching.

And far better to watch than to be watched.

I listened to the lesson. I would not be so proud, so bold, as to think that it did not apply to me. But in the listening, with my head bent slightly in a posture of penitence, I could see. Well enough to know that Goody Blake was going blind, though no one knew it yet but me. It had to do with the way she cast her hands out before her as she walked and sat. I did not know how she could bear the knowledge of it. I doubt if she had gained forty years, and she had a little one still tugging at her skirts.

Goody Metcalf would have one soon. It did not show yet in anything but her smile and the way she slipped her hands beneath her apron to stroke her belly. It was her first. She would be allowed such indulgences.

The Hillbrooks were doing poorly. Their crops must have failed last year, though I had not heard it. Their property lay down toward the common at the farthest end of the town's holdings. And now, with Indian troubles, they would not want to linger long during the summer's harvest . . . if indeed they were allowed to go there at all. But they were wise. They had read the signs and planned for the worst. I could tell it by the way Goody Hillbrook had turned her cuffs inside out instead of replacing them with new ones. By the way she had resewn her skirts so their frayed seams would not show.

The Phillips. . . now there was a picture of prosperity. There was always work for a carpenter when a town was being established. And a good thing, for his daughters would soon be marrying. Did they realize Mary Phillips's gaze wandered toward Simeon Wright . . . even as her sister Susannah's steadfastly avoided him?

I wondered about that. Perhaps, then, she had some inkling of his character.

As I sat there listening and wondering, Susannah's gaze shot now and then toward John Prescotte. But not as often as one might think for a young woman all but pledged to be married. And not in the dreamy, thoughtless way of those mooning over their beloved. Nay, if anyone could be said to capture her full attention, it was Captain Holcombe, who marched round the meetinghouse with the precision of a beating drum. 'Twas to him that her eyes seemed unaccountably fixed.

Curious, that. Because Susannah was good. And kind and meek. Not like some who wore their religion as a cloak to be drawn on or cast off at will. Not like her sister. Neither like her friend, Abigail Clarke.

Those two were cut of the same cloth. Abigail had sat two years before, numbered among her parents' children, watching Simeon Wright in much the same way Mary did now. But Simeon Wright had never, not once, returned the interest.

Nay, his attention was directed to two women in particular. To his mother and to Susannah Phillips, though only one of them was aware of it. And it was not a benign or casual interest.

I am sure that to ask Mary and her friends of Simeon Wright would encourage coy twitters. He was a handsome man and gave off the appearance of being receptive to flirtation. Half of the girls in town might imagine, with some reason, that he had an especial affection for them. I am sure he had sampled kisses from more than half. But they missed the clues. They failed to read the signs. They never noticed that his smile did not reach his eyes.

Not like Thomas's. Not that he smiled very often. But who would, when burdened with a wife like me? I often wondered, on his behalf, what might have happened if he had not come to market on that day three winters ago. What might have happened, what his life might have looked like, had he not met me. Which of these girls might he have married?

I did not think upon it often because the burden of it was too great to bear. Neither did I look at Thomas often. Mostly because I did not want to see him looking at me. For he did. I could feel it. But they were most likely looks of sorrow and pity. What other kind could they be?

Meetings were a vast source of information, if only one would bother to look as I did. And I did it with almost reckless abandon. But I had no fear of being caught, for no one ever saw me. Crowded gatherings were the best place to render myself into nothing. To become nobody. And because I did, no one ever thought to turn their glance upon me.

❧

It was after the sermon and before the long prayer that the captain's name was mentioned. At a motion from the minister, Nathaniel stepped outside the door and returned a moment later with the king's man.

Captain Holcombe took off his hat, tucked it under an arm, and then strode down the aisle to the lectern. "After having taken stock of the town and its surrounds, I stand ready to reform the watch. I know you've already doubled the men, but I wish them to be placed at different points. I call a training day this Wednesday and monthly hereafter."

A ripple of unease passed through the congregation.

The deputy, Goodman Blake, stood from his pew and cleared his throat. "Every month?"

"Every. Each one. This one and all of them thereafter."

"For how long?"

The captain's gaze seemed to stop at the center of the room on the men's side.

I turned just enough to see at whom he looked. It was Simeon Wright.

"As long as there is a certain threat. As long as you are in imminent danger."

What could be said? The captain had been charged with our protection. He was only doing what the governor had asked him to do. He stayed, frozen in posture for several moments more, and then he seemed to relax. But just as he stepped away from the lectern, the minister spoke.

"Why do you not wish to join with us in this service?"

He stopped in his movement. Turned slowly toward the minister. "I am sure the savages would delight in catching us all under the same roof at the same time, but if it is all the same to you, I intend that they not be able to do it."

"You say that God cannot protect those at worship in His own house?"

He smiled. "Of course I do not mean to say He *cannot* protect you. I simply wonder if He will. In England 'tis given that those who act in stupidity reap only pain and sorrow."

While the minister was left gaping like a fish, the men's side of the pews erupted in rage. "He blasphemes!"

"Is he some papist come to plague us?"

"Royalist!"

"Cavalier!"

Simeon Wright took to his feet. "He only seeks to protect us from certain threat and imminent danger." He turned toward the captain. "You, sir: are you a member of the church?"

"This church?"

"Any church."

He threw back those enormous coattails with his hand and planted his fist on his hip. "I am a member of the king's Church of England."

An eruption of questions ensued. "The king's church?"

"What about God's church? Is not the head of the Church of England God?"

"How can we entrust our lives to—"

"Silence!" Simeon Wright held up a hand and waited for the congregation to fall silent before he continued speaking. "Since this man prefers the king's religion to God's truth, then perhaps the perfect place for him of a Sabbath is . . . outside, on watch."

The captain bowed. "My thoughts exactly." He straightened and proceeded down the aisle toward the door. But not before giving me a wink.

Which was witnessed by half the people in that place.

The captain stepped forward from the side of the meetinghouse as I limped out the door. "Mistress Phillips."

I frowned at him and kept on . . . limping. There were too many people watching, too many goodwives bent on finding a topic for their gossip, to allow the captain to speak to me in so public a place.

Unfortunately, he did not know it. "May I walk with you?"

I did not answer.

He fell into step with me as I followed my parents, despite my pointed lack of reply.

It was then I decided to seize the opportunity his boldness had provided. "You may not flirt with me."

He leaned toward me but kept his eyes on my parents, who were walking still before us. "Flirt with you?"

"Wink at me."

"Wink at you?"

"Must you repeat everything I say?"

"Only if I wish to understand what it is you are trying to tell me."

"I am not some. . . . some . . . scandalous woman for you to treat me so lightly."

His gaze darted from my parents and came to rest on me. "Scandalous? But I never thought you were. I simply thought you were exceedingly beautiful. And a gentleman is honor bound to . . . honor beauty when he observes it."

"Then cease your observations."

"I would rather pluck out my own eyes."

"Have you a knife? I will do it myself." That such bold words would issue forth from my mouth!

"Such coldhearted cruelty from one so fair. A very flower of Puritan orthodoxy. And yet so spirited. You fascinate me."

There was laughter lurking in his eyes. I could see it. And I did not like to be laughed at. I was vain as well as rebellious. But I was still an upstanding citizen of Stoneybrooke Towne. And the towns-people thought me good as well. "Find your fascination elsewhere. I am promised to John Prescotte."

"Betrothed?"

I could not lie. Certainly not on a Sabbath. "Not yet."

He smiled.

"But I will be."

The smile disappeared. "Truly?"

"Before the summer is over." Please, God, may I not have lied!

"Is he the young one, then? The one with the scraggly beard?"

I ignored his insults. "The one with more virtues than you will ever know."

"Who works like an indentured servant on his father's farm?"

I could not stop my face from flushing. "His father has been ill."

" 'Tis that which has stopped him from marrying you?"

"Are you an orphan that you do not understand such obliga-tions to family?"

"Nay. I am a son of a man who pushed me out into the world to make my own way when I was yet a lad. Despite the fact that he had gone lame. In both feet."

How had he managed to shame me when he was the one who had been seen winking?

"John Prescotte?" He sighed. "I wish you much luck then."

I could tell that he did not mean it. And besides, I did not need his luck.

8

TRAINING DAY DAWNED SULTRY. Even the notes of the cowherd's horn drooped in the air. The sun had barely cleared the tops of the trees when waves of heat began to shimmer in the distance.

After breakfast Nathaniel ran up to the meetinghouse with his drum. Soon we heard his signal. By the time we arrived at the training field, several stakes had been driven into the ground. Between them stretched some lengths of homespun and beneath, blankets had been spread out and babes laid down. For once Abigail had been freed from her burden. She stood within a loose cluster of other young mothers.

John Prescotte walked by. I might have smiled at him, spoken to him for a moment, but he did not look at me in passing.

Thomas shrugged out of his doublet and handed it to me, leaving me free to join the other women. And so I would. For a while. But then I planned to slip away into the wood for a brief hour to myself.

But before I could move, the captain came to stand just in front of me.

A moment later, he was joined by Simeon Wright.

They stood there the both of them, arms crossed, staring at the field before them.

Simeon Wright spoke first. "If it is all the same to you, the men might as well drill as they have before."

"With you as their captain?"

"Aye."

"*Is* it the same?"

Simeon turned toward the captain, brow furrowed. "I do not understand your meaning."

"Will the drills work in the event of an attack? By savages?"

" 'Tis the sole reason we train. To prepare for an attack. By savages."

The captain's teeth flashed. He bowed slightly. "Then by all means, please do as is your custom."

In taking their leave of each other, they nearly ran right over me. But I was used to that.

Following inspection, the line of men split into two at Simeon Wright's signal, each line advancing forward and then moving, one to the right, the other to the left, to take up a position of two lines in the middle.

At an order, the front line loaded their weapons.

"Give . . . fire!"

They fired and then, without waiting to see what it was they had shot, they filed around behind the second line. And the whole exercise repeated itself.

They drilled for some time, advancing for a distance to the beating of Nathaniel's drum and then stopping to fire; putting on bayonets and then taking them off, while the putrid smoke of gunpowder hung in the air. Finally, at Simeon Wright's order, they broke into lines and passed before us in review, a forest of muzzles protruding one and two feet above the men's heads.

The ties at the collar of John's shirt had loosed themselves and the material flapped open. As he drew abreast of me, he turned his head slightly, his gaze resting upon me for a brief instant before he passed by.

My cheeks flamed with a fire that had nothing to do with the heat. It shamed me, seeing him with his chest bared to all the world. And to me. What might people think? I supposed I would look upon such things as a goodwife, but that pleasure was to come after the marriage, not before.

As the men came to a halt, the women began to rummage in their baskets and pails for dinner. But before Simeon Wright could give the order to break ranks, the captain stepped up beside him. In the stillness of that moment, his voice rang out.

"And what will you do if the savages do not oblige you by attacking in a tidy straight line?"

Simeon's tone was dismissive. "The militia has always trained—"

"Aye. It has trained. But has it fought?"

They stared at each other for a long moment, wary, alert, as if they were stags in rut.

"Nay."

"Then may I suggest an alternate course of training after dinner." It was a command rather than a question.

Dinner was subdued, the men casting peeved glances at the captain as they ate.

The captain, however, seemed oblivious to their displeasure. He ate as if preparing for famine. And as soon as he had finished, he called the men back to training.

The captain, gripping his musket between his hands, walked out into the field and then turned to face us. "May I submit that this musket may be more useful as a club."

Clearly no one would stop him from suggesting such a thing, but the men's eyes filled with horror. One of them even ventured to question his wisdom. "But . . . how am I to shoot a deer or a . . . a bear . . . if I bust my musket over a savage's head."

"Better his head than yours. And in such a case, it is better to grasp the musket at the muzzle and wield the butt like so." He sent his weapon crashing into the grasses at his feet.

"Here now! If we use our weapons thusly, we will have none of them left."

The captain frowned. "Aye. Such an inconvenience. Such a trifle . . . one life. Or two. Or three. Or perhaps, the whole town's! Blacksmith?"

Thomas stepped forward. "Aye."

"Could you not see to some small repairs of the muskets should they be needed?"

"Aye."

"Then get to it, men! Two lines forming just here!"

The captain had them smashing hay stacks and lunging at the grasses for an hour. The effort required of the men began to show itself in the dampened shirts that clung to their chests. John's the same as everyone's. And soon, I was loathe to look at him.

The captain raised an arm for silence. He was given it, the men no longer fit for anything but gasping for air.

"The changing of the watch is heretofore to proceed at the normal times, but the posts are to be at the wood by the river, the ridge near the hay meadows, the minister's on the south road and at Wright's hill. Double guards will be posted. The one to walk in one direction and the other to proceed in the contrary. There will be no matches lit for the muskets."

"What—!"

"How can we be expected to fire them if—"

The captain raised a finger. "If you can see the glow of the match, then so can the savages. Much better to use the rifle as a club, up close, and raise your voice in warning, than to be killed from afar and then overrun."

"But—"

"Thank you for your time. Training day is to proceed from now as is customary. I will greet the first watch of the night at the meetinghouse."

That night supper was a dreary affair. The captain was standing watch, waiting for nightfall to change out the guard at the meetinghouse. Father was still flush from the sun and Nathaniel nearly fell asleep in his gruel. The babe had slept for most of the forenoon and now it fussed, demanding Mother's attentions. It was only in the clearing away of supper that the consequence of the captain's absence registered in my thoughts.

He had naught to eat. And none to bring him anything.

A glance out the door told me that night was almost come. I took several thick biscuits that had been put aside for the morrow and set upon each a nice portion of cheese. Wrapping them in a napkin, I slipped the bundle beneath my apron and moved to step out the door.

"Where do you go?" Mary's voice was accusing, as if I were leaving my responsibilities for pleasures.

I inclined my head toward the privy. "If I do not get there soon, then you will know." It was not a lie. Least not a real one. I would visit the privy that night. Eventually.

Her shadow waved me away.

I moved in haste. It was not unseemly what I was doing. Not exactly. But I would not wish to explain it to any passing by. They might think something . . . different. They might not understand.

I gained my destination in time to see the group of men part, a pair in each direction. It appeared to me that the captain and John Prescotte started off together. I stood, hidden in the darkening shadow of the building, and reconsidered.

For certain John Prescotte would not understand my actions. But how could a man be expected to keep watch for a night with nothing in his stomach to sustain him? John's own mother would never let him stand watch without first feeding him like a prized pig.

I trailed them, perhaps too closely for my own good, unwilling to leave myself a lone target for any savage. John broke away first, disappearing into the wood.

The captain kept on, walking some distance until he too hid himself between the trees. And I was not quick enough to track him.

I stepped from meadow into forest. Stood for a moment, listening, hoping to be given some clue to the captain's position. There was no sound save for crickets and the low hooting of an owl. A dainty shivering of leaves as a breeze passed somewhere above my head.

"Captain Holcombe?"

The darkness around me went silent.

9

"OVER HERE."

What sweet relief to hear his words! I turned in the direction of his voice and began to walk. Soon I perceived him in the gloom. But then I blinked and realized I had offered my purloined food to a squirrel.

"If he does not want it, may I have it?"

I turned toward the sound of his voice and extended my offering.

He took it from me, spread the napkin on the log beside him, and ate in silence. Then he withdrew a flask from his doublet and held it to his lips, drinking with great gulps.

"Do you think . . . are we safe?" Though the meadow was lit by stars, darkness had fallen in the wood, and I could see little within the shelter of the trees.

"Safe as a babe in a cradle. I have not heard nor seen anything this day."

"At all?"

"Not one thing."

I wished that I had not been so hasty in bringing the captain his supper. Wished I had not brought him supper at all. I sent a glance into the wood. "Well . . . I will leave you, then."

"Wait a moment, and I will send you back with the cloth." He wiped his mouth upon it and folded it. "How is it that a woman such as yourself was sent to bring me food? Why not your brother?"

"Because he is foolhardy and prone to shrink at shadows." And besides, no one knew that I had come.

"Many thanks. The young John Prescotte sits watch just the other side of me."

"I did not know it." Why did the captain's presence always seem to provoke me to lie? If souls are judged by their fruit, then surely he was a devil.

"Go over to him. Make him feel better about the scandalous wink I gave you earlier."

"There shall be no more talk of winks between us."

"Go on. 'Tis a night for courting. A waxing moon. No savages on the prowl."

" 'Tis also a night for ruining reputations. And I will not squander mine." I had done enough damage to it already. I reached out to retrieve the cloth from his hand. It should have been an easy task, but he held on to his end.

"You cannot tell me you are so virtuous a woman as that."

"I am."

"When your beloved sits just there, in the shadow of the night? Alone?"

"What would you have me do?"

"Bestow one kiss upon the poor boy, at least. Perhaps two."

Kiss him? I only wished to marry him, not entice him to seduction like some immoral woman. "And distract him from the watch?"

He considered me for a long moment. "I will tell you a secret. From here I can watch both his position and my own. Go on." He said it as if he were doing me some great favor.

His words made me feel very young. And they raised up an obstinate spirit within me. "I do not wish to."

His sigh sounded of exasperation. "I will tell no one."

" 'Tis not that you will tell or not. 'Tis simply that it must not be done."

"Do you love the boy or not?"

"Lust is better left unprovoked until the marriage bed."

"Have you never kissed him?"

I could not lie again. "Nay."

"And he has never tried to kiss you?"

"Truly, I must decline to—"

"Were you mine, I would be well familiar with your sweet ways by now."

I did not like what he was insinuating. And the thought of it, of him, sent a not unpleasant sensation through my belly, as if I were sliding into some deliciously cool stream. Why should the thought of kissing the captain provoke such a feeling when the thought of kissing John provided no reaction at all? He was a devil indeed! I gave one last rather violent tug on the cloth.

He let go, and I fell sprawling onto my backside in the brush.

"Oh, pity! Here." He extended a hand to help me.

"Captain Holcombe?" The voice was followed by a snapping of twigs and limbs.

Frustration and resentment vied for control of the captain's face.

"Captain?" The voice was louder. I could identify it now as John's.

"Oh, for—!" He let go my hand and stood with indecision for a moment. And then he pressed me to the ground, throwing his cloak over me. Scrambling to sit beside me, he propped an elbow between my ribs, leaning against me as if I might have been a log.

"Ow! Could you—"

"If you do not want that boy to accuse you of something worse than consorting with the likes of me, be still!" he hissed.

"Captain Holcombe?" John asked.

"Aye, lad."

"Is all . . . are you all right?"

"Aye."

"I heard a great rustling . . ."

An elbow ground down into my rib. "Just . . . uh . . . stepped upon something, lad."

"Can you watch from there?"

"What's that?"

"Do you not have trouble seeing from there?"

"Oh. Aye. Well. We must attend to the . . . necessary every now and then, must we not?"

I drove a fist into the small of the captain's back. He grunted in response.

"Pardon me? Was there something else, Captain?" John's voice was tentative.

"Uh . . . aye. Aye, there was." He settled against me as if he meant to enjoy himself. "You are a man unmarried. If you were courting a girl, would you not wish to take advantage of a night such as this?"

"Advantage? How so?"

"If I were such a young man as you, I would . . . well . . . I mean . . . with the moonlight and a girl close at hand . . . I suppose I might want to kiss her."

"You would?"

"Why? Would you not?"

"Of course not."

"Nay?"

"Nay."

"Come on, lad. Man to man. Of course you would."

"Of course I would not. There will be . . . would be . . . enough time after marriage to undertake all of that."

"*All of that.* You make it sound like work. Not one little kiss? To know what to look forward to?"

"Nay."

He wouldn't? Not even one?

"Oh. Well." The captain slumped against me as if his argument had been exhausted.

I pushed back.

"Was there nothing else, Captain?"

"Hmm? Oh. And also, I had a wish to test you."

"Test me?"

"Aye. Had a savage truly crept up on me, were we truly wrestling upon the ground, no good would have come of announcing your presence. And were there other savages about, surely you would be dead by now."

"Oh. So . . . I failed, then."

"Aye. In more ways than one. Now, back to your post. Better luck next time. Off you go. Step sharp!"

There was more rustling and snapping of limbs as John retreated.

"Boy walks with all the grace of a blind ox."

Boy? He addressed John as if he himself were so very old, but the captain was of an age with Simeon Wright. And John was as much a man as they! I sat up and shoved at him to do the same.

"You can thank me later."

"For tumbling me into the brush and then grinding your elbow into my ribs?"

"Hush. I would hate to have him return, in silence this time, and find you here with me. How would you ever explain yourself? Do you not find it curious that he mentioned no intentions toward you?"

"I do not. 'Tis none of your business."

"I am a man unmarried. Of course it is my business." The captain shrugged, made as if to speak, then shrugged again instead. "Well . . . have you your cloth?"

"What? You were going to speak."

His lips pursed, his eyes narrowed, but he shook his head. "I do not wish to say."

"What is it?"

He opened his mouth, glanced at me, and then closed it. "Nay."

"Tell it to me this minute or I shall scream."

" 'Tis simply, my dear, that you deserve better."

"Nay, I do—" I halted, realizing he nearly had me disagree with

73

him, telling him that I did not deserve better. But then, I did not agree with him. John Prescotte was good enough. Was better. Was fine. He was better than fine! I gathered my thoughts. "I do not agree with you."

He pulled me up. And then he stepped close. "You deserve someone who would want to kiss you given even the very slightest of opportunities."

I could not think of anything to say to him. My ears had gone thick with a curious buzz, so I turned my back to him and left. Took two steps before I realized I had started off in the wrong direction. Turned once more and walked past that man and headed home.

But as I walked, I turned John's words over in my mind. Although we had both said the same thing in reply to the captain's baiting, there was a very great difference between not wanting to kiss your intended and knowing that your intended did not wish to kiss you. God curse the man for putting a question mark into my head where none had the right to be!

But as soon as I had thought it, I knew that I had sinned. No man deserved to be cursed. And so, as I walked along, I prayed.

"Dear God, please forgive me. A man such as the captain, controlled by carnal lust, though he chose his words deliberately for the purpose of teasing and baiting, and though he sees chastity as no virtue . . . though he mocks our ways at every possibility and turns every good thought into a jest . . ."

Was it even possible for God to save such a man?

"Though his time with us is short, may he see his errors and revel in your grace and become a convert to your truth."

Even though he lies incessantly.

"May it be done through your wisdom and according to your mercy. May I see him on the far side of eternity, a redeemed soul."

Though you would not make me speak to him, God, would you?

"Amen."

Would you?

10

THOMAS RETURNED FROM THE watch at the rising of the sun.

I was ready for him, pulling his doublet from his shoulders and offering him a jug of water with which to wash his face. The biscuits I placed before him were enriched with a precious handful of wheat flour, and the cheese I offered was the creamiest that was left us.

He followed the food with a cup of cider. And then he stood and took his doublet from the peg where I had hung it.

"Can you not take even a small rest?"

He turned round and looked at me, his face without any expression, red-rimmed eyes looking into mine. Smudges pressed into the space beneath his eyes made his skin seem even paler. "Nay. But thank you for thinking of me."

I blushed, for I *had* thought of him.

One corner of his mouth lifted in an attempt at a smile, and then he was gone. Out the door and to the smithery.

Aye, I had thought of him. And worse, I had shown it.

The captain came back the next morning as Nathaniel and Father were headed out. Mother placed his food before him as Mary and I began our labors. I endeavored to ignore him as we prepared for the day's task: cheese making. I poured a quantity of milk into a kettle, Mary added some rennet to it, and together we hung it above the fire.

As we worked we stepped around several tool handles that Father had placed in the ashes to season. Had that been the only thing he had subjected them to, none of us would have minded. But he had soaked them first in manure for a full two weeks before he had brought them in to Mother. And manure smoked just as well as wood. Maybe better. Worse. Mother had muttered at her work throughout the whole of the day that he had laid them down.

Once the milk and rennet began to bubble, it was Mother's task to watch it work. And it was our task to begin the preparations for dinner. By the time we sat to eat, the whey had been set aside for use on the morrow and the cheese wrapped in dry cloths.

Supper was nearly upon us when I went outside to get some firewood. The captain surprised me with his presence near the fence. "Would you wish to walk?"

I eyed the garden before us, looking for some task that needed to be done, but I could see none. Mary and I had worked too hard at weeding that forenoon. "Why?" The thought of his comments the previous night still had the power to pink my cheeks when I remembered them. Not that I had very often. Nor failed to follow them quickly with some thought of John.

"For the pleasure of another's company on a pleasant summer's evening."

Surely he must be jesting. "There is more than walking that needs be done this day!"

"And I am sure that with your industry, you shall accomplish it. But why not take two minutes to accompany me? To walk beside me. To appreciate the beauty in the evening that lays itself before us."

"It can be appreciated from inside the house with a ladle in my hand as well as here, idling with you."

"Must you always be so busy?"

"Have you not heard that idle hands are the devil's workshop?"

He reached up a finger to scratch behind his ear. "I seem to recall being told the same. By a knobbly-headed Puritan with a great air of nothing better to do than to find fault with me. And if I recall correctly, he was doing naught himself. Just as you are now. So why not walk a turn with me . . . since you seem to be doing nothing at all in any case?"

I did not know whether to be galled that he had called us Puritans knobbly-headed or to be shamed that he had discovered me to be absent some useful activity.

He took several steps away from me toward the hill.

I followed him so that I could speak to him . . . once I had determined what it was I wished to say. "We have not, all of us, knobbly heads!"

"Nay. I spoke a mistruth. Some of you are roundheaded and blockheaded as well. Come. Perhaps you misread my intentions. I do not wish to accost you. I simply wish to come to know you better."

"Know me?"

"Aye."

"Know what?"

"From where have you come—"

"Boston."

"And where are you going?"

"To gather firewood. Now, if you will excuse me."

"Why can you not be restful? And where are your manners? Do you not wish to know more of me?"

He seemed so certain that he was a fascination that for an instant I longed to tell him that I did not. But it would have been a lie. And so I said nothing.

77

"Where I am from, for instance? Do you not wish to know that?"

"Where are you from, then?"

"Gloucester. And you do not have to ask so meanly."

"I do not have to ask at all."

"Is there nothing more you wish to know of me?"

Aye. There was. I wished to know how he could laugh so easily when life was so difficult. How he could be so confident when all was so uncertain. And most of all, I wished to know . . . everything. Everything about who he was and why. But I could ask him none of those things. And so I asked him something else instead.

"You are a soldier for long?"

"Aye. Too long." My question must have disappointed him, for he turned from me. But then, just as quickly, he turned back. "You know, you do not have to live like these people."

Like *these* people? *These people* were me! "How else would you have me live?"

"Less . . . gravely. Can you never be restful?"

"I can. As I occupy my hands with a task, then my mind can dwell on other things."

"Such as?"

"Such as . . . God's great love and His benefits. His care for me and all of His children."

"Do your thoughts never go to such things as the setting sun or an evening's first star?" He swept his arm forward toward the valley.

As I followed his gesture, I gasped at the beauty of what lay before me. The sky glinted as if dipped in gilt. "I have never seen such a sight." I was always too busy with preparations for supper.

"I thought not. Or you would not have protested so greatly."

I tore my eyes from the sun's setting to fix them upon his own. Fascinating. They had gone purple in the shadow of the evening. I blinked. And then I remembered who I was and what I was about. "I have dawdled long enough."

"Nay. I daresay you do not dawdle enough."

Was he daft as well as vain? "We must none of us waste anything that God, in His goodness, has granted us. One day we shall have to stand before Him and account for it all."

"Really? You believe that? That God is some glorified clerk, tracking all the minutes of one's day? As if He has nothing better to do?"

"You say He does not care what we do with our time?"

"I say I hope I do the things that please Him most, but I can count on the fact that I will fail to. Most abysmally at times."

"Which means you must simply try all the more to please Him."

"Nay. It simply means that I rejoice all the more in His grace, knowing how truly wretched I am. Do you not believe in grace? Is that why you must work so hard?"

"Aye. Nay. Of course I believe in God's grace. But we must none of us rely upon it."

"Why? Because God is not trustworthy?"

"You twist my words to make them mean things I did not say!"

"I make them mean exactly what you say. You seem as if you know the right answers, but I ask you, Susannah Phillips: Do you know the right questions?" His eyes softened, changing from purple to periwinkle. "Do you not think that my time here and your time now is being put to good use?"

He seemed to almost pity me. I had liked it better when he had professed an interest in me. He wanted my own words? Well then, he would have them! "I cannot think how it could be, seeing that we do nothing but engage in idle chatter."

"There is no finer moment in life than one spent speaking to a beautiful girl on a beautiful night. You cannot tell me that even here, right now, God does not instruct me on the goodness of His grace and His benefits. 'Tis here, at this moment, that I know He truly cares for me."

"And how do you know it?"

His teeth flashed in the gloaming. "If He did not care for me,

He would not have sent me here. And, I daresay, did He not care for you—"

"No matter what you think of our customs, Captain, you still do not know how many days you have left on this earth. I should think you would care more for tending to your soul than coaxing a smile from me."

"But who is to say that coaxing a smile from you would not be the chiefest end and greatest glory of all my days?"

"You will not have it this night."

"Pity. Then I suppose that I shall have to live one day more."

I turned from him, marched toward home, and picked out my firewood. But just before entering the house, I turned my face toward the sunset and savored its last lingering traces.

The next morning, in a change from our normal tasks, Mother set Mary to the making of our biscuits.

"But why cannot Susannah—"

"Because Susannah knows very well how to do this. And if I read the signs correctly, she may soon be leaving us."

I blushed.

Mary frowned.

"So tell me, if you please, what is the first consideration?"

Mary and I grimaced at each other and answered in unison. "Always set aside some of the mother dough for future use."

Mother beamed. "Such good girls, I have."

Mary measured out a portion of the mother dough and put it back into its crock. Mother and I watched as she added flour and water to the dough that remained on the board in front of her. Kneading it with awkward movements, she pushed at it, folded it in upon itself, and then turned it.

Mother intervened, showed her how to do it more ably. "One and push. Two and fold. Three and turn. 'Tis a dance of your hands with the dough. And if you do not lead out, the dough knows not what to do."

As Mary worked, Mother watched her with ill-concealed apprehension. " 'Tis my pride and joy, that mother dough. From my own family back as far as can be remembered. From my mother and my mother's mother. And her mother before her. And her mother before her. To think that I join my hands with theirs whenever I make biscuits. . . ." She turned to me, her eyes both bright and sad. "When you are married, I will give some of it to you, joining your own hands to mine . . . and then you shall pass it to your own daughter." She shook her head as she swiped at the corner of her eye with the edge of her apron. "A sentimental fool is what I am."

"And you've the best biscuits in town." Mary's dough was growing glossy, and she pushed her words out to the rhythm of her kneading.

"The best we've ever tasted." I could match Mary's pride with my own.

Mother smiled and let go of her apron. If the sin of vanity could ever be found in her, it would be linked to the pride she took in her biscuits.

Later, as I turned a pot over the biscuits for baking, the fire flared, sending out sparks of copper and gold, in precisely the same shades that had laced the sunset the evening before.

The captain thought I knew all the right answers but not the right questions? Who was he to judge? He was a stranger forced upon us who would soon be leaving. What did he care about who I was or what I thought?

I was Susannah Phillips, aged twenty years, soon to be betrothed to John Prescotte, an able and honorable man. I could see no questions there.

Least none worth asking.

❧

I heard Thomas's axe ring out just as I finished shaping my biscuits. After scraping dough from my hands, I stepped outside.

Swiping at flies from the chickens' coop, I walked around the back of the house toward the smithery.

Thomas had stripped to his shirt and was chopping at the woodpile.

I knew a moment's regret for causing him undue work. He might have ordered his logs from Simeon Wright and avoided some of the chopping of it . . . and all of the hauling. Indeed, he had spoken to the man about it, but the price that had been quoted was much too high. Thomas had called it extortion. Though I had agreed with him, I begged him not to bring it to the attention of the town's deputy. The less notice Simeon Wright took of me . . . of us . . . the better.

And so, Thomas had acquiesced.

But if the need for chopping wood were my fault, then at least I could help him with it.

As he took a pause to wipe his brow with the forearm of his shirt, I handed him a cup of ale. After he handed it back to me, I placed it on the stump before him and bent to collect an armful of wood.

"Do not bother yourself with that."

"You bothered yourself with me. 'Tis the least that I can do."

He moved and bent to squat across from me, taking one of my hands in his. " 'Tis that what you think of yourself? A bother?"

I pulled it free and added another length of wood to my pile.

"You will ruin your hands with splinters."

"And why should I save them?"

"Because they are beautiful."

Beautiful? My hands? I nearly smiled. Wanted suddenly to laugh outright. My hands were work-scarred. My palms calloused from carrying heavy pots and pans. My forehands scarred from encounters with the pressing iron. My knuckles reddened and raw from the lye soap I used for washing.

He placed a hand on top of my pile, to stay me from rising.

"They are." He reached out to touch the back of one of my hands. "Your fingers are so . . . slender. Hands so neat . . ." He was looking at them as if he wanted to kiss them. But he did not. He raised his eyes and caught me looking at him. "Thank you for using them, for putting them to work on my behalf. Both inside the house and out."

My eyes darted toward the ground. I knew not what to say.

At length, he withdrew his hand and rose. Took another gulp of ale.

I added one last piece of wood to my pile and went to stack it next to the smithery.

When Thomas had completed his work and I had finished helping him, I returned to the house. Taking some unguent from a pot in the cupboard, I rubbed it into the calluses of my palms. Placed some on the cracks of my knuckles and around the dried edges of my nails.

My hands. Beautiful. Imagine that.

11

AS JUNE TURNED INTO July, the men's labors turned to the harvesting of hay. Town ordinance decreed that it be brought in no later than the tenth of the month. But thickening skies and the threat of rain ordered it be harvested as soon as was possible. A frenzied labor by all in town over the course of several days led to a speedy harvest. And as the last sheaf was placed atop the stack and the roof lowered upon it, thunder rumbled in the distance and lightning split the sky.

It was with thankful hearts we came that night to supper. And with hungry stomachs we devoured the food. None spoke until the meal was finished. And even then, it was the captain who broke the silence.

"What is it you people hope to do here?"

Father answered as if he were asked such questions every day. "Live as God commanded."

"Aye. 'Tis that which I've been told over and over and over again. But to what end?"

"To make here a new Zion. To live as a City on a Hill to which all may come and know of God's great love."

"Even the savage?"

"Certainly the savage."

"Even though he skulks in the wood and wishes you harm?"

" 'Tis expected when a man has not had his heart renewed. He is less than he might be. As are all of us. But he is a man. Like you. Like me. He wants only a reformed heart."

"And then what?"

"And then what . . . what?"

"And then what would he do? Once his heart is reformed?"

"Live in harmony with his fellow man. Leave behind his heathen ways. He would do what we all must: work for the glory of God." Father said it as a pronouncement. A conclusion to a matter, and it was taken as such. At least by me. And Mother and Mary and Nathaniel.

But the captain would not let the matter expire. "Has there been much success? In converting the savage?"

"Some."

"Perhaps more would present themselves if there were some merriment. Some laughter in this City on a Hill."

"Small is the gate and narrow is the path, Captain." Though Mother's words were pointed, she said them with a smile.

"Aye, Goody Phillips. 'Tis well known, that. But I must say that your City on a Hill will find itself bereft of citizens if there is no happiness, if no gaiety can be had within its walls."

"There is a time for laughter—"

"Aye. After all the work is done and all the labor finished. In the moment between wakefulness and sleep once one is abed. 'Tis well and good to be about work and to do it earnestly, but is it not said that the master himself took a rest from His labors? Even He feasted."

"Aye, He feasted, but it was as He was about His business, Captain. 'Twas always holy work that He was about. And we have our feast days. And corn huskings and stump pullings."

The captain threw up his hands. Pulled his pipe from a pocket. Then he rose and walked to the door. "I surrender. Even your merrymaking is couched in work. You have worn me out with all the talk of your labors. Farewell. Work well. For I am certain you will do nothing else this night!"

He probably never heard it, poor man, over the noisome rains, but we burst into laughter—all of us, Father included—once the captain had taken himself outside to smoke his pipe.

The next morning after breakfast, Father and Nathaniel went to Thomas Smyth to see about some tools. Mary and I began on the morning's tasks. As I was kneading dough, the door flew open and Nathaniel came in at a run. "Savages! The savages have come!" He dove underneath our bed, pulled out the drum, and disappeared through the door before we could react.

He must have started drumming as he ran, for that ominous, imperative beat was heard scant seconds later.

"To the garrison house!" Mother swept up the child with one hand and grabbed Mary's arm with the other.

"But the—"

"To Wright's hill. Now!"

But the fires and the mending and the dough! And what about a blanket for the babe and food for the rest of us? And the Bible and . . . and the captain's pipe? I could not save everything from the savages, but I could take one thing. I grabbed the pipe from the mantel, concealed it within my skirts and then ran out the door.

Mother and Mary had already taken to the road along with the portion of the town that was to rally at Wright's hill. I raced to catch up with them. And then, together, we sped up the hill, passing those less agile or more aged. The door to the Wrights' was already open by the time we reached it. Several others had gained that fortress before us, but the rest were behind us. We were thrust through a small sitting room and into the kitchen and we did not stop until we reached the back wall. Once there, we had need to push back against the crowds that were pressing in upon us.

The Wrights' servants worked to close up the shutters. The men

among us in the garrison took up their muskets and pounded up
the stairs to the second story.

The child started to cry and that set all the other babes in that
place to crying. Mother tried to soothe him, but we soon realized
that pleas were useless. The babe had soiled itself.

"And me without any clouts! You did not think to bring any,
Susannah?"

She had said it with such hope, but I could only disappoint her.
"I did not think to grab any." In truth, I had scarcely thought at all.
Not of clouts. I clasped my hand tighter about the pipe, unwilling
that she should see it. Unwilling that she should discover how truly
thoughtless I had been.

"But did you put out the fires?"

"There was not time!"

The same conversation was being repeated between mother
and daughter all around the room. And now, everyone strained for
a sniff of outside air, hoping that the scent of woodsmoke would not
soon be curling from the roofs of houses caught fire. To our terror of
savages, fear of being rendered homeless had just been added.

In that crowded, dark place, we stood straining for some news,
some indication of attack. Some gasped as the logs in the fireplace
crackled. Others jumped as the men on the floor above us began
to pace.

We knew that Nathaniel had taken refuge at the meetinghouse.
'Twas where he had run with his drum. Father did not appear among
us, so I could only assume that he had gone there as well. Mother
seemed confident of both our safekeeping and theirs, although she
kept glancing toward the sitting room. My own gaze kept sliding
in that direction too, but mine was in search of the captain. What
if he had been discovered on his watch? What if the savages had
already taken him?

Simeon Wright was among us and he was captain of the guard,
at least until the king's man had come. But his presence did little
to put my fears to rest.

Goody Baxter, Abigail's mother, found us and stayed for some moments to talk. Before she left to return to her own family across the room, she squeezed my arm and leaned close to whisper in my ear. "I have seen you glancing toward the door. Do not worry. The Prescottes have probably taken refuge in the meetinghouse. 'Tis closer."

The Prescottes? But why would . . . John! I had not thought to think of him before that moment. My cheeks flushed with shame. My first thought ought to have been of him, but it had not. My first thought, my only thought, had been of the captain. And his pipe.

Some goodwife I would be!

I vowed that my thoughts would not be far from John for the rest of the day. And, indeed, I whispered a prayer on his behalf. And that of his family. If his father's house was burnt, then John's attentions would have to go to rebuilding his family's home, rather than ours. And who knew, then, when he would find the time to wed?

After several hours the children began to grow restless. Mischief began to break out among siblings. And then it seemed that all of them became hungry at once. Mother left the child with Mary and me as she moved to help Mistress Wright at the fires.

At length, a blessing was pronounced, we were bid to sit, and food was passed round the room. Dinner came from several buckets filled with dried blueberries from which everyone took a handful. And another filled with biscuits, one for each family with the promise of more to be provided later.

With their hunger sated, many of the smallest fell asleep. Without any apparent threat, without any sightings of savages, a festive air began to prevail. Mary slipped away after the babe fell asleep in my arms. I watched her wend her way through the crowds to talk to her friends. With the child breathing heavy and with the air growing stuffy and stale, I must confess that I, too, fell into a sleep.

❧

Being confined to the meetinghouse during an Indian attack was even worse than being confined there of a Sabbath. The windows had been shuttered, the door secured. There was little space to be had and no air. I tucked myself into a corner and made myself as small as possible. Even so, it did not stop sweat from damping the back of my neck nor dripping down the front of my shift. But at least I was not at Wright's hill. I would fain discover myself in the middle of a band of savages than to find myself locked up there.

The babes might have been crying, the children working all kinds of mischief, but for the captain. He had tasks for all to do. While the men kept watch, muskets at the ready, the women were intent upon making food for dinner. Without the convenience of a fireplace, the meal was compiled from all any had thought to bring. The boys were set to work dividing up gunpowder and counting out musket balls; the younger girls were put in charge of the babes. Though the mood was grave, there was no panic and little anxiety.

❧

I woke with the echo of a strangled snore sounding in my ears. My strangled snore. From my position on the floor, I scanned the crowd for Mary, hoping that she would soon return to relieve me. I could not see her for several moments, but then back in the corner the door to the Wrights' lean-to opened. Mary's head appeared, her gaze darting round the crowded room. There was something furtive in her look.

I kept myself still, wanting to see more than to be seen.

She emerged from the doorway, cheeks in high color, her coif riding far back on her head. She nodded to Goody Metcalf as she pulled the door shut, then stopped to talk to one of her friends. Eventually, she worked her way round to us. I began to stretch out my arms to give her the child but stopped. "Your shift."

"What of it?"

"The strings."

She looked down and saw what I had seen. Her strings had come undone. She shrugged and then took up the ends and tied them off in loops.

"You ought to be more careful." I gestured her to lean down and took hold of the edge of her coif, pulling it forward.

She looked at me then with the most uncommon stare. I might have called it brazen. Her gaze wandered to the lean-to door, and as it did, the door opened once more. Simeon Wright stepped through it and headed up the stairs to the floor above us.

Simeon Wright? Had he . . . and she . . . ?

I turned to find Mary watching him and it seemed to me that there was a sort of hunger in her stare.

It was not long after that we heard the sound of a musket's report. And then a second and a third. There was a moment when the room went completely and utterly silent, and then the children began to wail and the mothers began to hush them. The rest of us waited. And prayed.

After those first three shots, there were no others. No shouts from outside, no exclamations from inside. There was simply . . . nothing. Hours followed. Hours of straining to hear something, anything, in that near silence.

Eventually word got round that it was Simeon Wright who had begun the fusillade. He had spied a savage creeping up the hill and had killed him.

Supper was long in coming and when it did, it was pottage eaten from the kettle and the biscuits that had been promised earlier. Mothers bedded down their infants afterward and curled up on the floor beside them. I passed the night in uneasy sleep, waking often to the sound of restless shifting all around me. And once in a while to the scuff of boots upon the boards above my head.

The next morning a knock pounded upon the door. "Open up! 'Tis Captain Holcombe! 'Tis safe. There are no more savages."

Praise God! It was a thought echoed by all in that place.

I cannot say that I was sorry to depart the Wrights' house. Grand though it was, I would happily leave it for another goodwife to possess. With no occupation, save waiting, and nothing to do but wake and sleep, I might have soon gone mad. And there was a feeling about the place, a sort of moroseness that did not rest easy within me.

Though Mary dragged her heels, we left among the first, before the savage's body could be hauled from the path. We had to step around him as we walked down the hill. His flesh was bared, though his waist and loins were wrapped in some sort of animal skin. It could be seen quite plain that a hole had been drilled through his heart. But he had no weapon, save an axe.

'Twas that axe upon which the captain was gazing as he knelt beside the body. "Why do you suppose he brought an axe to an attack?"

His question was put to no person in particular, but it seemed to me a daft one. " 'Tis lethal in the way of weapons."

"For a tree, perhaps. But not for a person. 'Tis gruesome work to hack a body to its death. And dangerous."

"Perhaps an axe was all he had. 'Tis forbidden to sell them muskets."

"Aye. But . . . he was just one? Alone?"

I shrugged. "The only one killed."

" 'Tis strange . . ."

As the captain stood, I cast one last glance at the Indian. His unseeing eyes gazed at the rising sun with such peace. It was hard to find anything disturbing about him . . . save the thought that his fellows might, even now, be lurking in the wood.

I was grateful to spy our home in the distance, still standing. Through some deft maneuvering, I succeeded in slipping the captain's pipe from my skirts and replacing it upon the mantel without his notice. But that evening as I passed him on my way to the necessary, he paused in his smoking and raised it by way of a salute. "My thanks."

I nodded and continued on my way before he could say anything more.

91

As we walked the road from the meetinghouse to the smithery, Thomas was told it was Simeon Wright who had prevented the Indians' attack. It was his shot that had broken their courage and sent them fleeing through the wood. Though I did not think much more about it, Thomas came into supper that night with thoughts to spare.

"I might have thought with all of us in garrison they would have tried to burn the town."

I was used to Thomas's strange ideas. His long hours at the forge gave him plenty of time to think. Burn the town? That would have required some work and many torches.

"We might have at least been looted."

'Twas strange now that he brought it to mind. I nodded. I had eyed the houses as we had passed by that morning. Nothing had seemed out of place.

" 'Tis odd."

We ate in silence for a while, but then he spoke again. " 'Tis odd, too, that the savage was not armed."

"He had an axe." 'Tis what had been reported.

"Aye. An axe. Not a hatchet. So what then had he meant to do?"

Who could know the mind of a savage? "Chop down all our trees?"

Thomas smiled. "I wish he would have. With no access to the common, he might have done us all a favor."

12

ONCE OUR NERVES HAD settled from the savages' aborted attack, all thoughts turned to flax, from which we made our linen. After Father and Nathaniel had pulled up the plants, bound them together, and whipped off the seeds, 'twas Mary and me who loaded them onto the oxcart and took them to the brook for retting.

After binding several bundles together, we slipped off our shoes, raised our skirts, tucked them into our waistbands, and then waded into the stream. On the far side, we submerged the bundles in the calmer waters.

Some in town retted their flax in one of the nearby ponds, but though it took longer to ret flax in moving water, Mother insisted the result smelled fresher and stayed cleaner. Mary and I gave no protest. The air under the tree-shaded brook was refreshingly cool. And so, after submerging each bundle, we lingered in the stream, letting the water run through our toes and over our feet. But though the respite was pleasant, I could not let us long remain idle. Not when there was so much work to be done.

"We should go back."

Mary only looked at me. And then she closed her eyes and

tilted her head back, the sun-dappled shadows making freckles on her face. "You first."

I gave her arm a gentle shove.

She shoved me back. Harder. But in doing so, she lost her balance, swaying on her feet for a moment. As she swayed, her hat fell from her head. "Look what you made me—"

I did not stay to listen. Her hat was already being carried away by the water. I lunged for it, but it had gained a swifter current and moved out just beyond my reach.

Behind me, I could hear Mary sloshing about in an attempt to join me. I held out a hand, which she soon joined with her own. Two were better than one when it came to both gaining and keeping a balance, and so together we started off to fetch the hat.

"Faster, Mary!"

"My skirt is drooping."

"Then fasten it!"

She dropped my hand for a moment to hike her skirts up higher, to tuck them more tightly into her waistband. By the time she had finished, the hat was disappearing round a bend in the stream.

She surged forward, yanking on my hand.

"I do not know if we should—"

She tugged me along, despite my words. "That old ox wouldn't move if you lit a fire beneath its tail."

" 'Tisn't that. 'Tis the savages . . . we've ventured beyond where we ought."

"And if we happen upon an Indian, I have no wish for him to see me unhatted. Hurry!"

She seemed to be putting much more emphasis on her looks of late. I was not sure I liked it. But I gave up my qualms and resolved to follow her.

As we splashed around the curve in the stream we saw the hat, stuck upon a stick, several paces farther down the stream. 'Twas Mary who recovered it. She shook it free from water droplets and placed it on her head. But then she paused. She took it off and plunged it into the brook, lifting it out, crown half filled with water. And then with a quick motion, she clapped it onto her head. She gasped as the water rushed down from the crown over her ears and forehead and down her back.

But she looked so refreshed and the stream running over my feet was so cooling that I did the same.

We stood there for some while, gasping and giggling, water making trails down our backs and fronts. And then, emboldened by our folly, we moved to the edge of the stream, grasped the slim trunks of saplings to pull ourselves up, and sat on its edge.

"We should go back." I felt the call of duty.

" 'Tis what you said that started us on this chase."

"Nay. 'Tis you who shoved at me which started us off."

"And only because you pushed me first."

"I tapped at you."

"You *pushed* at me."

"But not with any mischief in mind."

As we had been talking, I had kept one ear listening to the wood. And now I realized with a flush of dread that I heard nothing. Not one bitter with its calls for plum pudding, not one creak of a tree, and not one hush of the wind blowing through the woods' leaves. It was strange. Unnatural. As if everything was holding its breath. As if one hundred pairs of eyes were watching us.

And then I heard the snap of a twig.

We both heard it. Could not help it as it had the sound of a gunshot.

Mary grabbed at my arm.

We shared a look.

Then we clutched hands, jumped straight back into the water, and started to run toward the other bank.

But midway in flight I paused. What was to say that whatever it was I felt watching us was not on this side of the river instead of the side where we had sat? Or, perhaps, on both?

I leaned away from the bank ahead of us.

Mary bent toward it.

Like a coil stretched too far, we came back together again. But without stability, without balance, and with much fear. We wobbled first one way, then another, and finally fell onto our bottoms in the stream.

And behind us rose the most unexpected sound of laughter.

I turned, expecting to find a savage partaking in unholy glee, but discovered the captain instead, bent over, hands at his knees, laughing at us.

Mary pushed up from the brook and stomped over to him. "Some fine savage you turned out to be!"

"You thought me a savage? Is that why you leapt from the bank? I simply wished to join you, but you jumped up like partridges. I have never seen two people move so quickly in my life!" He paused in his mirth to wipe tears from his eyes.

Rage fired the words that burst from my tongue. " 'Tis fine and good for you to laugh while we're the ones paying for your slyness. You might have hailed us!"

"Oh, come now. Let me help you out." He straightened and offered me his hand.

"Nay."

"Come. You'll catch your death."

Mary marched past me and grabbed the hand he offered, but instead of using it to climb out of the water, with a quick tug she pulled him right in with us.

I only wished I had been the one to think of it.

"You nearly scared the life from us!"

"And my getting my boots wet will atone for it?"

Mary stood there, hand upon a hip, glaring at him. " 'Tis a start."

They exchanged glares for several moments, and then Mary whipped her hat from her head, scooped a portion of the stream into it, and dashed it into the captain's face.

He blinked while rivulets of water ran down his beard. And then he took the hat from his own head and bent to do the same.

Mary was forewarned and stepped back in the time it took him to arm his weapon.

Unfortunately, two of his steps were the same as four of hers, and in a moment's time Mary shrieked and bent, outraged and sopping, to fill her hat once more.

They kept at each other for several minutes, and then, just as I had determined to leave them behind and return to the cart alone, the both of them turned on me and dragged me into their fight. Mary held my arms while the captain poured the contents of his considerably large hat upon me.

And spluttering, dripping, I tore my hat from my own head and bent to do the same.

But by the time I had done it they had both, laughing and gasping, turned from me and started upstream. And so I was left by myself, drenched and muttering, following their backs all the way to where we had first set out the flax for retting.

I climbed out of the stream, skirts fast about my legs, refusing any offer of help from that man. I could not think where to place my hands, whether I should use them to block the view of my legs or my chest or some other part of my body now outlined with wet, clinging garments.

"Oh, do not be such a goose. You'll dry."

I did not bother to honor him with a glance.

"Mary, is your sister always so proper?"

She turned to him with a saucy glance. "Only with men so dark and handsome as yourself."

I stiffened in outrage, forgetting to hide myself.

His teeth flashed white against his browned skin. "Dark and handsome? Is that what she says about me?" He turned from Mary to me, a question etched between his brows. But before I could think how to answer, he took his sopping hat from his head, swept it toward the ground, and bowed. "Do not be offended. I shall take myself off. Good day to you, Mistress Phillips."

I would have liked to have kicked out at him and his fancy hat, but I would only have succeeded in tripping myself up in my skirts. And given my sister a story to tell to the townspeople. So I settled for turning my back on him and busying myself with the ox instead.

Mary joined me at the ox's head and together we pulled him into a walk. "If that captain were one of us, I would marry him in a minute."

"You wouldn't!"

"And why wouldn't I?"

"Because he is arrogant and glib and . . . and *rude*."

"But he's so strapping and brawny and merry."

"Merry? What does being merry have to do with being godly or kind or good?"

"He is those things, all of them." She smiled as she slid a glance at me beneath her lashes. "But he is also so much more! Would it not be something to be the wife of such a man?"

"But . . . but . . . merry? You would pledge yourself to a man for laughter? Laughter does not place food on a table. Laughter does not bring any money into a household. And laughter cannot mend a fence or build a barn."

"Aye. But what kind of a home would that be without it? And what do you plan to do with John after you finish feeding him and cleaning his house and mending his shirts? I fear, Susannah, that you might actually have to talk to the man."

"Of course I would talk to him. Don't be foolish."

" 'Tis not me, I think, who is playing the fool."

She dropped back behind the cart, plucking at the grasses as she walked. And so I continued on, trying to put her idle thoughts behind me.

Halfway to the fields, we began to think the better of displaying ourselves. Our skirts had not dried as quickly as we had hoped.

And our waistcoats, instead of hiding our womanly curves, seemed to emphasize them all the more.

"If we stop by home, just to change clothes . . ." I was trying to calculate whether the extra trip would be noticed by Father.

"But Mother would see us."

" 'Tis better than Father," I reasoned.

"And Nathaniel."

Agreed in purpose, we turned the ox toward home instead. But almost wished we had not once Mother saw us.

"And look at the two of you! Daughters of scandal, that's what you are!"

"We were retting the flax and—"

She held up a hand. "I do not wish to hear it. Change your clothes and return to helping your father and brother. One would almost think you had decided to shirk your responsibilities and go bathing on a hot day."

We dared not look at each other for fear all would be lost. And so we changed in silence, and it was only once we were away from the house that we finally looked toward each other and burst into laughter.

 **13**

AS THE DAYS OF July grew hotter, so did Thomas's work. In anticipation of the end of the retting of flax, he began to prepare scores of pins and nails in the smallest of sizes for hackles, on which the fibers would be combed in preparation for the spinning wheel.

The ring of his hammer on iron and the hiss of hot metal kissing water were constant as he drew the nails out to a taper and then upset them to form a head. At the end of a day's work, I stood with him in the smithery sorting the nails into piles according to their sizes and then counting them. Nails were gold. The most tedious of a blacksmith's labors, they yielded the greatest return. Only two houses in the town had been built with iron nails. Thomas's and Simeon Wright's. The rest were held together with wooden pegs.

It was during such a sorting and counting that a woman hailed the smithery and then stepped inside. Susannah Phillips had come to Thomas bearing several hackles.

"Good day, Susannah Phillips."

"Good day, Thomas Smyth. I've come to you about our hackles."

Thomas reached and took them from her, and then turned the

boards first this way and then that, holding them up to the forge's fire for light.

He looked first at the board having both the smallest and the most pins driven into it. "I cannot straighten these. They will break in the doing. But I can replace them."

She frowned. " 'Tis what Mother said, but I know that she had hoped . . ."

Thomas put the first board aside and took up the second. If the first had eighty pins the inch driven into it, the second had eight. "These others here, I can pull out and then straighten."

She let out her breath in a huff. "Then what else can be done? Please do with them as you must. When shall I retrieve them?"

"On the morrow if you wish."

She moved as if to turn, but then she stopped. "Please give my best to your wife."

Thomas looked at me then, confusion drawing his eyebrows together.

I did not speak, did not move.

"She is right here. And has been all this time."

"Where . . . ?"

Thomas put out his hand and plucked the arm of my waistcoat. "Just here."

She looked toward me then, and still it took her a moment to register my presence. "Oh. Well. Greetings, Goody Smyth."

I nodded.

As she left, Thomas stared after her in wonder. "She must be going blind."

I shrugged. I was used to it. Depended upon it. Poor Thomas, it was only he who saw aright.

⁓

By the time our flax had been retted, beaten, and scutched, the scorching days of July had drawn to a close. The morning of the last day of the month, Mother sent me to the miller with a portion of

newly harvested grain. Upon arriving, I joined the tail of a long line
of women. We waited, all of us, for the first fruits of the harvest to
be milled. But we did not wait silently.

"They say there's a new milliner come to Newham."

"From England?"

"From Boston. But she gets her goods direct from London."

From Boston! I still considered Boston my home. I had been
born there, had lived my life there, had in fact left half of my heart
there when we had moved. But I knew, even after all of this time,
that it was safe in my grandfather's keeping.

Three years it had been since I had last seen my mother's father.
And in all that time, no one had ever called me Susannah in quite
the same way, or listened to me with such gravity, or bothered to
read the Bible to me in Latin just so I could hear how it sounded.
He was a minister and often about God's work, but he seemed to
have all the time in the world for me.

Not unlike the captain.

In fact, strange as it might seem, I suspected that should provi-
dence ever give them an opportunity to meet, they would find
much to admire in each other. I heard myself sigh. I missed my
grandfather. I let my thoughts drift toward Boston as conversations
swirled about me.

"My girl says there's apples ripening in the wood."

"And what would she be doing in the wood with savages lurking about?"

" 'Twas that captain who told her."

"I hear Goody Metcalf is with child."

"So soon after her wedding?"

"No sooner than is proper."

"And when will you be wed, Susannah Phillips?"

All eyes turned toward me, and caught mooning, I could do
naught but blush and sputter.

" 'Tis not a fair question." God bless Goody Blake! "Is it not for
the man to do the asking and the deciding?"

"But come now, Susannah, there are ways to hurry a man along. . . ."

Somewhere, one of the women hooted. Were it possible, my cheeks grew even more red.

" 'And now, my daughter, fear not. . . .' " The quavering voice that spoke the words paused for a moment, then began again. " 'I will do to thee all that thou requires: for all the city of my people doth know that thou art a virtuous woman.' "

In front of me, the women stood on the tips of their toes, straining to see who it was that spoke. And then, as one, they fell back from the line, revealing Mistress Wright. She was standing there, frail and hunched, and she was looking straight at me.

" 'A virtuous woman is a crown to her husband: but she that maketh ashamed is as rottenness in his bones.' " She stood still as a stone for one long moment, watching me, and then she collected her sack, left the line, and walked slowly toward her home.

It was some time before anyone dared to break the silence. But even then, no one said anything else to me about John Prescotte.

Those heat-soaked days of August soon gave way to the more moderate temperatures of September. The captain still left every morning on his watch. The men still stood double watches with double men, but there had been no other signs of savages since the attack. And so we were able to put to the side that threat, for a far greater danger had been loosed upon us. The pigeons had come to nest.

They came by the thousands, winging overhead hour after hour. And after they had come, they settled in the wood. It seemed a benign invasion, but then they began to litter the ground with their droppings. So great was their output that it seemed an early frost had come. So many were their numbers that several trees broke from their weight. And then finally, nests built and wood occupied, they turned their attentions to our crops. And that we could not abide.

At church the following Sabbath a day was chosen on which the town would launch an assault upon their number.

On that morning Father and Nathaniel left the house, clubs in hand. Mary and I trailed them, taking a half dozen sacks and our own clubs with us. They went to trap a single bird; Mary and I went in hopes of clubbing its brothers.

Pairs of men and boys spread through the wood looking for a bird to snatch. Some, like Father, did it by launching a net over a nest. Others did it with persuasion, by laying out a line of grain and enticing the creatures down from their nests.

Once Nathaniel had clambered up a tree and brought down a bird, Father took a needle to hand in order to sew its eyes shut. But once needle had pierced skin, the creature shrieked and beat its wings in panic.

Nathaniel clutched the bird tighter.

Muttering, Father finished the job. And then he fastened the bird to a platform by its feet. "You can let him go."

Nathaniel dropped his hands as the bird's wings beat a tattoo against the air.

Father looked round at Mary and me. "Grab your clubs and hold yourselves still."

We did, all of us, until at length the birds began to stir from their nests, to rid their wings of sleep and take to the air. At that moment, Father raised the platform up above his head and then dipped it down toward the ground. Upon the going down, the pigeon fluttered its wings, looking for all the world as if it were coming to rest.

Seeing one of their own flapping toward the ground, the group of pigeons decided that he knew something they did not. And, as a group, they dove and joined him, settling themselves down upon the ground. And it was at that point the slaughter began.

'Twas not difficult in the way of sport. The birds followed each other as a group. Too late they learned of their folly. They were easily entrapped by a net thrown over them and then just as easily felled by the blow of a club. From that first group alone we must, all of us, have bagged a dozen or more birds.

After a long morning's work, we returned home for dinner. Mother met us in the yard, hefted the bags from our hands, and placed them beside the door. "They'll rest there well enough until we've readied for them."

We had turned to go inside when Nathaniel spied a woman hurrying in our direction. We waited until she made her approach.

It was Mistress Wright, Simeon's mother, come over to offer us her bag of birds. "From Simeon, my son."

Mother smiled. "We have some bags already."

"And we have five. Loaves and fishes. Feed the masses."

As Mother did not move to take it from her, she pressed it into my hands.

I could do nothing other than take it. As I did, I saw that Simeon Wright was watching us from the road. And so I tried to smile in his direction.

I handed the bag to Mother, and she placed it with our own. After dinner Father hauled a board from his shop and set it upon two trestles. Mother doled out the sacks, one for Mary and me, another for herself. Then she turned her pigeons out upon the board and began plucking the feathers from them. "Such small birds to cause such devastation."

"If only the trapped bird could warn them off." It seemed a piteous end to a creature so sleek and soft. Even if they did try to eat our grain.

Mother snorted. "And a good thing that it cannot."

"They can see the slaughter, but they follow one another to it anyway. Why can they not see they have judged incorrectly?"

She shrugged. "Because the scene is so deceptive. They cannot fathom that things are not what they seem."

" 'Tis pitiable."

Mother bid me back to work with her nod.

She finished her sacks and Mary and I finished ours soon after. That left only the sack from Mistress Wright.

Mother clucked over it as she lugged it to the board. "As if we did not have enough of them already." Mother frowned. And then she shook her head. "The poor woman. She never has been quite right. But at least her nonsense is from God's Holy Word." She threw the sack up on the board and then took it by the bottom corners and dumped it. A dozen birds fell out, but they were strange in the way of pigeons. They had been clubbed so hard that they were, all of them, rendered nearly flat.

Mother looked at them askance. "I do not know what I should use these for. There seems to be hardly anything left of them!"

In the end, we could think of naught to do but bury them. And I wondered what Mistress Wright, in her fine house on Wright's hill, had done with all of hers.

14

IN THE COMING DAYS, Mary and I worked with Mother to dry and pickle food for the winter. As I walked about on errands here or there, I could see the men tying shocks of Indian corn together. They would winter there, those shocks, like companions in arms, autumn mists swirling around them, winter snows drifting down upon them. And they would emerge, in spring, wizened old men.

It gladdened me to ponder the coming spring. To think of all the celebrations it might yield. A new marriage . . . and even, perhaps, the possibility of a babe growing in some secret place within me. Chased about town by an autumn breeze, I both savored the coming months and worried over them. If John Prescotte did not soon do his asking, then I might be doomed to spend another year as a maid.

And so, the weeks of September came and went. And with them, my dimming hopes of marriage.

One morning Mother put a tray of biscuits on the table before us, cast a glance to see that we all had what was needed, and then sat in her place on the bench. "Can you spare me Nathaniel?"

Father grunted.

" 'Tis a good day to go a-leafing."

"A better one would be some day in the next week. He's to be helping me turn spoons in the shop."

The captain was looking with some interest between the two of them. "Of what do you speak? And where is it to be done?"

Mother turned her attentions from Father toward the captain. "The leafing? Why, it must be done in the wood. Where there are oak trees. 'Tis children's work. They collect them in the common."

He was already shaking his head. "Not this year. Not with savages about."

"Then you'll be arguing with all the goodwives in this town."

A shadow of a doubt passed over his face. A chink in the mien of his normal confidence. "Perhaps, if they were accompanied. And stayed closer to town."

"Aye. Perhaps. Though you'd have to do a bit of persuading to make it so."

The captain tore a piece off from his biscuit. "Perhaps the Indians will quiet for the winter. Is it not a thing that can be delayed until then?"

"Not if you want to keep eating those biscuits. 'Tis those leaves they will be baked upon. And my supply has dwindled. At an alarming rate."

He looked down, with apparent regret, at the portion of biscuit that remained. Then he looked up, acquiescence written in the sag of his shoulders. "I will see what can be done."

That Sabbath, he stood before us all in church. "There will be one day on which the community will go a-leafing. Myself and John Prescotte will take the children into the wood—"

Simeon Wright shot to his feet like a spark. " 'Tis folly! They must not go to the common! 'Tis too far, the threat of savages too great. I must protest this dangerous scheme . . . for the sake of our youth."

The captain was watching the man with seeming curiosity.

"Aye. I agree with Mister Wright. And the children will not go

108

to the common. I have located a grove of oaks much closer to town, and 'tis from there the harvest of leaves will be gathered. But just on this one day. I cannot guarantee any person's safety who wanders the wood alone. We leave at first light and will return as soon thereafter as possible. Perhaps the millwright would like to come with us. For purposes of protection."

Despite appearing an advocate for the children's safety, Simeon Wright looked very much as if he would like to forego that pleasure. But after looking round at the gathered townspeople, he agreed.

Beside me, Mother muttered. And beside her, Goody Ellys did as well.

As we walked the road toward home, Mother took my arm and pulled me close. "You're to go a-leafing with that captain and make sure he does not hurry the children needlessly. There are leaves to be gathered and the harvest must be done in full or there will not be enough to last. He might know this if he had any sense, but I doubt he ate a decent meal in his life until he came here."

The morning of the leaf harvest I kicked at Nathaniel to push him from bed.

"Why do you hurry so?"

"If we do not meet the group at the meetinghouse, we will not be allowed to go."

"I know plenty of oaks in the wood. We can go where we want."

" 'Tis not safe and you know it. Get your lazy bones from bed!"

He sat up, then thrust his arms into the air in a leisurely stretch just to vex me. I thrust out a finger and poked it between his ribs in response.

"Susannah? Mary! Be up and about before the captain returns." Since the captain had come to stay with us, our mornings had begun somewhat earlier than before, did we wish to avoid his presence while we dressed.

At least he took his time outside. He claimed to be looking for signs of savages. I do not know what he expected to see each morning.

I wondered if he weren't a bit disappointed each day to see smoke curling out of our neighbors' chimneys in the way it always had. They were annoying, these Indians, even in their apparent indifference. Surely if we had not seen them since the attack, the threat could be said to have diminished.

I stood beside Nathaniel as Mary swung her legs over the edge of the bed. We took our clothes from their pegs, pulled up our hose and tied them on, stepped into our petticoats and then our skirts, hers a watchet blue, mine a murrey red. We re-tied the strings of our shifts and donned our matching russet-colored waistcoats. I was just fastening the last of my buttons when the captain stepped in through the door. I took Mary by the hand and pulled her into the parlor so we could pin up our hair in privacy.

"Why the hurry? I wager—"

"Wager!" No one in our town, no one in the colony, had any right to gamble.

Mary rolled her eyes. "All right. Fine. I . . . *imagine* that he's seen a head of hairs uncovered before. Or several."

"It makes no difference. He is a man."

"Though not one of ours. So 'tis not as if he would decry our virtues."

That such words would come from my sister's mouth! " 'Tis not about him. 'Tis about us. And how we might be modest." Though now I wondered. Had he? Had he seen a woman's head uncovered? When? And whose was it?

I stared at nothing for some moments before clearing my head with a shake. I was wasting my time on debased thoughts. Time which had been gifted me from God. I chose to direct my thoughts instead toward higher places. Toward how very low I had fallen. Had not once nakedness been our glory? But with Adam's fall, it had turned to shame. I thought on how very good God was to appoint creatures to aid us in covering ourselves. On how in clothing myself, I covered my shame. . . .

I did not know when she had left me, but Mary was nowhere to be seen in the parlor and everywhere to be heard in the kitchen. And so I had allowed my thoughts, as pure as they might have been, to overtake my responsibilities. Responsibilities which were, in themselves, a form of worship. Why did righteousness have to entail such work? And why was it I always failed when I tried to be good?

It was going to be a long day, indeed.

"Are you ready, then?" The captain took his musket to hand and waited for Nathaniel and me. As my brother went to walk out the door, laden with sacks, the captain held him back with a hand. Leaned his head out and looked round. Then he stepped to the side of the door and motioned us to follow. " 'Tis safe. There are no savages about."

We walked, the captain and Nathaniel together, me slightly behind.

The captain looked over his shoulder to speak to me. "How much time will the children want?"

"They are to take as long as they need."

"For being under threat of Indian attack, you people seem to take your safety quite lightly."

"Whether you choose to believe it or not, our time is in God's hands. 'Tis He who will determine the length of our days."

He had slowed in his walk so that Nathaniel was now ahead of him and 'twas me he walked beside. "And never have I doubted that. But 'tis I who will keep you alive while He does the deciding. Is one hour long enough?"

I stopped in my steps. "One hour? For each family in town to gather enough leaves for each day's baking?"

"Two?"

"The work will take as long as it takes."

His mouth turned grim and his grip tightened on his musket.

We met John Prescotte and Simeon Wright at the meetinghouse, and all of the children with them. Several of the goodwives, women like Small-hope who had no children, or those with children too small to be of use, like Abigail, were also in attendance.

I approached my friend with hands stretched toward her child, determined to put past offenses behind me. I missed Abigail and was saddened that the sweet friendship of our youth had altered in the wake of her marriage . . . and my continued maidenhood. I prayed it would not remain so.

"Do you want me to hold him for you? To free your hands for your sacks?"

She smiled. "Many thanks." She looked round at the crowd. "I see John Prescotte goes with us."

I did not say anything but could not keep a blush from spreading across my cheeks.

"Is it only the children he wishes to keep an eye on?"

I shrugged. "And how would I know?"

"I have the feeling—"

Her words were interrupted by the approach of Simeon Wright. He nodded to me, lips curving into a smile. "Have no fear of savages this day, Susannah Phillips. I will be watching you closely."

Abigail looked up sharp at his words.

Watching me closely? I hoped not. At least not too closely. I wanted to exchange a few words with John if the moment presented itself.

Simeon moved off and Abigail stepped closer. "Perhaps Simeon Wright has an eye on you as well."

"Simeon Wright? I cannot think so. He has his eye on every girl."

"But actually speaks to very few."

"Then I shall let some other girl have him."

"Will you, now?" There was a queer note to her words. But as I tried to discern the nature of it, the captain shouted for everyone's attention.

Susannah Phillips could not know the depth of jealousy hidden inside her friend . . . if friend, Abigail Clarke could still be called. A jealous woman could do much harm and no good. 'Twas what a suitor for my father's hand had taught me. She had seen how reviled I was of my father, how he shamed me, and instead of rescuing me, she abandoned me. Bereft of her attentions, she had left me in worse straits than before. Beware the reach of a jealous woman. Her suspicions, though rarely justified, are never satisfied.

The captain shouted for our attention, and now all had gone still.

"There is no one—not one woman, not one child—to be wandering about the wood. If you cannot see me, you have wandered too far. You must gather all the leaves you can as quickly as you are able. If you see a savage, you are to send up a shout. At a shout from any person, all women and children are to rally to John Prescotte."

John looked surprised and pleased at those words.

" 'Tis Simeon Wright and myself who will defend you." Any pleasure John Prescotte had taken in those first words was dissolved by those following. Poor boy. 'Twas not that he was incapable. Nor that he was incompetent. It was simply that he had not had a chance yet to prove himself a man. He was tied to his father's estate. But the loyalty of a woman like Susannah Phillips could do much to aid him there.

Looking at Simeon Wright studying her, I wished—and not for the first time—that Susannah and John were already married. He was a strong lad and a good one, but too untested to understand the danger that lay before him.

If they did not marry soon, I feared they would not marry at all.

15

WE WALKED, ALL OF us, into the wood. The captain at the lead, Simeon Wright at the end, and John Prescotte in the middle. Next to me. "Good day, John Prescotte."

"Good day, Susannah Phillips."

"Do you—"

"Would you—"

John laughed. "You first."

I shifted Abigail's babe away from us to my other hip so that I could speak to him more easily. "How is your father's health?"

" 'Tis . . . not what we had hoped for."

Oh.

"But I am convinced that he shall soon regain his strength."

Then he had more confidence than I.

Around us, the children scampered up and over a rocky rise.

John climbed a few steps, sliding a bit on fallen leaves, then turned and offered me his hand. I took it, noticing its strength and its warmth. But when the climb was over, I let it go. We walked on together into the wood, John, the babe, and I. I could not help but hope that John was right—that next year, the scene would be real, and John and I might be joined by our own babe. That the next time I went a-leafing, it would be for baking biscuits at my own hearth.

Once we arrived at the captain's grove, he stood in the middle of it and put the children to work picking up leaves. It was easy work and the leaves, still glossy brown, slipped underfoot, but this year there was no singing and little talking. The children picked, but as they did, they looked round the wood with wide eyes. Their actions were hasty, flustered, and most of them pulled twigs and other debris into their bags along with the leaves.

"You do us a disservice."

The captain turned his head toward me, though he kept his glance trained on the wood before us. "How so?"

"There will be twice as much work to do once the children are home. They are putting every kind of thing into their sacks just to get the task done. They go about it with no discernment, no skill."

He grabbed me by the elbow and turned us both around, eyes sweeping the wood that had formerly been behind us. "I should think I am doing you a favor. Such sorting would be better accomplished in the safety of a home rather than the treachery of the wood."

"Have you seen something, then?"

"Just because I see nothing does not mean something is not there. And make no mistake: there is something."

"But—"

"I do not yet know what it is. But have no fear. God brought me here for you; of that I have no doubt. And if ever I cannot protect you, He will."

A blush stained my cheeks before I could remind myself that by *me*, he meant *we*. Us. All of us in Stoneybrooke. And the curious thing is that I had known no fear until he had mentioned reason to have it, but even as a terror rose up inside of me it vanished, leaving only the warmth of certain surety behind.

"You would do better to transfer your attentions to the children. To help them fill their sacks so we might leave more quickly."

His words had an air of gravity that his demeanor usually belied.

I scanned the group for Abigail. When I located her, I set her child at her feet.

"Wait—why—?"

"The captain wishes to return us all to safety. Sooner rather than later."

"But—"

"I shall return for the babe once I have helped some of the younger children."

I moved away from her protests even as I wondered at her persistence. Surely she could not deny the younger ones the benefit of my help? Locating the slowest among them, I helped to fill first one sack and then two. Filling the third led me a bit farther away from the center of the grove. And filling the fourth led me farther still.

"Come away here. There are plenty of leaves just there past the gully."

I started at Simeon Wright's voice so close to my shoulder. "There are plenty here." Or there had been.

"Too few to bother with. I have just come from the gully. The place is littered with them."

I looked back over my shoulder and could barely see the captain through the brush. " 'Tis too far."

" 'Tisn't far at all. I am going even if you are not."

"But you're to be one of the watch."

"I am watching. And I will do it from over there." His eyes, a chilling blue, bored into mine. Then, suddenly, he smiled. And I could see, for a moment, why the girls in town admired him so. It was breathtaking, that smile. "I would never let anything happen to you."

The words were right, but the tone was wrong. He said them not with chivalry, but rather as if he owned me. As if I were some coveted possession.

He took a step toward me.

And there was something in the way he did it that made me take a step back.

116

He reached out and took hold of my arm, but he did it rather familiarly and much too tightly.

I tried to free myself from his grasp. "If you would—"

"Susannah?" It was John.

Anger flared in Simeon Wright's eyes, sending ice into my veins. As he released me, he turned to speak to John. "We had just realized that we had come too far. I was trying to get Susannah to turn back."

❧

As Susannah and John moved away from Simeon Wright, I breathed deep in relief. I had been standing against a tree, unseen, unnoticed. Had Simeon managed to move her down into the gully, I do not know what I would have done.

Screamed to bring the captain running? Run to get the captain myself? But for what? To bring shame down upon Susannah's head for allowing herself to be caught in an indiscretion? In what I assumed would have been an indiscretion.

I do not know what I would have done.

Prayed, surely.

I slumped against the tree, weak with relief. But a small movement in the brush caught my eye.

❧

"Susannah? I do not mean to doubt you, but—" John's words were overcome by a scream.

We stood, staring at each other for one short moment, and then he grabbed my hand and ran with me toward the grove. I am sure his thoughts were the same as mine: Savages!

Simeon Wright wasted no time in passing us, musket gripped between his hands.

As soon as we reached the grove, John moved to gather the children. I set myself to work in aiding him. The captain motioned

Simeon to stand watch over all of us as he moved off to squelch the screaming.

It was coming from Abigail, and she would not be quieted.

The captain grabbed at her elbow and pulled her to her feet. "Speak, woman!"

" 'Tis my babe—my babe is gone!" She clawed at his hand, trying to free herself from his grasp.

"Shut your mouth or you will bring the savages down upon us all!"

"My babe—"

The captain dragged Abigail toward Simeon and thrust her into his hands. "Keep them safe. I shall go look for the child. Where was it last seen?"

My friend held up a trembling finger. Pointed to the spot where she had been gathering leaves. "Just there."

As the captain disappeared into the wood, all my feelings of security and safety went with him. Though I longed for nothing so much as to be where he was, I went to Simeon and took Abigail's hand in my own. "Perhaps I could . . . ?"

He nodded and pushed her toward me.

I took her within the crook of my arm and turned her away from the direction the captain had gone. Her hand was sodden and clammy. It turned within mine as if searching for something more substantial to cling to. "He was there . . . and then he wasn't. How could he . . . how could . . ."

I did not dare to utter the only word that made any sense. How could it be anything other than savages?

John came then, musket in his hands, to stand beside Simeon. I saw him mouth the same word I was thinking.

Simeon scowled and shook his head.

I only wished the captain would return. Then I might begin, once more, to feel safe.

John ushered the children toward Simeon and took up a position in front of them, Simeon guarding them from the rear. The oldest

COVENANT ENTERPRISES

| 06/09/10 | 11:56 | F | 5 | 9245 |

8@ 2.00 ROBES	$	16.00
SUBTOTAL	$	16.00
SALES TAX @ 6.000%	$	0.96
TOTAL	$	16.96
TENDER Cash	$	20.00
CHANGE	$	3.04

946-8800 TOLL FREE:800 678-1346

COVENANT ENTERPRISES

| 06/09/10 | 12:00 | F | 5 | 9246 |

COVENANT ENTERPRISES

COVENANT ENTERPRISES
08/09/10   12:00   F   3   9248

children stood, faces pale, eyes looking every which way. The youngest began to sniffle. At that sound, the few women among us took the youngest ones and placed them behind their skirts.

I turned my attention back to Abigail. "Why did you not leave the child with your mother?"

"But why would I? Because I cannot be trusted to look after him myself?"

"Nay! I only meant—"

"Why should I not be able to gather my leaves and keep the child as well? Do I not keep just as fine a house as before I had him? Is our food not as well prepared? Our affairs as well managed?"

Though I knew for a fact that they were not, I tried to soothe her. "I did not mean to say—"

"I can do it. I can do everything. Why does everyone think that I cannot?"

" 'Tis no shame to ask for help, Abigail."

"Why should I have any need for help? I am a good wife."

"Of course you are."

The defiance in her face crumbled, and her chin began to quiver. "Then why does it always feel as if I am not?" She let go my hand and slipped from my embrace to her knees. She lowered her head toward the ground and began to pray.

And as she did, I prayed my own prayers. If anyone could understand how she felt, it was I. I thought back through the years of our friendship. Years of shared hopes and dreams. Years of shared love and laughter. She was a year older than I, and so I had lived and learned of life while watching her. We had both set out to become good women, good wives, and she had achieved both ends. At least, I thought she had. She had become everything I hoped to emulate. We shared both a past and a future. But if Abigail, my friend and example in all things, should feel so inept, so wretched, so despicable, how could there be any hope at all for me?

16

LIKE JOHN AND ABIGAIL and Simeon, I, too, heard the scream. But that movement in the brush gave me pause. Was it . . . could it be . . . ?

Using trees to shield myself, I crept as close as I dared.

And then one last step closer.

It was then the thing saw me. He grinned a big toothless grin gone black with dirt and leaves that he had shoved into his mouth. And then he burbled.

"And to think I thought you a savage!" I nearly laughed at my own fancies.

The mite stretched out an arm toward my face.

"How did you get here?" I put out a hand and touched his own.

He clasped on to it and then pulled into a sit and, from there, gained his feet.

"Did you walk?"

The child bent and picked up an acorn. Put it to its mouth.

"Nay. You will not like it."

He spat the thing out and screwed up his face.

"See? 'Tis nastiness, just as I told you."

He dropped my finger and took a few tottering steps before falling back onto his bottom and then pouncing forward into a surprisingly fast crawl.

I lunged at his trailing leading strings to halt his escape. "Your mother must be missing you by now."

He stopped at that thought. Sat upon his bum and put two fingers into his mouth. "Mam, mam."

"Aye. Let's go find your mam-mam, shall we?" I picked him up.

He put a hand to my collar and clutched at it, smearing it with dirt.

I leaned down to kiss its pudgy cheek.

"Mam, mam."

"Nay. I am not your mam." I was no child's mam. Perhaps would never be.

As I held him close, I chose a careful path over roots and around bushes. But in the going, I came to discern the approach of a sharp snapping and cracking of twigs. Placing a hand over the child's mouth, I paused, both to determine what it was and to look for some place to hide. 'Twas only Captain Holcombe who came into view, a knife clutched in his hand.

"You found him, then!"

"The babe? I did not know it had been missed."

"Then you are the only one not to have heard his mother screaming."

" 'Twas Abigail?"

"The same."

"Then she must be frightened."

"As are we all. With savages about." The captain made a quick search of the area before gesturing me to lead out the way he had come.

As we broke out into the grove, I spied Abigail Clarke and started her direction.

She was kneeling upon the ground, rocking forward and backward, hands clasped beneath her chin, eyes closed, lips moving.

I had almost reached her when her eyes sprung open. She fixed them fast upon me and then let out a shriek. Scrambling to her knees, she launched herself at me and wrested her child from my arms.

" 'Twas you who stole my child?" Her voice rose to a precarious pitch.

"I did nothing—"

"Why would you do it?" She had sheltered the head of the babe within her arm but he beat at her in protest.

"I did not—"

She glanced around wildly, then locked her gaze on the captain. "She stole my babe!"

"She did nothing of the—"

"Why would you do it? Because you have none of your own?"

The captain had reached her, grabbed hold of her shoulders, and shook her. "Cease your accusations!"

"She stole my babe."

"She did nothing of the sort."

"Then where was he found?"

The captain looked toward me.

I could do naught but answer. "In the wood. Toward the gully."

"Liar! How could he get there? He cannot walk."

"But he can." Perhaps not very far, but he could crawl like a serpent.

"He cannot!" Abigail set the babe on the ground and pushed him off her leg with a foot when he would try to cling to her.

He swayed once, twice, then landed upon his bottom and collapsed in a fit of tears.

"Look there! He cannot stand. You lie!"

I moved to pick the child up and give it comfort.

His mother intercepted me. "Do you dare?" She held out a quaking finger to stay me. "I know about you. I know everything. Henry told me about . . . about your *father* . . . all about how he—"

The captain stepped between us, his back toward me. "There is no need to be ungracious. The woman found the babe and was on her way to return it when I happened upon them. No one has done you wrong."

Abigail stepped around the captain and fixed her eyes upon me. "Stay away from my child!"

The captain bent to pluck the bawling babe from the ground, thrusting it into Abigail's hands. "Then take care of him yourself!" He stood for a moment, weight shifting from foot to foot, then turned toward Susannah Phillips. "And you—take care of her!"

❧

Putting a hand to Abigail's shoulder, I guided her to the shade of a tree and bid her sit. And she did for some time, babe clutched to her chest. But then, once he had wriggled and fussed and cried, she released him from her lap. From there, he crawled out past her feet and over to a bush. Quite quickly.

"The babe is fine."

"No thanks to her."

"Perhaps it was as the captain said. Perhaps she meant to return him."

"You do not know her, or you would not think it."

Together, we watched the child. He grabbed a stick, patted it upon his thighs. Let it drop. Clasped the limber trunk of a bush. Pushed to his knees. Wobbled there a moment before gaining his feet. He chortled, triumphant as he took several steps. Then he dropped to his knees and shot away in a crawl.

"The little—!" Abigail flew into the wood after it and soon reappeared, child toddling along at her side.

"It appears that he can walk. So you were wrong, then."

She settled herself back on the ground. "About what?"

"About Small-hope."

123

"Her? Nay. She is not one to be trusted. 'Tis true, all those things Henry told me."

What things Henry had told her I did not know, but I did not like her insinuations. Pushing to my feet, I looked round to find Small-hope, but she had disappeared.

❧

As quick as I could, I filled up my sack with leaves and then fell back into the wood and went home. Only the captain noticed my leaving.

"Hey there! 'Tis not safe. Wait for the rest of us. 'Twill not be much longer."

I shook my head.

He stepped closer. "She did not mean it."

Aye, but she had. She did. I turned away and he let me go. As I set my feet to walking, I put my thoughts into motion. There was only one way Abigail's Henry could have learned of my past. Only one way word of my shame might have reached him, and it was through the one person in Stoneybrooke who knew me.

Through Thomas.

As the wood crackled and snapped beneath my feet, as I put distance between the leafing party and myself, I flung away my fear of savages. What could they possibly do to me that had not already been done? My shame turned to anger. My anger to rage. As Thomas's house came into view, I wanted nothing more than to scream. To lash out and beat upon him, the person responsible for perpetuating my shame. But when I saw him, I could not think what to say. And so I just stood there in the door to the smithery, sacks fisted between my hands.

Thomas paused in his work, looking up toward me with soot-rimmed eyes. "What is it?"

"How could you?"

He glanced from me toward a twisted mass of iron meant to hold a taper and smiled. "I know. 'Tis not a candlestick such as I would have made, but 'twas Goody Metcalf who ordered it done." He shrugged and bent to his task once more. "What else am I to do?"

"How could you tell Henry Clarke of my . . . my father . . . and—"

His head came up sharp at mention of that name. "Henry Clarke? Why would I tell him anything at all?"

"But—Abigail knew. She said she knew everything. She mentioned my father and . . ."

He left his tongs in the fire, something I had never seen him do, and came around to stand before me, to reach out a soot-blackened finger and turn my face up toward his. "I have never said one word about you to anyone. Ever."

His words were no surprise. They fit everything I knew to be true about him. The one thing I could not understand is why I wanted so much to believe them. "But . . ."

"Am I the only tradesman from Stoneybrooke to visit your old town of a month? It is not as you imagine, Small-hope. You were never unseen."

Nay. His words were true. I guessed that I was not.

I had never been unseen.

But if I had been seen, then why had I not been helped? The answer was too evident. I had not been helped because I had also been despised.

And, therefore, all too easily ignored.

❧

As Mother cleared supper from the table that evening, she placed a hand to the captain's shoulder as she leaned forward. "I thank you for allowing the children to gather leaves this day."

The captain glanced at me.

I looked away.

"I still think it a foolish idea."

"No matter. There was no harm done, now, was there?"

"A child disappeared. We assumed it to be Indians."

Mother's head snapped from the food to him.

"He had simply wandered."

"Whose child?" She frowned as if she wanted to berate its mother.

"Abigail . . ." The captain looked to me to supply the knowledge he lacked.

"Clarke's."

"Abigail Clarke's?" Mother shook her head. "Why did she bring the child with her when she could have left him at her mother's instead? What happened?"

It was the captain who answered her question. "He had wandered into the wood. 'Twas the sharp eye of Goody Smyth who found him."

Mother nodded and went back round the other side of the table and sat down upon the bench with some satisfaction.

"But if it had been savages? It happened all too easily and no one noticed." The captain had no need to labor to make his point. "It could have been all of our heads. In an instant."

"Thank our God that it was not." Father had pronounced his benediction. "So have you trained the militia to your tastes, Captain?"

"Nearly."

"Then you will be leaving us soon."

Leaving? But it seemed as if he had just arrived. And what was it he had been saying in the wood? About being here for me? For us?

His eyes never ventured from my father's. "Aye. Though 'tis a pleasant place, Stoneybrooke."

" 'Tis pleasant enough. For us."

" 'Tis Virginia for the likes of me. I only wish I had been able to spy one of those Indians that run so rampant through this wood. One who was alive." He collected his pipe and tobacco from the mantel, shook some tobacco into the bowl, tamped it down, and took a light from the fire.

He stepped to the door, intending no doubt to smoke outside.

Mother reached out a hand to stop him. "You can smoke in here. No sense in making yourself a target for the savages."

He must have had no idea of the favor she had granted him, for he smiled as if her words were in jest. "I have no doubt that I will be as safe as a Frenchman at His Majesty's court." He bowed. "But thank you just the same."

Father's words halted his steps. "So you have come to believe as we do?"

The captain pulled the pipe from his lips. "I have ever believed thus. I may not think of God the same as you, but that does not mean I think of Him any less."

Father frowned. "Bold words . . . for a king's man. But what I meant to say is that you have come to believe as we do about the threat? That our times are in God's hands?"

"I already know of my end. It has been decreed from the beginning. Do you not know what our savior said? All they that take the sword shall perish by the sword." He smiled then, but it was a smile without mirth. "You cannot blame a man for trying to delay a destiny such as mine a while longer." He clamped his pipe between his lips and let himself out the door.

And I do not know but that a sword pierced my own heart at his words.

17

I AWOKE TO HEAR a scrabbling near the fireplace. Parting the curtains, I saw my mother kneeling before the hearth, tapping at the cinders with a stick. As I perceived a change in the tone of the stick upon the stones of the hearth, she pounced with a pair of tongs, pulling first one of my father's handles and then another from their beds of ashes.

My father appeared beside her, scratching first his head and then his belly. "I thought they had two more weeks. . . ."

"You placed them here on the first day of July and 'tis today that they are seasoned." Holding the tongs well before her, she stepped outside.

My father trailed her to the door. "Are you certain? Because I thought—"

She must have deposited them somewhere, for when she entered, they did not come with her.

Mary and I rousted Nathaniel from bed and raced to pull on our clothes.

After a breakfast of cheese and porridge, Father and Nathaniel went out to the shop.

The captain took his musket to hand and began to rummage through his bag.

Mother raised her head from her mending. "I'm of a mind to have Mary read a bit of Sibbes to us as we work."

Mary? Mary was always given the easy work!

"Captain? Before you leave us, could you get *The Bruised Reed* there, just above your head?"

The captain looked up from his bag and pushed to his feet. Standing in front of the shelf, he cocked his head first this way and then that. He put his finger to the spine of one book, and then let it trail to the base of another.

I glanced at Mother. She frowned and nodded toward the captain.

I went to stand beside him. Cleared my throat when he took no notice of me.

"Oh. I beg your pardon."

"If I might just . . . ?" I reached up toward the volume.

He moved his hand at just the same time and it came to rest upon mine, his fingers curling in upon my palm. "Ah. The Sibbes. Of course."

His touch was both hot and tender. I withdrew my hand.

He took the book from the shelf and handed it to me. He left soon after, and we did not see him until supper. Afterward, before taking to bed, I went to do the necessary. As I walked back toward the house, I found him leaning against the wall, face lit by the glow of his pipe.

"Good night, Susannah Phillips."

"Good night, Captain."

I moved to open the door, but I could not do it. I had to speak to him about what I had been thinking all day. "I could teach you to read."

He nodded. Exhaled. "I know how to read. Perhaps not with as much ease as you, but I can do it when I must."

"To read with ease, you must read at length."

"And 'tis that which I lack. The time."

"But how can you hope to gain knowledge of God's Word if you do not read it?"

"I am certain that He is God enough to tell me what it is that I need to know when I need to know it. The printed page is not the only path to knowledge."

I gasped at his arrogance. "You think that God would lower himself to speak directly to you? When He has already gone to the trouble to give us His Word within the Bible?"

"If He is God, then surely that is the least of what He can do." He was not mocking me.

"I tremble for your soul, Captain."

"Then you must pray for me."

"Why?"

"You must have a very special place in God's heart, being so upright. So righteous."

Righteous? Me? "You err. We are none of us righteous. Not one." But that did not stop me from trying to be.

"Perhaps not. But still, you have one advantage over me."

"And what is that?"

"You are so much better looking."

My cheeks flamed before I could think of anything to say. He thought me . . . he'd said . . . "You have no right to say such things!"

"Then perhaps you should pluck out my eyes as you promised to do some months ago."

I moved swiftly to open the door and this time, I did it.

The next day Mary came back from the miller's, eyes dancing with excitement. "Simeon Wright is having a husking bee!"

A husking bee? "For corn?"

"For what else?"

"He works with wood."

"Which does not mean that others are not welcome to use his space to their benefit."

There was something in her tone that made me look at her more closely. Something almost . . . proprietary. "Have you set your cap for Simeon Wright?"

She shrugged.

"Have you?"

"What if I have?"

"He is . . . old."

"Old-*er*. 'Tis not a crime last time I checked."

"I know, but . . ."

"But what? Am I not of an age?"

"You are. Of course you are."

Her mouth dipped down into a frown. "Ah. I see how it is."

"How what is?"

"You want to be the first."

"If you think this is about me—"

"Isn't it? Isn't it always about you?" Her eyes were bright with challenge.

"Nay. 'Tis not about me at all. 'Tis about you and whether you would be happy with such a man."

"With such a—oh! You mean with such a handsome man? With such a respectable man?"

"Nay. With such a . . . such an . . ." I could not think of the word I wanted.

"I cannot say that he is indifferent . . . at least not to me."

"Mary!"

"You have your fun with John Prescotte and I'll have mine with Simeon Wright." She whirled on her heel and walked past me.

The captain almost ran into her on his way around the corner.

"She would have been a menace at Newburn against the Scots."

I shook my head.

"She's a proud one."

"A stubborn one. She's set her cap for someone."

"Simeon Wright?"

I looked at him.

He smiled. " 'Tis not so hard to divine the bent of female ambition."

"Then you are the first man I have known to say it."

"She has not grown so old as she thinks."

"And 'tis that which worries me."

"Your parents are wise."

"But they do not see all."

"Oh . . . they see enough."

I puzzled on his words as I went about my business.

⁂

The night of the husking bee came too quickly. I did not wish to go. Why would I wish to enter Simeon Wright's lair?

I spun excuses as I worked.

Perhaps I could be feeling poorly. Perhaps I already did.

But nay, I was always the model of good health.

Perhaps I could be feeling my courses.

But nay. They had come last week and Thomas knew it.

Perhaps I could have some business, some work to attend to.

Nay. What could be left that had not already been done? The winter's strong beer had been made. Bayberries gathered. Candles dipped.

Perhaps . . . perhaps I would just have to go.

Thomas came in for dinner as I was pulling the pottage from the fire. I heard the door open. After several moments, I heard it shut. He always moved slowly. I knew it was because he had no wish to frighten me. He was like that, was Thomas. But it infuriated me that he would think I was so fragile. And it infuriated me even more to know that I was both more and less so than he thought.

"Are you well this day?"

"Aye." Though it pained me to say it.

"Are you . . . happy . . . this day?"

I could not keep my eyes from darting in his direction. Could he know my thoughts? I said nothing as I placed a trencher between us and sat beside him.

I kept my eyes on the table before me as I ate. But it did not stop me from knowing when Thomas had finished. I rose and took the trencher to the fire and filled it up once more from the pot. Set it before him.

He touched my hand as I took it away. "This is your home, Small-hope. Yours as well as mine. I did not bring you here to be my servant."

My intake of breath sounded like a shout in the silence.

"I did not mean . . . I meant . . . I only wish that you would be . . ." He sighed, withdrew the napkin from his shoulder, and set it on the board. And then rose and left the house.

18

IN SPITE OF MARY'S odd moodiness, it was a fair walk to the sawmill, made fairer still by our joining with neighbors as we walked along. We passed the Wrights' house on the way. It had been built away from the rest of ours, made of brick rather than wood, with real glass windows rather than oiled paper, and a brick chimney rather than one of plastered logs. A testament to the wealth of its owner, it seemed to have everything most of ours did not. And servants aplenty, brought with them from Boston, to attend to their every need.

This day, the mill had been silent. No rumble of logs. No whine of blades. Though the scent of new-cut wood perfumed the air, the floor had been swept of all shavings.

Mary entered the building as if she were already its mistress. I prayed that would never be true. I just could not shake the idea that . . . that something . . . There was something about the man I could not like. Could not trust. But my sentiments were soon pushed away by the hum of the activity.

Head-high heaps of corn had been placed about the room. Benches ringed the mounds, and buckets stood at the ready to receive the husks.

Mary spied several of her friends and moved to join them at one bench.

I spotted Abigail at another and walked over to sit on a bench beside her.

She smiled as she saw me. "Susannah! Sit here." She put her babe from her lap, adjusted his cap, and sat him on the floor. He rocked for a moment, and then rolled backward, thrusting plump legs into the air and grabbing at his toes. "Has John Prescotte—"

"Hush!"

She blinked. "Are you not—"

"Aye. But he has not yet spoken to Father . . . and may not yet be able to this autumn."

She leaned close and spoke with a lowered voice. "And why not? Did I not just see him pacing off his land for a house?"

"Did you?"

She gripped my arm. "Aye. And just this day—" She glanced up and behind my shoulder, let go my arm, and leaned forward to draw an ear of corn from the pile.

I puzzled over her actions until I realized that Simeon Wright had taken a seat on the bench next to ours.

Next to me.

Abigail waved at our friend Rebecca, who stood at the center of the floor, bouncing an infant in her arms. She came over to sit beside Abigail, bending to pick up an ear of corn before settling the child between her jouncing thighs. "She's got colic. I don't know what to do. I tried Mother's cure, but it does not work."

Abigail frowned.

I leaned toward them. "Our child had the same. But Mother bound him round his middle and gave him an infusion of anise and fennel. It seemed to work."

Rebecca and Abigail looked at each other. Looked at me, uncertainty in their eyes. Then they turned and looked round the building. After locating my mother, they waved her over.

Mother obliged and came at their gesture. "And what is it you're wanting, Goody Parker?"

"The babe has got the colic."

Mother set our own babe on the floor and bent to look into the other child's face. She took her from Rebecca and jiggled her up and down for a bit, then put her to her shoulder and patted her back.

The child let out a great belch.

"What she needs is an infusion of anise and fennel."

"Anise and fennel? How much of each and when will I give it to the child?"

Was that not what *I* had just recommended?

Abigail and Rebecca made a place between them for Mother to sit. Which left me with Simeon Wright to talk to. But only if I stayed there beside him. Looking round, I spied Mary clustered in conversation with her friends.

I gathered my skirts and rose. Smiling in what I hoped was an apologetic way, I moved to walk past Simeon Wright.

He stared up at me for a moment, eyes bright, his knees barring my exit.

I felt my smile falter.

But then he swung his legs to the side and let me pass.

With a breath of relief, I walked toward Mary. But as the group around her jostled, I saw her face for a moment. Her eyes were throwing daggers at me. I would gain no welcome, no harbor from her.

Just as I was wondering where to go, John Prescotte called to me. "Have you nowhere to go Susannah Phillips? And no corn to husk? I've found a red ear." He held it up for me to see.

A red ear. A red ear meant that he could kiss any girl he wanted.

The men seated around him looked up from their own ears at his declaration.

"Leave me a look at that, John!" One of the men sitting beside him was looking at the ear of corn with a curious expression on his face.

John tossed it to him. Then he stood and approached me, a smile playing at his lips.

'Twas not seemly to be kissed in the center of a room in the middle of a corn husking, but I leaned toward him as custom dictated and closed my eyes.

With a caress of exhaled breath, his lips found my cheek and pressed a kiss into it. My cheek marked the spot with a rapidly spreading blush.

"Did you use blackberries or beets?"

"What?" John turned his eyes from mine toward his friend.

"Did you use blackberry or beet juice to turn it red?"

"Beet."

"He stole a kiss!" The loud protest caused heads to turn throughout the mill.

John looked at me, brow raised, and shrugged.

I wanted only to disappear. As I stood there, wishing I could vanish, Simeon Wright's voice sounded from a corner. "A contest! For the men."

With one last glance at me, John left to join the contest.

Relieved, I slid into the place he vacated and turned to watch. But as the contest was assembled before me, I could do nothing so much as remember John's kiss. His lips had been . . . clammy. And his breath had been . . . unpleasant.

Though why should they not have been? Had he not just been talking to his friends? And had he not also eaten supper before coming?

And . . . he had kissed me on the *cheek*!

But why not? 'Tis not as if we were betrothed. 'Tis not as if we were even truly promised to each other. And in truth, 'twas not as if I had even wanted him to kiss me. Had I?

Had I?

Of course I had. Though if I hadn't, 'twas only because we were not yet married. There was a time and a place for such things and they were not at a corn husking. But though I should have been shocked and shamed at such an exhibition, the devil inside me kept insisting that the captain had been wrong. John Prescotte *had* wanted to kiss me! And when no opportunity had been forthcoming, he had made an opportunity to do so. Had I been a lesser woman, I might have figured out a way to tell him.

As it was, I delighted in my knowledge.

My mother, Abigail, and Rebecca had already left their seats. They stood now, babes in arms against the far wall, watching the contest being assembled in the middle of the room.

Room was made for more benches; a pile of ears was placed in front of each man. The boys stood beside the mound at the center, ready to deliver more ears to the men who would have need of them.

Simeon lifted his arm for silence. "Half of an hour."

The men groaned but not one of them protested.

The minister stood, holding his beloved sandglass above his head. He went nowhere without it. "I shall be keeper of the time." Surely more than one of us wished he would volunteer to do the same of a Sunday, though I would be the first to deny it.

Simeon nodded and made a place for himself beside John.

The minister stood as tall as he was able. "Now . . . begin!"

The men worked quickly, most with the bucket between their feet. At first the women talked quietly and the children made a play at husking at one of the other mounds. But gradually, as the contest drew on, as men began to slow at their labor and the competition became more grueling, conversation ceased. Some of the men now paused with every ear, flexing their hands, or wiping sweat from their brow.

But at least two labored as if impervious to fatigue.

John worked quickly, face slick with sweat. Fingers slipping on the husks now and then, he ripped them away with something like bitter determination.

Beside him, Simeon worked with apparent ease, methodical,

precise, and not a little ruthless. He snapped more than one ear in two during his efforts.

And finally, the minister called out, "Time!"

Conversations began again as the ears were counted. And the tally was given with some ceremony by the minister.

"It is Thomas Smyth, the winner!"

⟨❧⟩

Thomas Smyth, the winner. Everyone seemed as if they were surprised. But why should they be? How could a blacksmith not be stronger than the strongest man among them?

But, oh! Now Simeon was looking round at him. And now the man was turning his head to look at me with his iced blue eyes.

I stepped behind the bulk of a mound of corn to hide myself.

Why could Thomas not have left well alone? It was not his contest. Not his fight. Simeon meant to show Susannah how good a man, how strong a man he was. What he had not meant to do was be humiliated at his own game.

And now Thomas had begun something.

Please, God, it would end in nothing.

Please, God?

In the silence that followed the minister's announcement, only one person clapped. 'Twas the captain. And the sound was loud. Rhythmic. Mocking.

"Well done, Simeon Wright. Well thought. And now not a man of you can handle his musket! Whatever would happen should the Indians choose this night to come?" He had been advancing upon Simeon and finally he stopped. But not without one last word. "You might pause to think on that."

19

THAT SABBATH SIMEON WRIGHT stood in the midst of us in the meetinghouse and announced that more signs of savages had been seen.

There was an immediate outcry.

" 'Tis not my doing! I only thought that all should be warned."

I almost pitied the poor man. For certain it was not his doing, but I understood why the townspeople would protest. Though we had not forgotten the attack, we had chosen to ignore it. Had not the savages run away? In this critical time for storing up food, the men had begun roaming farther from town in their hunt for game. There had been talk of organizing a party to fell some of the trees in the common, to lay up a supply for the winter. Of course, the captain still organized his double watches. But the men had been grumbling about the inconvenience of it for near onto a month.

As Simeon Wright returned to his seat, the minister took to his lectern. With the opening up of the Bible, the protest quieted and then died out.

As we broke between sermons for dinner, the captain met us at the door to the meetinghouse. "They tell me sign of savages has been observed."

Father nodded.

"And who was it observed those things?"

"Simeon Wright."

The captain turned from us, eyes sweeping the crowd. He spun on a heel and marched straight toward Simeon Wright.

Conversations broke apart at his approach. Men stepped out of his path. Boys trailed in his steps.

"Mister Wright!"

Simeon dropped his arm from his mother's shoulders and turned around. "Good day, Captain Holcombe."

"I am told you saw more signs of savages."

Simeon placed the heel of his musket on the ground and rested the muzzle against his shoulder. "I did."

"I would like to know this: Why is it to you alone that these savages always appear? Are you some special friend? Or enemy?"

Simeon's face flushed. The knuckles gripping his musket turned white. "Nay. Not to my knowledge. But is it not providential that I have noted signs of their presence? In order to warn you all?"

"Providential, indeed."

Several days later, the presence of even more recent signs of savages worked its way through town like a rushing wind. By the time it reached our house, by the time we hurried to the road, half the town had gathered at Goody Blake's.

I spied Abigail and walked over to join her. "What is it?"

" 'Tis said to be the mark of an Indian's foot."

"Where?"

"Over there. By the window. Where the pigs have left their mess. 'Tis thought he was sent to spy on Goody Blake."

"Truly?"

"Why else would he have stood there?"

I tried to shake the chill from my spine. As the crowd grew, I left my friend and worked through the people, trying to get closer to the window. Standing on the tips of my toes yielded no success.

But I saw Nathaniel crouched down upon the earth with some of the other boys.

I went to him and prodded his shoulder with my knee. "What do you see?"

He looked up at me. The protest writ upon his face dropped away once recognition lit his eyes. " 'Tis a footprint. And not from any shoe of ours."

"But how do you know it?"

"There is no mark from a heel."

I let him go back to his peerings and moved as close as I could toward the front of the crowd. Having no luck, I settled on a place at the extreme edge of the multitude, toward the corner of Goody Blake's house. It was there I overheard a conversation between the captain and Simeon Wright.

"There now. You cannot tell me 'tis not proof of that which I have seen!"

"I tell you no such thing."

" 'Tis the print of a savage for certain."

"Perhaps. Though 'tis curious how a savage who can keep himself from sight for months on end would simply happen to stumble into these pigs' leavings, conveniently located right here, by Goodman Blake's house."

The crowd had begun to quiet and the captain's words to reach more ears than just mine.

"Perhaps they grow careless."

"And 'tis another curiosity, that. Why should they grow more careless as they creep closer? 'Twere me, I think I would take ever more care not to be seen."

"These savages do not think as we do."

"Nay. But I could not say, with any sort of certainty, that their thoughts are any less than ours." The captain broke from Simeon and walked to the window. He squatted and appeared to examine it, spreading his hand alongside it, as if to measure its length. "Such a long foot I have rarely seen!" He placed a hand to the ground and turned to look behind him. Toward me. And Simeon Wright. " 'Tis almost as if you have a double, Mister Wright, loosed in the wood to harass us."

"Those Indians come in all shapes and sizes."

"No doubt." He pushed to his feet and addressed the crowd. "There is nothing more to be seen here." His eyes fastened upon several of the men. "Back to the watch."

But Simeon Wright would not be told to leave. "Will you make no new rules, Captain Holcombe? Upon this evidence of savages creeping about the center of the town?"

"What would you have me do, Mister Wright? More than has been done?"

"I do not think it wise to continue talk of felling trees in the common."

"Not even with a guard?"

"And leave the women and children without protection?"

At Simeon Wright's words, mumbling swept the crowd. And soon protests could be heard. "How are we to survive this winter if we have no logs to burn?"

"And how are we to mend our fences?"

The captain held up a hand and the men were silenced. "If you've need of lumber, then go to Wright's mill. I am certain he has laid up wood in abundance. Enough for all of your needs. Is that not so, Mister Wright?"

"I suppose I could spare a log or two."

The captain nodded as if the words confirmed something. And then he pulled his hat farther down on his head. Gestured to his watchmen and started off.

Those at the front of the crowd took one last look at the print and left. Those standing farther back soon came to be at the front. There was naught to say. And naught to do but to return home and pull our latch strings inside behind us.

The crowds dispersed rapidly, neighbors pulling cloaks fast about their shoulders and hurrying their children on the path toward home. Thomas touched my arm and began walking away. But I could not move. I was watching Goody Blake.

After all had left, all but us, she had squatted beneath her window. Her eyes had grown worse. I had known it, this past month, by the hesitation in her steps. She could hide it within a group of neighbors, for when speaking to another, which of the women actually looked into the eyes of those to whom she spoke? But now, alone, she stretched out a quaking hand and patted the mud, feeling for the footprint. When she felt it, she put down a knee into the pig-fouled earth and bent so her face was almost soiled by it. And there, as she fingered the length and breadth of the impression, her face grew pale, her fingers grew even more unsteady.

At last, she lifted her head from the droppings and then turned her beautiful, failing eyes toward the window. And I could almost hear her thoughts. Could almost feel her fear. 'Twas one thing to be spied upon by a savage, but 'twas another thing entirely to know that you could have done nothing at all because you could not have seen it, would never have known. If there was a savage come to Stoney-brooke, he could pick no better place to begin his . . . savageries . . . than Goody Blake's.

But the Indian could not have known it. Of all the houses in Stoneybrooke, why had he felt compelled to choose her window to peer into? To make a prison of the one place where the woman was still able? Could still feel secure?

❧

By the next Sabbath, the meetinghouse had been adorned with wolves. Two of them. Someone would be collecting a generous bounty of ten shillings apiece! The creatures had been fixed to the wall with nails driven into their back paws, their heads left to loll at the ground. Whoever had killed them had done a thorough job of it. Their skulls had been crushed beyond recognition and their front legs hung at odd angles from the bodies. Birds rose from their corpses and flew away at our approach. But only to the top of the roof.

At the break between sermons, I went to find Abigail.

She was leaning against the wall of the meetinghouse, babe suckling at her breast. Beside her, Rebecca crouched in the dirt, her own child playing at her feet.

I had just come to stand in front of Abigail, just opened my mouth to greet her when my words were cut off by the approach of Simeon Wright.

"Susannah Phillips." Several heads turned in our direction, drawn our way, no doubt, by Simeon's loud voice.

He was trailed by my sister.

"Mister Wright."

From the shade beneath the brim of his hat, his eyes glowed blue. He flashed his teeth in a smile. "My mother would like to invite you to supper Wednesday next."

"She . . . would?" Simeon's mother was rarely heard from and rarely seen, so I could not keep from searching for her behind his broad shoulders. A small step to my left revealed her lurking in the shadow cast by the corner of the meetinghouse.

"She would. You and your father. Family. I have a . . . proposition . . . to make."

"A proposition?"

"I wish to speak of your future."

"*My* future?" But how could he know of the plans between John and me? We had barely dared to speak of them yet betwixt ourselves.

"What is this, Simeon Wright?" It was with some relief that I recognized the voice of my father come to join us.

"An invitation to supper. Next Wednesday."

"We are honored."

Simeon nodded at my father. Nodded at me and then left us without another word. For such a tall man, he moved easy on his feet through the door. Like a fox.

I turned to resume my speech with Abigail, but in all that had followed from the start of our conversation, she had found conversation with Rebecca instead.

" 'Tis good. The captain will take his meal with him this night to the watch . . ." Mother turned round to look at the house as if she had forgotten something.

"Shall we go, Mother?" Father moved toward the door as he spoke.

She cast another glance round the place and then, finally, she smiled and withdrew her cloak from its hook. "Not without my cloak." She looked at Mary and me. "And not without yours either."

It seemed too hot, this sun-warmed day, to need them. "But—"

Mary's protest was cut off by Mother's words. "You'll thank me on the way home."

We walked down the road past a half dozen houses. I would rather have turned into any of them than continue on to where we had been invited. I had been there once, during the attack, and I had no wish to go there again. Mary, however, seemed to have no such misgivings. It was only on the climb up the hill that her pace began to slacken.

The house was set just beneath the high point of a ridge, overlooking a meadow that stretched up from the river. Had we crossed over the ridgeline behind the house, we might have seen the mill in the valley below.

A manservant opened the door at Father's approach. We were shown, all of us, into a room that I could see served no purpose but for sitting. Such a room was a luxury none of the rest of the houses in Stoneybrooke had. It was furnished with a settle, several chairs, and a small cabinet I took to be a sort of instrument . . . all of them things that I had failed to note when we had been quartered here during the attack. Still, I clung to my opinion: Though I was happy to think one among Stoneybrooke might someday be a goodwife here, I was content for that person not to be me.

As we passed into the kitchen, a hand reached out and plucked at my arm. I turned at the movement and found Simeon's mother beckon. Her smile beamed out of her withered face like a ray of sun. She took my hand in her own. " 'Because the Lord hath heard I was hated, he hath therefore given me this son also: and I called his name Simeon.' " She looked at me in expectation.

I could not think how to reply to such strange words, and so I nodded and quickly followed my sister through the door.

Once in the kitchen, we were seated upon benches, as was the custom. But for himself, Simeon Wright had a chair. A splendid chair with spindled legs and a carved back. It was positioned at the head of the table. And it was from there he commanded the meal to be served.

Silent servants leaned around us to place the food upon the table. No trenchers for the Wright house; each one of us had our own plate cast from pewter. Even Nathaniel and the child.

Once we had all been served, the servants withdrew to the corners of the room. And then, a silence befell us. It was not a wordless silence, for Simeon entertained us all with stories of the Puritan struggle against King Charles and news of Boston. Nay, the silence was more of a posture. It was a watchful silence, a waiting silence. A silence conjured chiefly by Mistress Wright and the servants who sat and stood as if they might be found wanting at any moment.

I could not understand the mood.

Simeon himself was expansive, seemed almost to sprawl in his chair. His demeanor was that of a man with plenty of leisure and ample good will and time enough to spend them both as he pleased. And obviously, it pleased him this evening to spend it with us.

Across from me, his mother made not one sound. Not that I expected her to speak. She seemed too intent upon eating to save any energy for words. But she made no attempt to follow the conversation, no attempt to listen to her son's words. Though her gaze shifted now and then to him, it was a furtive gaze, as if she hoped he would not notice her. It seemed odd to me. As odd as a woman with a forearm the size of a sapling to eat enough to satisfy a man five times her weight.

Once the meat and sauce had been finished, once the flummery had been served, Simeon requested that his mother play the small organ that stood in the sitting room. " 'Twas my father who removed it from a church in England. With his own hands. To purify the worship."

Mistress Wright had started at Simeon's request. Raised her eyes to look at him and then quickly lowered her gaze toward the table. "Nay. Please do not ask it of me."

"For our guests."

She shook her head.

Mary and I shared a glance. 'Twas uncomfortable to be witness to a family disagreement.

Mother laid her hand upon Mistress Wright's. "Please. Do not worry yourself on our account, Mistress Wright. We will be no less welcomed for not having heard you."

The poor woman flinched at Mother's touch.

Simeon's smile stretched even wider. "I must insist."

His mother blinked. Stilled. Then she took a great breath, rose, and walked to the sitting room.

The rest of us followed, arranging ourselves behind her in the shape of a crescent moon. For several long moments, she simply sat there, hands upon her lap.

"Mother!" Simeon reached out in front of her and threw open two doors, which revealed a sort of cabinet containing wooden tubes. The insides of the doors had been painted with scenes of maidens frolicking in a garden.

Mistress Wright placed trembling hands to the instrument and began to play. The last time I had heard an organ was in my grandfather's house. It had always seemed to me a music even sweeter than that of birds. I did not recognize the tune she played. It was something insubstantial, light and gay, which did not fit the season or the gathering chill of darkness outside any more than it fit our sober group. A hesitation between each note soon overcame the tune and worked a tension through the room. I am certain it was as much work to listen to the song as it was to play it, and it was with some relief that I greeted its conclusion. When she started on another, I do not know that I breathed until, at last, she had finished.

The third song must have been well loved. It was played with a growing confidence. A growing grace. And in the playing, Simeon's mother seemed transformed. Her shoulders raised themselves, straightening her hunched back. Her chin lifted, imparting an illusion of assurance. A smile so worked itself upon her face that she appeared, for that moment, quite pretty. And youthful.

But then Simeon moved to shut the cabinet, stopping his mother from playing when she might have begun another song. And in the closing of those doors, he seemed to lock away his mother's substance, returning her to us quite as haggard as before.

The final note extinguished itself almost immediately, leaving no lasting impression.

"That was beautiful!" My mother's face glowed with pleasure. "Wherever did you learn to play?"

Mistress Wright's eyes strained to meet my mother's, but they did not. Instead, she answered while looking at the floor. "In England. Before I was reformed."

Simeon stopped her words with laughter. "Before the *church* was reformed. 'Twas my own father that did the reforming. It was he who chased out the Anglican priest, Mother's father, and installed a proper Puritan minister in his stead."

He led us back into the kitchen, where we regained the seats we had left. His face changed from hilarity to levity as he straightened himself in his chair. He cleared his throat, folded his hands on the top of the board, and addressed himself to my father. "I wish to ask you for Susannah's hand in marriage."

20

I FELT MYSELF BLANCHING. My hand in marriage? But ... he wanted to marry me? How could that be? What about Mary? And what about John?

My father nodded. I kept waiting for him to say something, to say anything at all, but he did not.

"If it seems good to you, we can be married this fall. Before the onslaught of winter. You and I are already partners in business. Why not join our families as well? Is there not special compensation to be given to relations?"

If I could have spoken, I would have said "nay" and that would have been the end of it. But I had no right. It was not my place. Later Father might ask my opinion and if he did, then I might tell him my mind. But not here. For now all I could hope was that an agreement would not be made.

My father's eyes sought my face, and I only hoped my eyes would plead my case for me. "I will think on what you have proposed."

My body went weak with relief. He had agreed to nothing. Perhaps, then, if John spoke soon ... perhaps all could be set right.

After Simeon's Wright's astonishing announcement, there was little left of which to speak. The abruptness and enormity of his declaration seemed to have stolen from anyone's mind all but the dullest material for conversation.

Mother prodded Father with an elbow.

He nodded once more. "Thank you, Simeon Wright, for your hospitality."

"It was our pleasure, was it not, Mother?"

Across from me, a change came over that woman's face. As if a curtain had fallen, as if she had closeted herself away from us. She straightened and cast her eyes to her lap. " 'Be not forgetful to entertain strangers: for thereby some have entertained angels unawares.' "

Her odd reply was overshadowed by Simeon's hearty laugh. "Have no fear. When we are wed we shall see to it, Susannah Phillips, that your parents are no strangers here."

I should have had no fear, not from a proposal that could be so easily dismissed, but I did. I could only nod. And in my haste to be gone, I had already stood away from the bench.

We made short work in leaving. Mother collected the babe from Mary. Father took up his musket from the wall by the door and we were gone.

I was trying to lift that mantle of fear from my thoughts when Mary fell into step beside me for a moment. "You always spoil everything!"

I glanced over at her, startled at the vehemence of her speech. "What have I spoilt?"

"Everything. First born. First loved. First courted."

"You speak of John Prescotte?"

She looked at me as if she thought me daft and leaned close to me. "I speak of Simeon Wright!"

"But 'tis not Simeon I want. 'Tis John."

"It did not look it from where I was standing."

"If you want Simeon, then take him."

" 'Twas not me he asked for."

"But John Prescotte—"

"And it was not he who asked for you."

Bats swooped and flitted through the darkening light of the dusk. Out in the woods beside us an owl sent out a mournful hoot. I walked on in silence, though my thoughts spun themselves into the yarn of a plan quickly. There would be no way to speak in private once the captain returned to our house. With the hour growing late, that time was nearing. It was on this walk home that my plea must be made.

"Father?"

He stopped in the road, Mother beside him. "Simeon Wright has asked for your hand."

"Aye."

"He is a good man. Pleasant of character. Godly. And 'tis true—we are already partners in business. Since my wood burnt this spring, 'tis Simeon to which I turn for my trade. 'Tis he who controls my trade. I might wish his price a bit fairer—"

" 'Tis extortion what he demands!" Mother's tone was accusatory. Strident.

Father laid a hand upon her arm. "And 'tis not for you to say, Mother. We have an agreement of sorts, he and I . . . and it seemed to me that he did make a promise to be fairer."

In spite of Father's reliance on Simeon Wright, I knew that I must speak while there was still time. "I had hoped . . ."

Mother reached out a hand for mine and drew me toward them. "What had you hoped?"

"I had hoped for John Prescotte."

"He has not spoken to me."

Yet. He had not spoken *yet*. "Perhaps if he did . . . ?"

Father did not reply.

Which could mean any one of several things. It could mean that John's proposal would be entertained if he spoke. It could mean that Simeon Wright's proposal was as good as accepted. Or it could simply mean that Father had not yet made up his mind.

We walked on a few more steps in silence.

"I suppose I could speak to his father."

Mother turned and beamed a quick smile toward me.

I was afraid to return the smile. Afraid to speak. Afraid to hope in the words he had just spoken. As we walked down the hill, I felt a weight shift from my shoulders, heard a melody in the beating of my heart. And then I remembered that I had left my cloak at the Wrights'.

I paused as I considered whether to go back for it or wait until morning.

"What is it?" Mother stopped at my hesitation.

"My cloak."

"What of it?"

"I left it. Back there."

"At the Wrights'?"

"Aye."

"Then you best go back and get it before night falls for certain. Nathaniel? Accompany Susannah back to the Wrights'. She's forgotten her cloak. And be quick about it!"

We turned from the group as smartly as if we were marching at a training day review and climbed back up the hill.

In the gathering gloom, the Wright home could only be seen as a dark silhouette against the sky. Not one light glowed from those costly glass windows. Whatever tapers had been burning when we left must have been extinguished directly thereafter.

I clutched at Nathaniel's arm to stay him. "Do you think . . . they could not yet be sleeping?"

"Nay. Let's be about it. Maybe we can still catch up to the others before they reach home."

He closed the distance to the house at a run and rapped at the door. He was still waiting for it to be answered when I joined him.

"Perhaps they did not hear you."

"I knocked twice."

The latchstring had not been pulled in, so they must not yet be bent on retiring. I pulled at it, and once I heard the latch lift, I pushed the door open. "Hail and hello!"

153

We waited, Nathaniel and I, on the doorstep, exchanging glances.

On the wall opposite, I could see my cloak hanging.

"Hello?" No use wasting time. I stepped through the doorframe and went to retrieve my cloak. Quickly in, I meant to go just as quickly out, but Nathaniel had followed me and as I turned in the gloom, I walked right into him.

He yelped. "Watch what you're about! You've stepped on me."

"Then stop following me about like some newborn duckling!" I grabbed at his arm, pulling him toward the door. "Hush. Let's go."

We walked back through the sitting room, but a noise from the kitchen stopped us. It was the sound of Simeon's voice . . . and his mother's whimper. I could not understand the words he was saying, but the tone was sharp, the words terse.

As we passed in front of the entrance to the kitchen we could see them thrown into profile by the embers of the fire. Simeon was talking to his mother, finger raised as if to make some point in particular.

She was listening to his speech in a meek attitude, hands tucked away beneath her apron.

As we watched, Simeon raised the whole of his hand above his shoulder. As he swung it down toward his mother, he caught sight of us.

I flinched, expecting somehow that his hand would reach out to strike his mother's cheek.

Mistress Wright must have thought so as well, for she cringed.

But Simeon only placed his arm around his mother's shoulders and turned her toward us. "Our guests have returned."

"I left my cloak."

He smiled, the fire gleaming off his teeth. "And have you found it?"

"Aye. Thank you."

"Do not tarry long in the night."

"Nay."

Nathaniel and I were in such a hurry to leave that we nearly tripped over each other in our haste. We left the house at a walk that proceeded to a run, and we did not stop until we had reached the bottom of the hill. Finally, once I knew the house no longer loomed behind us, I felt my pace slow to a walk.

Beside me, Nathaniel slowed as well.

I could not stop puzzling over what I had seen.

What I thought I had seen.

In the end, Simeon's movement had been the gesture of a man embracing his mother. But why had she shuddered at his touch? Why had his knuckles around her shoulder gleamed white in the fire's light? And why had I been so sure that he would strike her?

Had she not been certain as well?

Yet she had always been a strange woman, a bit addled in the head.

As I prayed that night, I fear my thoughts were not on my words but on Simeon's. And Father's. And the words that John might say.

The words that he *must* say.

But if I had expected Father to visit the Prescottes the next day, he did not do it. Neither did he do it the day after.

And by the day after that, my nerves were frayed as if from the sharp edge of a knife. At dinner that third day, I dropped a tray of biscuits. Mother took it from me and then set it on the table. "Father? You must talk to Goodman Prescotte this day or all of my hard work will be ruined."

He blinked as if he were annoyed at the request. But he nodded once, rose to his feet, put on his hat, and walked out the front door, leaving the rest of us to stare after him.

He did not return until supper.

Once the blessing of the food had been accomplished, Mother wasted no time in questioning him. "Is there to be a wedding?"

Beside me, the captain lifted his head from his meal.

"Aye."

We waited, all of us, for more details, but that seemed to be the extent of what Father wished to tell us. I was to be wed, but I did not know yet to which man.

"Well, tell us to whom, Father, and when, so we can get about the business of preparing."

"To the Prescotte boy. Is that not the one she wanted?"

Mary brightened.

The captain shot a glance of disapproval at me as if I were some prized student who had given him cause for disappointment. He shook his head before returning his attentions to his meal.

But I could not care.

I saw Mother nod in approval before I hid my head in my apron and cried in sheer relief. All was right. I had nothing to fear.

My prayers that evening were incoherent with gratitude and joy. The only clear phrase I could muster was one I repeated ad infinitum.

Thank you! Thank you!

I could only hope that God would decipher some higher and more complex meaning in them. As I lay in bed, my thoughts too busy for sleep, I listened to the conversation of Father and Mother through the thin walls.

"Speak, Father. Tell me when their banns are to be published."

"Oh . . . maybe not for a few months yet. No hurry."

No hurry! But I wanted to be married now. All the other girls my age had married. It was time. It was past time! And if I did not marry John, then what reason could be given for not wanting to marry Simeon Wright?

"And they are to live . . . ?"

"He's to start on a house this winter. I told him I would help him fell the trees and plane them, but he wants to do it proper. Take the trees over to the sawmill."

A proper house!

" 'Tis good, that. Shows determination."

"Hmph. Stubbornness."

"You do not think he'll do well by her?"

I held my breath, waiting for Father's answer. Beside me, Nathaniel let out an impossibly long snore.

I elbowed him, hoping that he would turn over. He grunted and snuffled, grinding his teeth.

" . . . do fine. As well as any of them."

" 'Tis he she wants."

"And what do I care of that?"

There was a shifting of the bed. The sound of a shared kiss. "You do care. You care more about your daughters than any man I know."

Father grunted.

"He's a good man."

"He'd better be. He'll have my girl to answer for!"

Mother said something I could not decipher.

And then Father's voice came again. Loud and vexed. "Why did Wright even have to ask?—and tie it to the price of his wood? And why was I sent like some message boy to prod around and get the Prescotte boy to propose? It was a torment to the soul. I might have kept on glowering at him like I have been."

"You haven't!"

"Aye, I have. And I could have put the whole thing off another month or two at least."

"Shame, Father."

"But then you had me go and ask him if he wanted to wed my daughter? It's not right, woman! Made me sound as if I was begging to be rid of her when all I want is to . . . well . . . 'tis more than a man can be expected to bear."

"You did well, Father."

He muttered something unintelligible.

Mother laughed.

There was silence for a long while, and then Father spoke again. "Are you willing, then, Goodwife Phillips?"

"More willing than not, I'd say." By and by their talk turned to kisses and their kisses into something else. And it was to that which I fell asleep.

21

THE NEXT MORNING I woke in expectation of some good thing. It took only the briefest moment before I realized what that good thing was. I was to be betrothed. Was as good as betrothed!

I pondered all during breakfast and later, during the morning's work, on how I might slip away for just a moment to see John.

"I have a . . . could I . . . ?"

Mother turned from her chores with a frown. "What is it you're saying?"

"I . . ." What was it I had been saying? I knew the end of it, but I could no longer remember the beginning.

She relented. Smiled. "Go, daughter."

I adjusted my coif and placed my hat atop it with care. Slipping into the parlor to look into the glass, I saw only relief at work in my eyes.

John was pulling turnips from his father's field and so he did not see me coming.

"John."

He lifted his head. Smiled as he saw me. "Susannah." He straightened.

"I did not mean to . . . I mean."

His brows drew together.

"I had been asked . . . I did not want to make you . . ."

"You made me do nothing. I had always intended to ask your father for your hand. Only . . . your father can be so . . . imposing . . . I was not certain . . ."

I smiled.

He smiled back.

"Surely I am blessed, Susannah."

I felt my cheeks color and suddenly, I did not want to look at him at all.

"I will start on our house as soon as I am able. I'll speak to Simeon Wright this week about the lumber for it. By winter, God willing, we will be wed."

I began calculating that day what I had laid aside for my hopes. And Mother with me.

"You must have bedding."

"I have it."

"And linens for your board."

"I have one."

"You must begin, then, on another. You have a cushion for pins? And a thimble?"

"Aye."

"And I will give you a paper of pins and a needle. Your Father will make you a great chest as a present, and we shall ask him to get you some stitching and sewing silk when he next goes to market."

I began to work on a shirt cut from linen for John. It pleased me to assemble the pieces, to stitch it together and know that it would clothe him. That it would be to him a symbol of my esteem. And it would make it plain to everyone what a good wife I was.

That Sabbath John walked into the meetinghouse with me. Though we sat on separate sides of the building, his glance warmed me as surely as he had been sitting beside me.

My hands were folded on my lap and my eyes properly downcast when the minister stood. "I announce the banns today of Simeon Robert Wright . . ."

Simeon Wright was getting married? Relief flooded my heart. But it was followed by curiosity. To whom? Surely not to Mary, so to whom, then . . . ? I raised my eyes and looked as far as I could without turning my head, to see if I could guess.

Beside me, Mary grunted.

" . . . son of Robert Wright and Arabella Howard Wright . . ." Arabella? Arabella was his mother's name? It was lovely. Fanciful. And completely at odds with the shell of a woman that sat among us.

" . . . to Susannah Elizabeth Phillips, daughter of John Phillips and Susannah Phillips, residing in Stoneybrooke Towne, Somershire County, Massachusetts Bay Colony, aged twenty years, single."

To me?

But—but—John! I half rose before I remembered where I was.

I leaned forward to see if I could spy Father in his pew on the other side of the aisle. He was blinking rapidly, as if he did not understand what he had just heard.

I glanced wildly about the room, looking for someone, some person, to tell the minister that he was mistaken. To tell him the truth.

But no one did.

Of all the pairs of eyes that were fixed upon me, only one set mattered. John's. And he looked at me with outrage, anger, and disbelief.

What had happened?

&

My heart beat heavy within me.

Susannah Phillips was to be wed to Simeon Wright.

Everything that was decent and kind in this town married to

160

everything that was dark and evil. I wanted to weep from the knowledge of what must come. I knew what would happen. I understood how it would start. Only one such as I could comprehend how a woman could be turned into a shadow, how she could be tied so tightly, so vastly overshadowed by a man that the only sign of her presence was a dull, flitting spot of shade upon the ground.

I lifted my head so I could see her.

Her hands were clasped in her lap. She sat straight, staring out past the minister into the misery she must see beyond. I knew how she felt, a creature entrapped. And there would be no release. No escape without much pain.

❧

The minister spoke for two hours, but I did not hear a word he said. Father had not accepted Simeon's proposal. How could he have when he had just reached an agreement with the Prescottes? Clearly Simeon Wright had misunderstood. Clearly he had mistaken Father's words for agreement.

And just as clearly, he must be made to understand.

As the minister brought his sermon to a close and we broke for dinner, I pushed through clustering women, intent upon reaching Father.

But John reached me first. "I thought we had an understanding! I thought we had reached an agreement!"

"We do. We had—"

"I was to start building a house, Susannah. *Our* house."

"It was a mistake."

"A mistake! No one announces banns mistakenly."

"I never told him—I never made him believe—"

"You? What have you to do with it? With anything?"

I opened my mouth to speak, but then shut it up tightly. What *did* I have to do with anything? Father could well have made an agreement with Simeon Wright. On his own. Without my knowledge.

But I could not believe it.

"You must trust me, John. This is not as it seems. It has always been my wish to marry you."

"How can I know what to believe? And how can you give your hand in marriage to two men? At the same time?"

As John turned and stalked away, Mother stepped close and put her arm around my shoulders. I wanted nothing more than to turn my face into her broad chest and weep from frustration. But I was no longer a girl.

"Your father will make all right."

But how had matters gone so wrong?

I looked around for someone to speak to of the injustice, but those who approached me only wished to congratulate me.

"Felicitations, Susannah Phillips. He is a fine man."

"A godly man."

"If my own girl were just a few years older . . ."

"A fine house you'll be going to."

" . . . strong sons, by the look of him . . ."

"Could there be any finer match?"

Aye! My own to John Prescotte!

I passed around my thanks for their good wishes and then broke from that circle of women to find my own friends. Mary was part of that circle, but she left as soon as she saw me coming.

"Good day, Susannah Phillips." The greeting of Mary's friend Hannah was polite, if cool. "I suppose you wish to hear our felicitations."

Another of Mary's friends spoke. "I, for one, cannot profess to what I do not feel. You have taken Stoneybrooke's finest bachelor. Did you not hear all the times I spoke to you of my own interest in him?"

"I do not want him!"

She shook her head. "False modesty is no virtue."

"You have your sweet temperament and your fair looks—could you not save something for the rest of us?" Hannah asked.

Sweet temperament? Fair looks? If I knew any oaths, I would

have shouted them. If I had a pair of scissors and thought that it might save me, I would have shorn my head myself. But still their angry stares made me feel so guilty that I turned on my heel and left. Surely there was no dearth of women wanting to marry Simeon Wright. Why could he not have chosen one of them?

I found Mother and Nathaniel and prepared to return to the house for dinner. Father left us in our going and went to speak to the Prescottes. He returned shortly after we began to eat.

Mother glanced up, her face lit with expectation. "Has all been righted, then?"

He sat down hard upon the bench. "They will not listen to reason. They choose not to understand."

"But what is there to be understood? 'Twas a mistake."

"They do not understand how Susannah's hand could be pledged to two persons at the same time, and I must confess that . . . neither do I." He looked at my mother, bewildered. "I did not agree to the man's proposal."

"Nay. You did not."

"But the Prescottes will not hear me speak."

"What do you mean they will not hear you?"

"They go on and on about not aligning themselves with persons of wavering minds. Of not being dealt with honorably or being able to trust in one who breaks his promise. But it was not I that broke it. I did nothing. 'Twas all Simeon Wright."

I could not refrain from speaking. "But what are you saying? What did they say?"

"They say John will not have you."

"But then—"

"They say the marriage is off. They retract the offer as they say I have retracted mine."

Mother stayed his hand when he would have put drink to his lips. "Surely they do not mean it."

Father scratched at his chin. "It seemed as if they did."

"Then you must go to Simeon Wright and tell him to retract the banns."

Father looked at her with haggard face. "For what reason?"

"She was promised to another."

"Perhaps she was, but she is no longer."

"One would almost think Simeon Wright did it on purpose!" Mother clearly was not pleased with this turn of events.

"Nay. It was a simple misunderstanding."

"Nothing simple about it. It leaves Susannah unattached."

"But betrothed."

"To the wrong man!" I could not keep myself from speaking. Why were they talking as if I must accept what had happened?

Father turned toward me. "Aye, Susannah, perhaps. But what am I to tell Simeon Wright? I am obliged to the man for my wood and if he chooses not to sell to me . . . ? I might have told him that you were already betrothed, but now I cannot. What reason would you give me now to make him wish to subject himself to ridicule?"

That there was no warmth in his eyes? That his mother was witless? That the man himself frightened me?

"He is a good man. A supporter of the church. A leader in the community. Head of the militia."

Mother smiled at me. It reminded me of the way she used to coax me out of a bad humor when I was yet young. "He is a godly, learned man."

Father took a drink from the cup. Wiped his mouth with his napkin once he was done. "What would you have me say to him, Susannah? Do you have any reasons to give me to stop what has been started?"

I had suspicions, fears, and vague apprehensions. But reasons? "I have none."

22

THE FOLLOWING DAY AS I was turning a chicken upon the spit, Abigail appeared at our door, babe toddling at her side, snowflakes clinging to her cloak.

'Twas Mother that saw her first. "Abigail Clarke! And you've come with snow."

" 'Tis just an early taste of what's to come. Surely it will melt."

I turned from my labors to find her looking at me. Her smile warm. "Congratulations, Susannah."

She chattered on and on about my dowry. About how many handkerchiefs I ought to bring to the marriage. And how many spoons. And then, at the last, when I was ready to weep with self-pity, she allowed that she was with child.

"And maybe, this time next year . . . God willing, Susannah . . . ?"

"Felicitations!" My mother was quicker with her congratulations than I was. But it was only because Abigail's announcement had revealed to me the full horror of what would happen when I joined myself in marriage to Simeon Wright. Of course I knew what would happen, had to happen, but I had not dwelt upon it. Not even in my thoughts of marrying John. There were so many things to consider—my dowry, the house, the banns—that the actual union had been last in my mind.

It was soon after that Abigail left. And soon after her leaving that I stumbled outside and began to walk. I did not know at first where it was that I wandered, but my steps led me to the one person who could help me.

"John."

He looked up from his work, but what had been an impression of quiet peace about his face vanished.

"It was a mistake." I clasped my hands in front of me, beneath my apron, so that I would not cling to him in the way I so desperately wanted to do.

"I fail to see how banns can be published without some sort of agreement between the parties." He turned from me toward his ox cart.

I stepped in front of it. "You have to believe me. Please, John."

"Do not ask that of me."

"They will marry me off to Simeon Wright."

"Is that not what you wanted?"

"Nay! I wanted you. I always only ever wanted you."

" 'Tis a fine way to show it . . ." He stabbed at the ground with his spade. "To have your banns published to some other man."

"It was not Father's fault. Simeon asked for my hand, 'tis true. But Father did not give it. He came to you instead. He chose you."

"And I agreed, as we had agreed, and then your banns were read . . . and . . ."

"You must help me!"

"I cannot help you, Susannah. I have no right. You are pledged to another man." He turned from me and returned to his labors, snowflakes salting the back of his doublet.

That night, the dishes tidied from dinner, I wrapped my cape around my shoulders and stepped outside. The snow had stopped and a clear coldness had blown in to take its place. Gazing up at the sky, I wondered what it would feel like to touch a star. And if in touching one, I might be swept far away from Stoneybrooke and up into a world where there were no men. And no maids. No promises that could be broken.

" 'Tis not often I have the pleasure of company of a night."

I sighed as I perceived the captain, standing near the wall of the house, smoking his pipe. The wind blew past me before it went on toward him and so I had not noted his presence. The snow that sifted from the clouds earlier in the day had turned the ground into a soft downy mattress.

I took a step or two away from him. Away from the house. I might have continued on were it not for the snow. Might have ended my journey in Boston. At Grandfather's house.

"Felicitations."

"On what?"

"Your marriage. Or is that not what you people say? Are you not allowed to be gladdened by such things?"

I lifted a shoulder and pulled the cape tighter about me.

" 'Twas a jest."

"Then it should have been amusing."

"Must you marry him?"

"There is no reason not to."

" 'Tis flimsy as far as reasons go."

"Then how is this: The man I wished to marry will not have me. Not any longer."

"Ah. The young John."

"You speak of him as if he were still a child!"

"And when he stops acting like a child, then I will speak of him as a man. There are things worth fighting for. You are one of them."

It was ridiculous that such foolish words would make me feel like crying.

"Your father should fight for you as well. Tell the good Mister Wright that he can stuff his underhanded proposal right down the front of his lace-collared shirt."

I choked on laughter as I tried to imagine anyone telling Simeon Wright anything. "Here, in this land, children do as their fathers ask."

He laid a hand on my arm. "And in England, fathers do not marry their daughters to brutes."

"Don't they?"

His grip tightened. "You should tell him yourself."

"Tell him what?"

"That you will not do it."

"For what reason?"

"For any reason at all."

"And offend the man from whom my father buys his wood? How can I do it when our own lands are destroyed? The arrangement has been made. I cannot break it."

"Not even if . . ." The captain's words trailed off, but his eyes seemed to speak just the same.

Why could he not have come earlier to Stoneybrooke Towne? Why could I not have known him sooner? But even if . . . I heard myself sigh. There was no use thinking about it. My father would never have given me over to a king's man.

He blinked. And then he smiled, but it was halfhearted in the way of smiles and only succeeded in tipping up one side of his mouth. "Here is a thought to cheer you: 'Blessed are the peacemakers . . .' "

He seemed to want me to complete the verse and so I obliged. " 'For they shall be called the children of God.' "

" 'Blessed are ye that weep now . . .' "

"I do not know it."

He sighed. "Do you Puritan folk know nothing? 'Blessed are ye that weep now . . . for ye shall laugh.' "

"Laugh? I am to laugh? At what?"

"At this." Staring as I was into his eyes, I barely saw his arm move. I only realized what he was doing after his snowball hit me on the throat above my cape and disintegrated as it slid beneath my shift.

I gasped.

And then I lunged toward the ground to take up snow in my

bare hands and roll it into a ball. When I threw it, it struck him right between the eyes.

He gasped. And then he ran around the corner of the house and disappeared.

I considered his character for one brief moment before deciding what to do. And then I gathered a mound of snow and shoved it into a bucket. Stepping softly around the other side of the house, I lifted my skirts and climbed upon the woodpile. And then I waited.

I did not have to wait for long.

The captain came around the corner backward, searching, I suppose, for me. Looking as he was behind him, he failed to see me in front of him. I upended the snow upon his head, causing him to let out a great shout in exclamation.

At that, the door was flung open and Father appeared, his musket at his shoulder.

Nathaniel followed at his heels. His eyes widened as he saw the captain and me. And then he scooped snow into his hands and flung a snowball at the captain before taking cover behind our father, who, unfortunately, received the snowball intended for his son.

The door opened once more and Mary and Mother appeared in silhouette. They stood and watched while we exchanged snowballs until our clothes were spattered with snow and the chill had turned our laughter to wheezing. But I returned to the house thinking that marrying Simeon Wright might not be the worst thing in the world.

❧

I had watched the snow filter down from the skies all day. It was not a snow to stay, for it was too early in the season for that. But it was a snow nonetheless. I used to hate snow. It was a harbinger of the times to come. Of days when all work would be done inside, when one would not be able to escape four walls that seemed to form a very prison. The worst things had always happened to me in winter, within the confines of my father's house.

But not anymore.

Since coming to Stoneybrooke, my days continued untouched by weather or season. I saw no one. No one saw me. I was mistress of Thomas's house and everything I put to my hand was, in his mind at least, my own. I rose from bed of a morning to my own work, and I went to my bed at night unmolested.

⟡

Though I went to my bed light of heart, my first thought the next morning was of Simeon Wright. And so was the next thought and the one after that. Setting my mind on God's Holy Scriptures was no help, for I began to wonder at His ways. Placing my thoughts into prayers did no good either, for I began to put my wonderings into words. And who was I to question what must be? What my parents were willing to allow? Surely they knew better than I. Surely those things . . . those . . . those . . . *things* about Simeon Wright that gave me pause were simply a lack of knowledge. Surely once I knew him, I would see him as everyone else, as every other girl in this town did. Surely I at least might be able to see him as Mary did. Had. But still, I confess my work shoddily done that day, as it seemed so often to get in the way of my thinking.

In fact, I nearly dumped the pigs' slops onto the captain's shoes as I walked through the door outside and caught him coming in.

He steadied me with a hand to my arm, and then he took the bucket from me and carried it out to the creatures' pen. "I hope your frown is not on my account."

I tried to straighten my lips. "It is not."

"On John Prescotte's account?"

What I could not do, the mention of John's name had done. My lips had grown straight as a pin.

" . . . or perhaps on Simeon Wright's account."

I snatched the bucket from his hand and dumped it over the rail into the pigs' trough.

"It must grieve God's heart to see you so despondent."

"Why should He care who it is that I marry?" And why should

the captain? He would leave as soon as he was able. With regrets, perhaps, and with my own as well, but in the end he would leave just the same. And it made something inside of me ache to know it.

"I wager He cares about you more than you think."

" 'Tis vanity to think such things."

"I would bet my life upon it."

"You wager your life on this or that. Is it worth so very little?"

"I do not plan on keeping it forever. I might as well enjoy it while I still have it."

"And it is for such as you that our Lord was sent to die!" I was quite certain that God had not intended His son's death to cover over a multitude of sins such as his.

"Exactly. His son. For such as me . . . and such as you."

"For mankind."

"Have you such a low opinion of yourself?"

"Have you such a high one?"

He laughed. "It seems we are of differing minds about it. But I wonder . . . which of us is right?"

"I am."

"Ah. And now who is arrogant?"

Why did the captain keep pursuing me? Why could he not just go? Far away from me? "You must be one such as our Lord spoke of in the Scriptures."

"Aye?" He narrowed his gaze as if he suspected some trap. "I have no doubt that I am but . . . what is it that you think He said of me?"

" 'That seeing they may see, and not perceive; and hearing they may hear, and not understand; lest at any time they should be converted, and their sins should be forgiven them.' "

"You make it sound as if He did not favor me."

I shrugged. "They are not my words. They are His. I merely repeat what you might find out for yourself, had you the ability to read them." I ducked my head in shame ere I had finished speaking. Had I truly said those words? My soul was darker than I had known.

I turned from the pigs and started back for the house, but his hand on my arm stopped me.

"Bang on a drum that is already quite slack. I can read. But it takes time. And how am I to be about it when I stand watch all day for savages?"

I hardened my heart against the pity that worked up inside me. With him it was always one thing or another. "One day you will stand naked before your creator, and what will you say to Him? What excuse will you use then?"

"Naked, you say?"

"As the day you were born. With nothing to hide behind but shame."

"That sounds terribly humiliating."

"Indeed!"

"Perhaps, then, I ought to practice."

Finally, he was becoming reasonable . . . at the very point he meant to leave me. Us. To leave us.

He set his musket down beside him. Took his hat from his head and held it out to me. "If you would be so kind?"

I took it from him.

"I thank you." He unfastened his doublet, drew his arms from its sleeves. "Can you . . . ?"

I took it from him.

He worked to loose the strings that tied his shirt together and then pulled the tails of it from his breeches and pulled it over his head.

He was disrobing. In front of me! "You cannot mean to—you cannot just—have you no shame!" I flung his hat and doublet back at him, turned, and hastily left the way I had come.

His laughter reverberated from the wood behind us, and it followed me all the way to the house. But 'twas not his laughter that bothered me. 'Twas my own reaction to the sight of his naked flesh. John's nakedness had caused me to turn away, but the captain's had . . . entranced me.

23

"SUSANNAH, YOU ARE TO go with your father to Newham. To fulfill my list of things we lack and to buy the items necessary to complete your dowry."

Mary looked up at Mother's words, envy evident in her eyes.

"What sort of items?"

"You'll need some fine lawn for a new collar and lace to trim it. A length of black stuff to be made into a gown."

"Black?" I'd never worn a black gown. Never thought I would be grand enough to own one.

"Aye. What's good for Mistress Wright is sure to be good for her daughter-to-be. You must ask for the best to be certain the dye is fast."

I nodded.

"And you'll need some silk for stitching and sewing. And another board cloth."

"But they must have them in abundance already."

"If you are to marry a fine man, you must take to his household items of value."

"But—"

" 'Tis decided, Susannah. We must not be shamed."

And so, several days later, I walked beside the oxcart with Father to Newham's fair, the cart packed carefully with the fine work Father was known for. Walking with us were others intent upon attending that same fair. Thomas Smyth led an oxcart heavily laden with his wares. Goodman Ellys led a cart bearing the surplus from his harvests, and Goodman Hillbrook had loaded his with dairy goods.

Newham was a bit over four miles to the east along the road to Boston, and a good two hours walk. I would have given anything to ride, but the oxcart was filled with wares too valuable to be displaced for reason of my comfort. Having risen in darkness, none of us were up for talking much. And due to the threat of savages, attention was devoted to the wood that brushed up into the path. I must say I breathed a sigh of relief as the shadowy darkness gave way to dawn's pale light. And another sigh as the thick stands of trees surrendered to meadows and the meadows to cultivated fields. There was no cover here for Indians. 'Twas then that the men traded their muskets for portions of bread and cheese. And then that easy conversation passed between the merchants.

My father turned to look over his shoulder and slowed the walk of his oxen so that Thomas Smyth's slower pair, last on the road, could catch up. They labored with their heavy load, tongues lolling in fatigue. "And what are you selling today, Thomas Smyth?"

I turned to hear Thomas's response and saw his teeth flash. "Oh, I've a chain for every goodwife who hopes to slaughter and drain a fatted calf or stout pig this month coming. And a hook for every need. And you, Goodman Phillips?"

"A thing or two. This and that. An ordinary bench and a stool. Some small tables and a cupboard." He put a hand to the oxen's yoke and clucked to set it straighter on the path. He had more than those few things of course, and his benches were only ordinary in the practical sense of the term. They had legs which had been turned on a lathe to produce fanciful bulbs and knobs. And the stool had a seat that had been smoothed to a shine.

"And you, Susannah Phillips? What do you do this day?" The pleasant conversation suddenly turned wearisome with his question.

Thankfully, my father answered. "She shops to complete her dowry."

"Felicitations, then."

I nodded my thanks, though I could not bear to give it in words.

We came, finally, to the town green, where merchants had already begun to gather. There was a smell of meat roasting and the sizzle of fat dripping into flames. Several pigs roamed the area, rooting in the mud and straw. Behind them, a swine reeve tapped a stick, no doubt trying to herd them out of town. Several small urchins skulked about; greedy gleams lit their eyes as they surveyed the wares . . . and the gullibility of the merchants attending to them.

I closed my eyes and imagined myself once more in Boston, my feet set upon the road to Grandfather's house. But then I sighed and opened them. No such pleasures awaited me this day. As we set up next to Thomas and Goodman Hillbrook, a woman passed by in a frivolous state of dress. Undress. She looked as if she had not seen a sad color in the short years of her life. Her gown was made from a shiny cloth that had been dyed as pink as a trumpet weed. Though she wore a collar in name, it was fastened far back on her neck and the line of her gown was cut so low that the tops of her breasts could be seen . . . which showed just how little her cloak was used for covering. There were so many ribbons sewn onto her bodice she looked like a buckbean. Her great puffed sleeves made it likely that she might flutter away in the morning's slight breeze, and they did not even cover the full length of her arms. She was wearing a hat . . . or something that looked like it, but her hair was visible to all and sundry, curling down from a topknot to caress her cheeks.

And I could not help but stare at her as she walked by.

But then I prayed for her soul. Only utter depravity would convince a woman to dress in such a manner.

After helping Father unload his wares I toured the market, Mother's list at the forefront of my thoughts. She needed several barrels of salt for preserving meats and making brines. A goodly amount of sugar. Some diverse spices. All of these I purchased and then ordered they be brought to Father's cart. Once I had done those tasks, then I was free to wander farther into the shops of the town to complete my dowry. I confess that I went about it with all the zeal of a man condemned to die. In the first shop I purchased some needles, sewing silk, and a sturdy pair of scissors.

Placing them into my pocket, I walked next door to the milliner's. The new one, come from Boston. As I stepped into the shop, I saw that before me had come that young woman I had seen in the market. She of beribboned gown and uncovered hair. She was looking at ribbons as if she had decided she needed more of them.

"Have you none in a bright carnation?"

"And who else in this town dares to wear that color, save you? Were I to have some sent, you would have to promise me you would buy it all. Every last thread of it."

"And why should I not if you had it sent in carnation? 'Tis my favorite color."

The milliner sighed and shook her head. "Have you not one somber thought in your head?"

"Why should I? You people have quite enough of them. And why should you begrudge me this one little, tiny pleasure?" I had heard those words before, or something quite like them! Had the woman grown a foot and changed herself into a man, she might have been the captain himself.

It was quite clear the milliner did not approve of the woman, but it was just as clear that she bore her no ill will. No great animosity. In fact, she seemed rather amused by her candor.

Beside the beribboned woman, I felt quite plain. Fairly simple. Rather dull.

The shopkeeper directed her attentions to me. "You would like . . . ?"

"I should like a length of lace."

She brought several styles up from a drawer and laid them upon the table for my view. But they were meager in both width and decoration.

"I had hoped to find something . . . more . . ."

The shopkeeper's brows rose. She gathered the examples she had just shown me and replaced them with others.

Still, they were not what my mother had hoped for. "Have you nothing . . . greater?"

Her brows rose higher still, but she only sniffed and returned the lace to their drawers and brought out two more. "This one is worn by Selectman Miller. And this one here, by his wife."

I might have chosen the first, but it was clear the milliner was suggesting the second.

"How much for the second?"

She gave my clothes a glance and then stated the price. "But it is not fit for a man below a . . . certain station."

"I am to be married to a man of great station." And if his station could give me the right to face a woman such as this with a smile upon my lips, then perhaps it would not be so very terrible a marriage.

She returned my smile and placed her scissors at the ready. "How much?"

"A man of great station?" The young woman turned round from her inspection of ribbons and looked at me with some interest.

"Aye." I did not mean to be a spendthrift with information that was mine alone to bestow.

"Pray which man? Of which town?"

"Simeon Wright. Of Stoneybrooke."

"Simeon. 'Tis a name that is difficult to forget." She addressed herself to the proprietress. "Is that not the one, Mistress? The one from Boston?"

The milliner crimped her lips together and nodded.

Why would being from Boston be such a dreadful thing? "We are all of us in Stoneybrooke come from Boston."

The young woman raised one slender eyebrow. "Are you not a brave one, then?"

"A brave one? Why must I be so?"

"To marry such a man."

"Such a man as . . . what?"

Again they exchanged glances. And it seemed to me that the milliner shook her head, ever so slightly.

The younger woman looked straight into my eye and, birdlike, tilted her head. "I err in dispensing gossip. And truly, I know not exactly what happened or what was said . . ."

Something had happened? Something was said? "If there is something I should know, please, make haste in the telling of it. Is there some reason . . . should I not . . . ?"

The woman stared at me one moment longer, and then she made a show of adding a smile to her face. "In truth, some reason can be found not to marry most men." But then, the smile slipped. For just an instant. "Only do you be careful. 'Tis said the men in that family are brutes. Is that not so?"

The milliner's eyes dipped toward her table, and she shrugged. " 'Tis what we have heard. But that does not make it so."

The woman returned her attentions to the ribbons, taking them to hand and stroking their shiny lengths. But just when I thought she was done with me, she spoke. "You have good taste. Selectman Miller is my husband. And I, his wife." Then she walked to the door, drew it open, and headed out into the chill with a flounce.

I could not help staring at her as she left. When I turned back to the milliner, the woman was shaking her head. "An impudent little thing without a pious thought in her head. She was on a ship bound for Virginia that landed in Boston instead. The selectman, newly widowed, took one look at her and proposed. That instant."

"She is not . . . a Puritan . . . ?"

The woman laughed. "One would not think it to look at her, would one? She told me she made an arrangement with the selectman. For want of throwing away perfectly good clothing, she is to wear the gowns she brought from England until they fall apart."

"Aye?"

She looked up at me with a twinkle in her eyes. "But she comes to me, now and then, to assure that they do not. Fall apart."

I shook my head as well, marveling at the glimpse of a woman I had mistaken for frivolous. She most likely ruled her husband as well as her home. "She is not . . . her virtues are . . ."

"She is the wife of but one husband, if 'tis that which you are asking."

I flushed in confirmation.

"There is naught but a faithful soul beneath all of that frippery. 'Tis not her fault the ship got blown from its course."

The ship. And it had been bound for Virginia! "And when was that?"

The woman's eyes narrowed in thought. "Must have been . . . in spring. Late."

I could see it. She was a perfect match for the only other person I had known come recently from England. The woman was the captain's equal in fashion as well as attitude. And the both of them bound for Virginia. What sort of people were there in Virginia that lived beyond the rules the rest of us pledged to follow?

And then, in the next instant, relief buoyed me. "But if she only arrived in spring, how could she know of Simeon Wright? We have been at Stoneybrooke, all of us, for these three years past."

The milliner looked up at me with something like pity in her eyes. "Good news is difficult to keep from traveling. And bad news, even worse." She held out the packet of lace to me.

I exchanged coin for it.

As I let myself out the door, I thought I heard her say, "God keep you."

It looked to have been a profitable day at market for all. Thomas Smyth's oxen were light on their feet compared to that morning. And Father had sold all but his cupboard.

We walked along beneath a sky cobbled with clouds. Father passed me a loaf of bread. I broke off a piece and handed it back.

"You are ready, then. For the wedding."

"I have a collar left to make. And a board cloth. And a gown."

We walked on several dozen yards in silence. "And after those, all is readied."

I nodded.

After going up one hill and down another, Father spoke again. "I have no misgivings about the man, about Simeon Wright, beyond the way he keeps his business. Some, I suppose, are shrewder than others. Still if I . . . if there is some reason . . ."

There was no reason. Perhaps if he had asked me what I felt about the union. If he had asked me whether . . . I was happy about it. But what had happiness to do with anything? And why should I doubt my own father's opinion? Had not God entrusted me to his care? And what sort of daughter would I be if I questioned my father's guidance? I, who longed to be good? This then, was one way in which I could do it: *Children, obey your parents in the Lord.* Was that not the first of the commandments that I had been taught? "He is . . . a selectman."

"Aye. Aye, that he is." Father's face seemed to brighten at that thought. "Chosen by the freemen of the town."

"He looks after his mother."

"He does. The poor woman."

"You do not . . ." How could I ask if *he* knew some reason, had some cause for the marriage to be cancelled? How could I question his provision for me? Give voice to the thought that he might knowingly pledge me to some man who . . . was not . . . good? I could not do it.

"Aye?"

"You do not . . . you do not know how good a father you have been."

He looked up at me then. For just a moment. Quickly. Then he fixed his eyes once more on the path ahead of us. "Well, now . . ."

The remainder of the walk home was spent in silence.

24

WE MET UP WITH the captain that night as we walked from the road toward the house.

He blew a ring of smoke in our direction. It quivered as an apparition in the moon's light before he pushed away from the house and came to fall into step beside us. Beside me. "And how was it, the market?"

" 'Twas filled with merchants."

"There were no consumers of fire? No one chasing after greased pigs?"

In truth, I did not know. Perhaps there had been. It seemed a pity not to have enjoyed the journey more. Who knew when I might next go? And then I remembered one thing. "I met there a Mistress Miller who had been married to one of the selectmen of that town."

He received that information as if it meant nothing to him.

"Newly married. She said that she had come on a boat that was meant for Virginia."

"A Mistress Miller?" He shook his head.

"She was . . . ." How did one describe, exactly, how she was? "She wore . . . she had many . . . ribbons. And bright, fair hair. With curls. She would have been called something else when you met her."

His eyebrow had lifted and his eyes twinkled. "Something else indeed! You remember to me Mistress Howard." He *tsk*ed. "That such a sad fate has befallen her."

Father had already walked on past us toward his shop. We trailed along after him behind the cart.

"What sad fate?"

"Hmm? Oh. To have married one of you. One of those dour men. She was such a girl for laughter and for teasing. I cannot imagine it."

"We are not all dour and grim."

"Perhaps not." He stopped to look at me. There was hesitation writ in his eyes, but finally, he seemed to have come to some decision. "Can you not call me Daniel?"

"Daniel?"

" 'Tis my given name. My Christian name."

I frowned. "I do not think so."

"You do not like it?"

" 'Tis not that. 'Tis simply that I would only call a brother by his Christian name."

"Well, that would not do! Please, say no more. I withdraw my request completely."

We had caught up to Father and so I did not complete my thought. But had I done so, I would have said this: that I would call only a brother by his Christian name. A brother or a husband. But Daniel? That was a name I truly would have liked to have said. And that thought did not surprise me as much as it should have.

The next morning after breakfast had been eaten and the men sent out to their tasks, Mother stopped Mary and me from taking up our work by placing her hand on my arm. "Your father is to take me to my parents' in two days' time. 'Tis time for the weaning of the child and perhaps I can be of some help to my mother. Her constitution is not what it once was."

There was a pricking at work in my stomach. And not only

because it was she who would soon see Grandfather and not I. "But Simeon—"

"Do not fear your marriage, Susannah. Just because he was not of us does not mean he is a bad man."

Nay. It did not.

"All that is needed is time to know him. Your father and I married with only my father's recommendation and ten words shared between us. Your father asked me, 'Was I willing, Susannah Morris?' and I replied, 'I am willing, John Phillips.' And now we are weaning our sixth child."

I knew the story of their courtship. I had heard it at least a dozen times. And the phrase "are you willing" passed often between my parents even now. But there was one thing about their marriage that she had never told me. And it was the one thing I desperately needed to know. "But are you . . . happy?"

"I am very content. As my own father knew I would be. He knows things, does your grandfather. God speaks to him. And knowing that, when he came to me about John Phillips, what else was there to say?"

Perhaps she was right. My trepidation could have everything to do with timing. It might not have anything to do with the man. How could it? Not when half the girls in the town wished to be wed to him. Mary among them.

Although perhaps that was not so great a recommendation.

"There is much to be done while I am gone. I know you will be about the doing of it. And I know you will look after my sweet babe. There will be time enough for brewing small beer, dipping candles, and making soap when I return . . . before you are married. 'Tis only for a week."

Mary and I shared a glance. We were both of an age that we could still remember the weaning of Nathaniel . . . and of a sister and a brother who had come after. Weaning was not a pleasant time. But it had to be done, and what mother could long withstand the cries of a babe?

184

"Will Father tarry in Boston?"

"Nay. There is too much to be done here."

We saw them off two days later. The child, though wrapped in Mary's arms, was already wailing as they left. Things would get worse before they got better. It was the way of babes and their growing. Two days to take Mother to her home and two days to return. We would be without Father for less than one week, even if our grandparents persuaded him to stay an extra day. But 'tis Mother's absence that we feared. Even if she only stayed one week, it would take another four days for Father to fetch her home. We would be left to manage the house for nearly three weeks on our own.

The first four days went well enough. It was the morning after Father's return that Simeon Wright knocked upon our door. "I've come to speak to you of Susannah." All eyes lifted from our breakfast.

Father gestured him to sit.

Simeon Wright shook his head, stood planted in the door.

"Aye?"

"I would have the day of our marriage determined."

Father's brow lifted. "Would you, now?"

" 'Tis what I've come to say."

"Well . . ." Father wiped at his lips with a napkin. "No marriage will take place without her mother. I need her here to manage the house."

"And so she shall. But why can the date not be decided?"

"It can be. Upon Goodwife Phillips's return."

Simeon Wright frowned. And then he shrugged. "Upon Goody Phillips's return, then. But I warn you: I will not wait one day more than I must."

Had he said it with any ardor, with any passion, it might have changed my thoughts toward him. As it was, he said it with all of the

185

interest of a merchant trading at market, coming to claim something for which he'd already paid.

" 'Tis not my intention to hold up a marriage. I simply have need of all of my children while their mother is gone."

After he had left, Mary pushed away from the table and busied herself with the child.

The day before Father was meant to fetch Mother, a heavy north wind began to blow. By evening it had brought snow. Father paced by the fires after dinner, opening the door once or twice to assay the accumulation. The swirl of falling flakes spun my eyes dizzy each time he opened it. Morning proved his worries well founded. The feeble light revealed that no one would be going east until the spring.

The previous year after the first heavy snow, a man new to Stoneybrooke had braved the drifts. He had insisted the road to Newham had been engraved upon his memory. But the fallen snow must have masked what his mind's eye knew, for he had never returned. And after the spring melt he was found, his body huddled into a hollow in the common, not one mile from where he had first started out.

I peered round Father's shoulder. The snow that had fallen looked to have reached my hip. It was early for such snows, but now the roads were impassable. It was as if what we had known had passed away in our sleep. We had awakened to something strange. Something new. The world had been reduced to the space of the village. And only that much if the road could be broken out between the houses.

" 'Tis God's good and perfect will. Perhaps your grandmother has need of your mother for a while longer." With that pronouncement, Father took the spade from the corner and handed the hoe to Nathaniel. But before our brother could follow Father into the day to clear a path to the necessary, the captain took the tool from Nathaniel and set out behind Father himself.

Mary, Nathaniel, and I stood in the door, watching. I felt very small. Very frightened. Very young. Our mother was lost to us. Perhaps for the entire winter.

I was to be our mother in her place.

The house seemed suddenly too big, the work too hard. I took a breath. And then another. Perhaps our misfortune was a blessing in disguise. If my mother could not be present, then I could not be married.

My father had given his word.

And Simeon Wright had given his.

Father and the captain chopped a path to the necessary and another to the barn. Once they had done that, they hitched the pair of oxen to a harrow. Halting the oxen by the door, they called for Nathaniel to come stand atop it, next to the captain, to weight it. With the snap of Father's whip, the oxen moved off, breaking a path to link us to the road.

I bundled the child in a blanket, and Mary and I came out of the house to watch them work.

Once they had broken through to the road, we waited there, all of us, until a shout from the top of Wright's hill informed us that all to our right had been broken out. Eventually they reached us, a harrow and a team of twelve oxen. Father unhitched his own pair from our harrow and joined them to the others. Off they went, from house to house, each man adding his own team to the group.

Behind them ran a string of boys, Nathaniel among them, ostensibly shoveling away at the drifts but throwing more snowballs than shovelfuls of snow. Just as Mary and I turned to go back into the house, a shout drew our attention. Simeon Wright appeared in a narrow sleigh pulled by a prancing horse. He was seated between an Ellys girl and a Baxter girl. They slid by, the girls smiling and giggling, Simeon seemingly indifferent to their foolishness.

Mary looked at me, a question in her eyes.

I spun on a heel, pretending I had not seen them. For how was I to know why Simeon Wright, betrothed to me, would parade around town with two other girls in his sleigh? How was I to know why he wished to shame me? To mock me? And why he had bothered to publish our banns when he so clearly desired others' company to my own?

I turned away from the spectacle and went back inside.

There were things we had held off doing, Mary and I, thinking Mother would soon be returning. That day, we started about the doing of them.

There was small beer to make and candles to dip. There was flax to be spun and meat to be salted. As if that were not enough, there were the myriad daily tasks required so that all of us might be clothed and fed and sheltered in comfort. And then, there was the child.

He still would not eat or drink as easily as I would have liked.

A stubborn mite, I knew he would not spurn us so well once hunger began to gnaw at his belly, but with such a great belly as he had, there was time needed for desperation to do its work.

That forenoon, Father arranged for a day-girl to come starting the following morn. Just to lend a hand, he told me. If he had feared my sensibilities, he need not have worried. They were not very tender, and I was after all the help I could get.

That night while Nathaniel tried to persuade the child from whimpering to smiling, the men sat on a bench in front of the fires while Mary and I picked through their hairs with combs. It would not have done for Mary to comb the captain's and so, as Mother's task, it was left to me.

It did not seem right, his being a man unmarried and a stranger, but I took a breath, took up the comb, and then parted that lovely hair straight down the middle. It was so thick, so heavy, it ran like water through my fingers. I imagined that it must feel like silk. For what other sensation could be so extravagant, so luxurious, so bordering on decadence?

I combed and parted, parted and combed, catching lice between my fingers and crushing nits between my nails.

Beneath my probing, the captain shifted.

It made me conscious of my hands woven through his hairs, my fingers kneading his scalp. I had not touched any man thus. Ever.

"Do you need me . . . want me . . . to turn?" His voice seemed somehow strange, stifled, as if it took great effort for the words to reach his throat.

"Nay." I added speed and precision to my work. And as I did it, I tried to talk reason into my thoughts. Why should his head signify anything different than Father's or Nathaniel's? Or John's? Had I not imagined myself doing exactly this when I had imagined myself married to John? It was something any goodwife would do. And yet . . . I was no man's wife. Not yet. But still the captain's welfare had been given over to my care. And had his voice not sounded rather faint? As if his head had been stopped up? "Do you feel the coming of winter in your head? I could make a plaster for you."

"Nay! Do not leave me."

He had perhaps spoken overloud, for I saw Father glance over at us.

"Least . . . not until the work is done." The captain must have seen him as well.

"In truth, your hairs are so long and they have entrapped so many . . ."

Father grunted. "Do as you must." He rose then, Mary having finished with him, and gave his seat to Nathaniel.

And so I continued combing and parting, parting and combing, catching lice between my fingers and crushing nits between my nails. Imagining myself a goodwife. A goodwife to . . . some man other than Simeon Wright.

25

AS I WAS MEASURING out mother dough into a bowl one morning, Mary bumped into me in passing.

The bowl struck the floor and broke.

"Sorry."

Clearly, she was not. It was not the first time she had done it. And my arms and legs were marked with bruises where she had kicked out at me in the night. The Holy Scriptures said the same fault must be forgiven seventy times seven times. But our savior could not have known that I would be pummeled in the process. "If you cannot be civil—"

"I said I was sorry."

"Stop punishing me for Simeon Wright's mistake! He is the one who spoke. He is the one who published our banns. It was a *mistake*. And I am the one who will live with it for the rest of my life!"

She looked at me long and hard. And then she spoke. "If you knew anything about Simeon at all, you would know it was not a mistake." Her words were edged with bitterness, anger, and . . . shame?

"What do you know of him?"

"More than . . . " She pressed her lips together. Shook her head.

I left off collecting pieces of the bowl and rose to my feet. "What do you know of Simeon Wright?"

"Only that he is pledged to my sister." She spat out that last word as if she hated the sound of it. " 'Tis enough."

"I cannot help it if you imagined some flirtation with him. I cannot help it that he offered for me. I cannot help it that I was made to accept."

"You can help nothing at all." She sped toward the door, grabbed her cloak, and left.

❧

Thomas came back into the house as I was readying to leave it. I had taken my cloak from the peg and was tying it beneath my chin.

"Where do you go?"

"To the Phillips's."

Surprise lit his eyes. And . . . delight? "I am glad you go to see them. You should be about more often."

I went about when I had to. I went to the meetinghouse with Thomas of a Sabbath and I went to the fields in the forenoon of a summer's day. I had tried to fall into the easy habit of the other women. Into a borrowing of this or a sharing of that. But I never knew what to say. Or what to do. And did they know me, I was certain they would never wish for me to darken their doorstep with my shame.

"Greet them for me."

I nodded and slipped out the door.

I was going to the Phillips's, but it was not as Thomas thought. Though I was going to see Susannah, I was also going to warn her. She seemed confused. Bewildered. As if all that had happened was somehow a simple mistake. A mistake that she could set right by following through with the marriage.

Perhaps she could.

But I knew that it would cost far more than she knew.

❧

Just a short while later, Mary came back in the house at a near run. She slammed the door behind her and pulled the latch string in.

"What—?"

"Hush!"

"Why?"

" 'Tis Small-hope."

"What of her?"

"She is coming down the road as if a demon chased her, and it looks as if she intends to stop here."

It might have been an inconvenience to entertain her, but there was no need to be rude. "Open the door and put the latch string back out."

"Nay."

"And why not?" Mother would never have put up with Mary's foolishness.

"She is . . . odd. And 'tis uncanny how she can just . . . appear. Out of nowhere."

"She is . . ." What was she? "Just . . ." What? " . . . different. 'Tis an opportunity here to be a friend to the friendless."

"Let some other household do it. If she truly wants a friend, she has Thomas. And 'tis time for her to be about the bearing of a babe."

"Mary!"

"They have been wed these three years." She stood close to the oiled paper of the window, then withdrew as a shadow passed in front of it. On the tips of her toes, she walked across the room to stand next to me. Hissed in my ear. "And if her womb is cursed, there must be some reason for it."

❧

When I reached the Phillips's, I realized the latch string had been pulled in. That was odd. Had I not just seen it, blowing about in the wind? Had not Mary just run into the house?

What could . . . why would . . . ?

Knowledge brought a flush of red to my skin: They did not wish to receive me.

I stood there for one moment, staring at the door, wishing I might let myself inside. My message was too important, the danger too great for Susannah not to hear it.

But I was not wanted.

I was never wanted. Small-hope. Small hope of ever truly finding a place for myself here. Of ever really becoming part of the town. Pulling my cloak tighter around me, I hunched my shoulders against the wind and started back the way I had come.

"How could you—"

"Hush! She might still be out there."

I *wanted* her to be out there. I put Mary's hand aside and crossed to the door, pulled it open wide.

There was nothing there but the wind. It blew a few snowflakes in across the doorstep. Looking down, I could see where Small-hope had stood. Her shoes had pressed an outline into the snow.

Of a sudden, I knew a strange desolation.

Running down the path, I called out her name. As I reached the road, I could see her in the distance, her slight form wrapped in her russet colored moth-eaten cloak.

"Small-hope!"

She gave no sign that she could hear me.

The next week the weather began to warm. The sun came out of a day and began to melt the snow. Drifts that had been shoulder-high soon shrunk to the height of my waist. Three days more, maybe four, and the roads might be judged clear.

Father might leave.

Mother might return.

In three weeks time, I could be wed.

I had counted on a three-month reprieve. Now I had not even half that.

Several days later after dinner, Father made an announcement. "Tomorrow I go for Mother."

My hopes sank to my toes and poured out upon the ground.

He looked toward me. "I must not delay. Not while the weather is so favorable."

"Nay, Father. You must not delay." I knew that he must go.

" 'Tis not that . . . well . . . hmph." He dropped his chin to his chest. Left it there for a moment. "What else can I do?"

Nothing. There was nothing that anyone could do.

He opened the Bible and began to read. It was from the book of Psalms. " 'The Lord taketh pleasure in them that fear him, in those that hope in his mercy . . . He giveth snow like wool: he scattereth the hoarfrost like ashes. He casteth forth his ice like morsels: who can stand before his cold?' "

Who indeed? And had I not already profited from God's snow and hoarfrost and ice? Why then should I hope to profit any longer?

I went to bed that night, dull of heart and tired of hoping.

But in the morning, I woke to a world gone white once more with snow. Father would go nowhere this day, nor this week, perhaps not even this month. And neither would Mother.

Some several days later, after the road had been broken out once more, I set Mary to work with the day-girl, showing the girl where the pigs were kept and where the chickens made their roosts. Not long after, I heard the door scratch the floor and looked up, surprised they had accomplished their tasks so quickly. But it was not the girls; it was Simeon Wright.

He had not knocked but had come through the door as if he owned the place. And then he sat down at the table.

"Good day to you, Simeon Wright."

He fixed his pale eyes on me in reply.

"Is there aught that I can do for you?"

194

"Nay."

I sent a prayer to heaven that the girls would come back soon, for I had no wish to entertain him on my own. I went on with my work for some moments, sliding the pressing iron back and forth across Father's shirt. But Simeon Wright's constant stare unnerved me. I cast an eye toward him as I was drawing the iron back toward me and it ran right into my other hand.

Abandoning the iron, I slipped the burnt finger into my mouth. Then I rummaged through the cupboard to find an unguent to smear atop it. Fumbling with the top of first one pot, then another, I finally found the right jar.

Mary came in through the door with the day-girl behind her, saw Simeon sitting at the table, and went right back out, nearly barreling over the poor mite in her haste.

It was only after I had applied the cream to the wound that I realized I had left the iron atop the shirt. I rushed to pick it up and found the shadow of its base imprinted upon the material. Permanently.

Now Father had only one shirt left: the one he was wearing.

From the table, Simeon spoke. "Have you naught to eat?"

I looked up from the burnt shirt. Blinked.

" 'Tis noon. Or nearly."

Nearly? It would be noon in . . . about one hour. I could not understand what it was that he was asking. It was our habit to eat a bit past the noon hour. About the time that Father came in from his shop.

"At Wright's hill, we eat at noon."

"And here, we eat a bit later. I could offer you something, but if you insist upon having it now, 'tis only a biscuit and some cheese that I could serve you." The pottage had just come to a simmer over the fire. As I looked toward it, I realized I needed to place the pudding atop it to steam.

Simeon rose to his feet and came toward me, staring at me with great intensity. "When you are mistress of Wright's hill, you will see that I am served. Well. At noon."

I moved to place some distance between us. "It will be my pleasure to do so. When I am mistress of Wright's hill." As I stood there calculating how many more steps back I could take until I trod into the fires, the door opened once more and the captain came through it. Relief turned my knees to water.

The captain's glance took us in. Settled on the space between us. Looked back toward the parlor. Up to the loft. "Have you no one to help you?"

"Nay." And bless him for noticing.

He came to my side in two quick steps. Taking the iron from me, he set it on the hearth. After pouring the dying embers from the iron's heater, he refilled it and then set the iron in it once more. "Do you need the pot moved? The fires stirred?"

Simeon moved off away from us and returned to the table, mumbling about women's work.

"If a man cannot make himself useful, then what sort of man can he be, after all?" The captain smiled at Simeon Wright, though it seemed to me, by the set of his shoulders, that he would rather have struck him.

True to his sentiments, the captain made himself useful indeed, hauling logs and piling them beside the hearth. In his presence, the burden of Simeon Wright eased and I was able to concentrate on my work once more. Enough to realize that I was woefully unprepared for dinner. And that I needed Mary and the girl to help me.

I rolled up the ruined shirt and set it to the side, then turned my attentions to the turnips meant for the pottage.

"What is it?" The captain had finished piling the logs and now he stood before me, gazing into my face. "You appear as if you had some great decision to make."

"And I have. I had hoped for Mary to climb up to the loft and get me some corn and berries, but I do not know when she will return."

"I can do it as well as she." And so he did.

But while he was up in the loft, the babe began to fuss.

I put aside the turnip I was slicing and went to get the child from bed. I set him on the bench across from Simeon and gave him a biscuit to keep him quiet.

All was well for a moment, but then the babe let out such a howl that I nearly cut my finger off.

I looked up from my knife to find Simeon taking to hand a portion of the child's biscuit and placing it into his mouth.

" 'Tis the babe's!"

He shrugged. "And I'm a man grown. With the needs of a man. It can wait until dinner."

Nay, the babe could not! No more than he. "In this place, children are loved . . . and fed."

"How curious. In my place, when I was a child, they were cuffed and caned and whipped. Especially when they wailed."

I might have laughed, but the words had not been spoken in jest. Frowning at the sudden presence of two children in the house, one small and one fully grown, I picked up the babe and moved him to the floor at the end of the table. And I handed him a piece of turnip as I did it.

The captain came down from the loft, bringing the corn and berries with him. He was setting them down upon the table when he lunged of a sudden at something behind me. "Nay—I do not think you'd like it much in there!"

I gasped as I saw the captain grabbing at the child who was intent upon a journey into the fires.

"Let it go." Simeon's words were strangely placid.

I turned toward him in disbelief. Let it go? Let the child be burned?

His eyes seemed indifferent to the babe's plight and curiously cold. "Could be it learns more from getting its hairs singed than it does from being stopped upon its way."

The captain picked up the babe by the nape of its collar and then secured him in his long arms.

Simeon frowned at the pair of them. "You do not stand watch today?"

The captain sat at the table opposite Simeon, set the babe on his knee and began bouncing him up and down. "I've watched the others on watch and they do well. And I will watch them again this forenoon. But I must ask you, Simeon Wright, why, in spite of everything I say and everything you've seen, you insist upon being out in the wood."

"I do not."

"Was it not you I saw early this morn?"

I looked up from my turnips with interest. Had it been? Simeon Wright had been the first to notice sign of the savages. 'Twas he who ought to be the most concerned about them. And he of all people who ought not wander about.

"*This* morn? I do not think you could have seen me."

"*Would* have seen you? Is that what you meant to say? Maybe not . . . I was standing a bit . . . concealed. I doubt any would have noticed I was there."

Simeon frowned. "Where was this you thought to have seen me?"

"Are you certain it was not you? With the dawning of the sun? Coming *back* across the bridge?"

Simeon shrugged. "Why would you have thought it me?"

"Because I could have sworn I recognized the glint of sun off your hair . . . but perhaps I was mistaken."

The captain mistaken? Surely not. And if so, then why would he be so cheerful about it?

The babe clapped his hands and began to babble in the way that babes do.

The captain took one of the mite's chubby hands into his own and pretended to nibble upon his fingers.

The child giggled, and so the captain took up his other hand and nibbled on that one as well.

"You are a fortunate man indeed, Captain Holcombe, if all you have to do in a day's work is play at child's games . . . and stand hidden in the brush, waiting for people to cross bridges."

"Then you are a fortunate man as well, Mister Wright . . . if all you have to do in a day's work is harass some woman trying to do her work."

Simeon's jaw tightened.

The captain ignored him and bent to press his lips to the child's belly to tickle it. "But if all I do this day is keep a child from the fires, then I consider it an honest day's work."

Without a word to the captain, with a nod to me, Simeon Wright pushed away from the table and left. And at his going, we breathed a great sigh of relief.

The captain opened his mouth to speak.

"Do you not say it."

"I—"

I held up a hand to stay his words, and then I walked straight out of the house to the edge of the wood. I had not bothered with a cloak, but still I made my feet take steps slow and deliberate because I wanted so badly to stomp them. I could not bear Simeon Wright in my house for half an hour's time. How could I be expected to live with him?

I wanted to weep, I wanted to yell. I wanted to curse God and die. But I did none of those. What good would it have done? And what purpose would it have served?

I let a lone tear trickle down my cheek instead.

26

I HAD BEGUN TO find sleep only with great difficulty. Began, in fact, to dread it. I would close my eyes and let my mind drift toward the edge of slumber only to have it snap into vigilance with the memory of some task I had forgotten to do that day or some chore I would have to see to in the morrow. It was torturous, that drifting away and then reeling toward wakefulness. I felt like some fish being jerked along by a string.

Eventually my thoughts would soften around their borders and the urgency of remembered chores seem not quite so urgent. I would slip into a dream of day, a dream of work. And I would repeat those tasks I had just so recently finished. I would instruct the day-girl in this and that and command Mary upon our daily routines and all would be accomplished in harmony and good humor. I would reach the hour of supper, I would place the biscuits upon the table and would realize, with shameful astonishment, that I was quite naked and had been for the entire day. I would look around at my family's faces wondering why no one had thought to tell me, why no one had warned me. And just as I began to use my hands to cover my shame, the faces of Father, and Mary, Nathaniel and the captain, would fade into white brightness and the form of Simeon Wright would come walking toward me through that haze.

And then it was just the two of us. Alone.

As he stepped near, a slow smile would begin at the edge of his lips and curl up into a sneer. And then he would come for me.

And I would wake, panting with fear.

Though the ground was blanketed with snow, the month was still November and November was the month of blood. There were pigs to be slaughtered and sausages to be made. Hams to cure and bacon to be put up. The tasks were common to every household, and so we assembled ourselves together to accomplish them.

I chose to carry offal to the fire for burning. It was dirty, smelly work, but it was also a task that I knew would ensure my solitude. The attentions of Simeon had pinched my soul. I did not wish to be where others chattered of mindless things. I did not want to hear their gossip or their laughter. I only wished to be alone.

As I walked to and from the slaughter, I set my thoughts beyond my work to the tasks that awaited me at home. When Father left to put our meat up, I would go with him to see to the fires and to check the porridge meant for supper. On the morrow, with the fresh swine's fat, it would be time for making soap. And later in the week, I would have to do a washing.

As I began to think of tasks to assign the day-girl, a shadow crossed the ground in front of me. I looked up to see Simeon Wright. Glancing around, I realized we were hidden from sight by the walls of the meetinghouse.

I hefted the bucket to my chest and wrapped my arms about it. The smell was offensive, but it placed a barrier between us. I smiled. "Good day, Simeon Wright." I looked over my shoulder in the direction I had come. Moved sideways as if I meant to return to the others.

He blocked my going with a swift step. "Good day." He put a hand to my arm.

I tried to pull it away.

He stopped me by hefting the bucket from me and placing it beside him on the ground. "You should not have to do such work. Not now. Not when you belong to me." He put his hand to my arm again. Only this time, it clasped tighter. And he put his other hand to my face. "You are so . . . beautiful. What is it about you? Why have you bewitched me?"

I closed my eyes, willing him to go away, but I could do nothing to block the burning imprint of the brightness of his eyes.

"My father always told me I was nothing. He always told me I would never make anything of myself. If only he could see me now." But for the caress of his whisper, the tone of his words might have been violent. "I have the sawmill. I have built a garrison house. And now I have you." He trailed a finger from my cheek toward my lips.

A numbing chill spread forth from his touch.

"I have always been watching you. Did you know that? I have always been wanting you. I knew you would make a good wife. But you never saw me, did you?" His hand cupped my chin.

I dared not move.

"Not in Boston, and not here either. Because of John Prescotte. But John no longer wants you, does he? So look at me now." He was whispering still, but the words had a peculiar sting to them.

I flinched.

His hand tightened. "Aye. That's it. Look at me. Now."

I did it. In truth, I was afraid for what he might do to me if I did not.

There was a strange smile playing at his lips.

"You will be the perfect wife. Chaste. Pure. As a lily among thorns. My father was wrong about me. I took you from John Prescotte. I won. You are no one's but mine."

Tears began coursing down my cheeks.

He wiped them away with gentle hands, then pulled my head to his chest and kissed the hair that had escaped my coif at the temple. "All will be well. You will be my wife. And I will be your husband."

I clung to him because he was the only thing I could grab hold of. My only partner in that madness.

"You will have fine gowns and servants and wealth in abundance. I will give you anything you want."

But he was wrong. He could not give me what I wanted because the only thing I wanted was to be free.

Soon he left me. But I could not wipe my tears away. Could not rid myself of the knowledge that I had clung to him, that I had willingly embraced him. And the thought of it soured my stomach.

I retrieved my bucket, tossed the contents onto the fire, and then walked back toward the slaughter. From this distance, the only way any would know of my plight was if I gave the secret away. But I would not do it. And so I wiped away my tears, threw back my shoulders, and walked among them, worked among them, and no one guessed. No one knew.

⋙

She was crying.

Susannah crossed the town green in front of me, but some paces off. I had seen her talking to Simeon Wright. And now she was crying.

To everyone else she might have appeared as she always did. But I knew differently. I knew how she felt. I could tell it by the way she held her arms pressed against her sides, as if everything within her threatened to leak out upon the dirt. As if in keeping her arms close she could stop up her pain and keep it hidden. And this one thing at least she was determined to do. And do well.

How could everyone look but fail to see?

How could no one understand?

If she would cry out, if she would speak, then we could help her. But I knew she would not do it. She had too much pride.

I, too, had suffered from pride in abundance, though I had not known it at the time. But pride goeth before destruction and a haughty spirit before a fall.

Very soon, I knew, she would have little left. Of anything.

Simeon Wright looked up from his labors, from slitting a pig. His eyes sought her. He did not move from his work but kept his eyes fixed upon her all the same.

Fly like a bird, Susannah Phillips! Fly swift, fly far.

❧

Once our animals had been slaughtered and the meat dressed, Father took it home where we submerged some of the pork in brine and placed our flitches of bacon in salt.

I stirred the fire, the one for the pottage, chopped up a pig's liver and added it to the broth, and then I put my biscuits in a second fire to bake. Father headed back to the town green while I stayed behind and tried to gather my wits. When I found myself jumping at every snap of the fire and turning at an imagined scrape of the door, I took myself back to the green as well. At least with all about me, I would not have to conjure my fears. I would be able to see them well enough.

To see it.

Him.

The next day soapmaking began. Mother was part of a group of neighbors that came together for a whang. They worked at a task as a group and so, in the course of a day, everyone's soap would be made, but none would have to do it alone.

It was hot work, but it was not lonely. We shouted across fires, keeping up a conversation all the while. Soapmaking was not a task I minded in the winter's air. At least it kept one warm.

Mary delivered food to us at dinner. Biscuits and cheese and a nice chill ale.

Later in the forenoon, after the remaining soap had cooled, Father helped me turn it into a last barrel. And there they sat: three barrels filled with soap. A soft clear jelly, a grained soap, and the soap that would eventually harden into a cake. My first barrels, and good ones all! They would be enough to last Mother for a year.

Though my arms were wearied from stirring the soap, the passages inside my nose seared by lye-scented fumes, and my eyes itching from the smoke of a dozen fires, still I must confess that I looked forward to the week's nitpicking that night. Aside from our evenings on the settle, during which we could not speak, it was the one time I spent with the captain.

With Daniel.

In truth, it was the only time that I could touch him. And I knew I was not alone in partaking of that pleasure. He had come to lean into me as I worked. I could feel, through my skirts, the broadness of his back and the shape of his shoulder's blades. And every time, he urged me on long past when I could find nothing more. And it was then, my fingers could do as they wished. They could slide through his hairs at their leisure and luxuriate in the feel of his scalp beneath their nails.

But that evening, as I worked through his hairs combing and parting, parting and combing, I found nits without number and more lice than I could count. The captain sat on the bench before me long after Mary had finished both Father and Nathaniel.

"Do you hurry, daughter." A reproach could be detected in Father's voice.

"I cannot—they have multiplied beyond comprehension!"

The captain's hands reached up to grab mine. "Simply do as always you have done."

"But—your hairs. They are so thick and so long . . ."

"Too long?"

"I do not . . . the moment I see one, it takes refuge elsewhere—"

"Then cut them. Cut the hairs."

"I cannot—"

Father took Mother's sewing box from the shelf by the door. He rummaged in it for a moment and then came toward me, Mother's scissors extended. "If you cannot do as he asks, daughter, then I will."

"Nay! I will . . . I can do it."

He handed me the scissors.

I took them, heavy, into my hands. And then I grabbed a lock of Daniel's hairs and I did it. I cut them. Hanks of those long, beautiful hairs dropped to the floor around us. I had the thought to save a length of it, but Mary stooped to gather them as I cut and then threw them all into the fires before I could stop her.

I was able to keep my tears at rein as I went about the task, but as soon as I was finished and I saw Daniel sitting there, his hairs as close-cropped as the rest of Stoneybrooke's roundheaded men, the enormity of the change and the cruelty of it overwhelmed me, and I fled the house.

All those long, beautiful hairs. The waste of them. The pity of it.

After a while, I heard the door slam. Looked around to find him walking toward me. Seeing him, without the cloak of his hairs flowing out behind him made me cry all the more.

He knelt before me in the snow and succeeded in wresting the scissors from my hands. "Here now! Does it snow? Or rain?" He glanced up at the sky. And seeing it cloudless, he looked at me.

I moved to hide my tears, but he saw them.

Laying the scissors on the snow, he put an arm around my waist and drew me down to sit upon his knee.

"Daniel . . ." Throwing my arms about his neck like a child, I buried my face in his shoulder and wept.

"They are but hairs."

I tried to laugh and only succeeded in wailing. "You are shorn."

"They will grow."

"But you look like one of us now."

"Rest assured, I will not act like one of you."

I did laugh then. But my laughter stilled as his eyes came to rest upon my lips. As he tipped his head first down and then toward me. But at the last moment, just before our lips touched, he hesitated.

'Twas me who closed the gap between us with a kiss.

He broke from it. "You should not let me kiss you. I might just want to stay. And you would not want that. I would not want that." He sounded as if he were trying to convince himself of the words.

And so I did it again.

We kissed for a few sweet moments, and then he drew us apart. "Was it so very difficult?"

"The cutting of your hairs?"

"The saying of my name."

"Daniel? Nay." And once said, I only wished to speak it another thousand times. What was wrong with me, that I could not stop kissing him, could not keep myself from lapping at his lips like some enamored pup? Surely this was not what a woman should do. How a good, godly woman would feel. But truly, I did not care. Not one whit!

"And so . . . does this mean . . . that you think of me as a brother?" He bent to touch his lips to mine once more.

"Nay." I reached up to kiss him in return. In gratitude.

"Good. Because I must confess that brotherly thoughts are far from my mind."

I leaned forward to kiss him again.

But he laughed softly and held me gently away. "However, I must not let them stray too far."

I went to sleep that night with the memory of his lips upon mine. And for the first time since Mother's leaving I slept peacefully, and without dreams.

27

IT WAS THE NIGHT for nitpicking, and I had already completed my task. Thomas's head had been picked clean and it was time then for me. I sat before him on the bench placed in front of the fire for light.

He put the comb to my hairs and began his work. He went about it ably, being neither too swift nor too slow. There were times when his fingers wandered about my head that I wondered he did not cuff me or strike me or simply crush my skull between those two strong hands in frustration. Or anger.

But he did nothing.

I wished, how I wished, that I could give him what he wanted. But I could not do it. Not even for the kind, patient, gentle man that stood picking through my hairs with a comb too small for his hands.

I loathed myself for not giving to him what he wanted, and I despised him for not demanding what was his, by right of marriage, to take. If he would just take me, just seize me and be done with it, then I might know how to live. But he did nothing. Nothing save being kind. And patient. And gentle. And good.

And oh, how it shamed me.

I woke the next morning light of heart with a smile upon my face, remembering Daniel's kisses. But my mood soon moderated as I went about my tasks, pulling Nathaniel from bed and peering into the lean-to, making certain the meat was curing as it should. I set porridge upon the table and took it away after breakfast.

As I worked at making dough for biscuits, I remembered that there was pewter to scour and asked the day-girl to fetch the scouring plants. Leaving her to accomplish the task, I turned my attentions to preparations for dipping candles. But in doing so, I glimpsed Mary's pile of mending and recalled that my own cap needed mending as well. Leaving the dough, I went to get my cap, but as I passed the bed, the babe cried out, having woken from his sleep.

I put aside all my thoughts to take him up and soothe him awake.

Upon Mary's return, I committed the child to her care. Instructed the day-girl on the intricacies of scouring. Returned, finally, to my dough.

It was after the kneading and the overseeing of the scouring that my thoughts returned to the fires. I grabbed several corn cobs from a pile and turned and tossed them into the fires for the purpose of curing the bacon.

But there were no fires. Not a one. Not any longer.

They had all gone out.

I grabbed a poker and stirred it through the ashes, hunting for a coal. Even the smallest one would have done, but I could find none.

I stopped for a moment and forced myself to think. I could try to spark a flint, but that rarely worked . . . least not for me. I could see if Father had a coal to spare. But why should he? He was not working in his shop this day. He was out chopping what remained of his wood. There was only one thing left to do, and it needed to be done quickly. There were biscuits to be made, bacon to be cured, and porridge to be cooked. I would have to beg a coal. There was nothing else to be done.

That my mother would live to see her eldest daughter begging a coal!

I sent Mary and the day-girl out for water and then I bundled up the babe, threw on my cloak, took the fire spoon to hand, and started off down the road.

Of whom would I beg it?

Goody Newman?

Nay. She was too much a gossipmonger. Word would be all over town that I had let my fires die before I even reached home with her coal. And then all would know me as I truly was.

Goody Turner?

Perhaps.

But her aid ever came with sermons and lectures, and I had neither the time nor the patience for them. Though perhaps, if I were truly good, I would look upon it as a sort of trial sent by God to test my character. But then, I was not truly good and I did not truly like her!

Goody Hillbrook?

She was a pious soul that took no pleasure in gossip, but seemed to pass it on as her bounden duty. And she was worse than Goody Newman, since she treated the passing on of scandal as a wearisome, though moral, obligation.

The babe squirmed, poking his head out from the shelter of my cape.

"Do you be patient. I promise you, 'twill not be long 'til we are warm at home."

And then I knew of whom I could beg a coal: Goody Baxter! Abigail's mother. Surely she would understand the misfortunes that could befall a young woman trying to manage a household on her own.

I stepped up to her door and pulled on the latch string.

She turned to greet me from bright, blazing fires. "Susannah Phillips! How do you fare without your mother?"

" 'Tis been . . . difficult."

She cocked her head to the side and peered at me with squinting eyes. " 'Tis not an easy thing to manage a household: a father, two siblings . . . and a stranger as well. You've the look of weariness about you."

"I have not much been sleeping." I shifted the babe to my other hip.

"And neither has my Abigail. That child of hers is a good one for bawling. Half the day and half the night. There does not seem to be aught to please him."

I nodded. I did not know what else to do.

"And how does this one do without his mother?"

"Mam, mam?"

I bent to kiss the child's head. "Aye, she speaks of your mam." I turned my eyes from the child to Goody Baxter. "He does not forget her as quickly as I would like."

"Then try some small beer, warmed. 'Twill work like a charm to sweeten its disposition."

"Goody Baxter?"

"Aye, girl, speak what's on your mind."

I revealed the fire spoon that had been hidden in depths of my cloak. "Could I . . . borrow . . . a coal . . . ?"

"A coal? Goodness me! You let me stand here chattering when you're in need of a coal?"

"I just . . . I did not mean to let the fires go out—!"

"But one thing led to another and then it was too late?"

I nodded, relieved that there was no judgment here.

"We've done it, all of us, a time or two." She reached out a poker toward one of her fires and isolated several glowing coals. "Bring your fire spoon here."

I did as I was bid.

211

She took it from me and scooped the coals into it. And then handed it back and opened up the door for me.

"Now go. And quickly!"

Stumbling through the snow, I walked just as fast as I dared, balancing the child with one hand and the fire spoon with the other.

By the time Mary and the day-girl returned with water, the fires were hot and high.

"Have you a wish to burn the house down?"

I lifted my eyes from the shaping of biscuits to my sister. "Only stirring up the fires for a bit of warmth."

A raised eyebrow told me she questioned my skills. "Stirring and adding wood to the flames are two different things."

I gestured to the cap to be mended, ignoring her question.

Though Goody Baxter's trick with small beer satisfied the child that morning, he was back to his old tricks by dinner, pushing food out his mouth and refusing to swallow. But this time, at least, the refusal was not accompanied by loud protests. Through the afternoon, the child was quiet. Not quite content, neither was he obstinate.

"Lay him on the bed, Mary. Maybe a sleep is what's wanted."

She did as I asked and then came back to the table to help me.

He woke for dinner but was silent and pale.

"Has he got a fever?"

Mary put her lips to his forehead. She left them there a long moment. "Nay. I think . . . ? Nay. He does not."

Her answer put my mind at rest. The child was simply as numbed by the cold as the rest of us.

That night as I lay sleeping, a sound intruded upon my dreams. It was a wheezing sort of noise that conjured the shape of a hoarse, rasping bullfrog in my night's imaginings. I begged it to tell me what it wanted, but it could do no more than wheeze and gasp in reply. As I turned and tossed to dismiss the image, I came to realize that the sound came not from a frog, but from someone in the bed with me.

I reached out a hand and pushed at Mary.

She protested groggily and then turned over and went back to sleep.

I could hear Nathaniel snoring, so it could not be him. . . . I sat up, reached over Mary, and put an arm out, feeling for the child.

The wheezing stopped for a moment. Started once more.

I thrashed about, trying to rid myself of the covers entangling me. Finally pushed myself over Mary's legs and felt for the child.

Pulling him away from the wall, I pushed through the bed curtains with my elbows and climbed over the rail at the foot of the bed.

Daniel rolled to his feet as I made my appearance. "What is it?"

"The child—he's choking!"

He grabbed a taper from a shelf and stirred the coals with it to get it to flame. Holding the candle in one hand, he took the child from me with the other and laid him upon the table.

The babe's eyes bounced back and forth, up and down, with each hard-won breath.

As Daniel held the taper, I brushed a string of drool from the child's chin and forced a finger inside his mouth, using it to pull open his tiny jaw. I had expected the light to illuminate the normal pink tones of the mouth, was looking, in fact, for a button or a piece of carrot or some other object stuck fast in there, but there was none. And all of his mouth had gone white: the tongue, the back of the throat, the flesh that bulged from the sides. I had seen a mouth such as that one before.

"Father!"

There was a rustling from the parlor and then a thud of feet hitting the floor. From our bed, Mary poked her head through the curtains.

As Father came into the room, I motioned him toward the child. "Look!"

He took the candle from Daniel. Bent to peer inside the child's mouth. When he straightened, his mouth was set in a grim line. " 'Tis the strangling sickness. The one that took our little Bess."

Bess had been five. This child was not yet even two.

"Is there—"

"There is nothing to be done. Not even your mother could save poor Bess. 'Tis in the hands of God."

"But . . ." I could not let my mother's child die. Not while she was gone. Not when that child had been left in my keeping.

Father placed a heavy hand upon my shoulder. "If you wish to help the babe, then pray."

I took the child from the table, sat upon the bench, and held him to my chest.

His heart beat against mine, fast as a baby bird's.

If only a way could be found to ease his breathing. As I sat there and rocked back and forth, the sound of little Bess's gasps passed through my thoughts like a ghost. I shivered in remembrance. It had been like this. Exactly like this. And then her breathing had become louder. And slower. And then finally, it had stopped.

Mary sat beside me and put a hand to the child's forehead. Frowning, she moved to touch his cheek. And then she grasped one of his tiny hands. "There's a cold sweat come to the skin."

"Bring something to wrap him in."

She grabbed her cloak from its peg on the wall and spread it on the table.

I set the child in the middle of it and wound the material around his small body. Eyes wild, skin pallid, he accepted our ministrations without complaint. After each breath, the tiny face would crumple, his mouth go open as if to form a cry. But then, lacking any energy, lacking any breath, his eyes would go round as a wheeze squeezed from his chest.

I sat, babe clutched to my chest, rocking, straining, swaying back and forth. Back and forth. As if my rhythm could somehow guide breath in and out of his body.

Back and forth.

Back and forth.

Only Nathaniel slept. He could sleep through anything.

Back and forth.

Back and forth.

Mary stirred the fires and added some logs to them.

Father, kneeling at the bench, praying with his head in his hands, began to snore. He woke when his head slipped from his fingers and struck the bench. He gasped. Then he looked, misery writ upon his face, at his hands. At the bench. At his knees. "I could not keep watch with you. Not even for one hour." Brokenly, he began to weep. "If only your mother were here."

I reached out a hand and patted him upon the back. "There would be naught for her to do." What had she done for little Bess that had proved to be of any good at all? In all of the potions, all of the poultices, all of the cures that she had made, not one had been of any use.

Back and forth.

Back and forth.

Father gave up on his prayer and slumped forward to the table. He fell asleep, head resting in the crook of his arm. And soon, Mary joined him.

Back and forth.

Back and forth.

I desperately wanted to stop, but I feared that if I did, then the child would cease his breathing. I shivered from cold; my thighs ached with the motion of pushing back and forth, my arms from the burden they held.

Back and forth.

Back and forth.

Daniel moved to the wall, removed my own cloak from its peg and then wrapped it around me. When that did not stop my quaking, he drew me up with a hand at my elbow and he led me to the settle. I placed myself there, tried to rock as before, but I was confronted with the stiff back of the piece and could not do it. I nearly wept in frustration.

He placed an arm about my shoulder and drew me to his chest.

And so we sat there, the babe, Daniel, and I. Waiting for death, praying for salvation.

The lift of Daniel's breath against my hairs highlighted the impossibly shallow breaths of the babe in my lap. Finally, I could listen to his gasps no more.

" 'I will say of the Lord, He is my refuge and my fortress: my God; in him will I trust. Surely he shall deliver thee from the snare of the fowler, and from the noisesome pestilence.' "

The child's body went stiff with the effort of breathing.

Daniel's arm tightened about my shoulder.

Trying to stifle a sob, I continued, speaking through clenched teeth. " 'Thou shalt not be afraid for the terror by night . . . nor for the pestilence that walketh in darkness. . . . A thousand shall fall at thy side, and ten thousand at thy right hand; but it shall not come nigh thee. . . . There shall no evil befall thee, neither shall any plague come nigh thy dwelling.' "

I felt Daniel press his lips to my hairs. " 'Tis a gift, a faith like yours."

Faith? Like mine? But I did not have any. I did not believe it. Not any of it! Those words promised no evil should befall me, neither should any plague come near my dwelling. But it *was* here. It *had* befallen us. There was a very real terror in this place this night.

How could I make God my habitation? A God who commanded of us all faith, all hope, and all loyalty—and then held His favor far beyond our grasp? What good was faith? What good was hope? But if I did not believe those words, if I could not put my trust in them, then what did I believe? Where could I turn?

If God was not on my side, then all was truly lost.

It was not so much faith that kept me rooted to the Holy Scriptures. It was a lack of any other option. If I did not believe this, there was nothing else to believe in.

Faith?

I had none. I merited no special favor from God; I could command from Him nothing at all.

28

THE NEXT MORNING WE understood that the Angel of Death had passed us by. And we all of us, tired as we were, rejoiced in that fact.

"Give us some butter, Susannah."

I felt an eyebrow rise at Father's request, but why should we not have a taste of sweet butter when we could so easily have been drinking of tears instead? I had just returned from the lean-to when a knock sounded at the door and it opened forthwith.

'Twas Henry Clarke, Abigail's husband, with skin as gray as ashes and the bruises of circles beneath his eyes. "I'm to see you for a . . . coffin . . ." His voice caught on the word even as my own breath stopped itself up in my chest.

"Abigail?"

His eyes met mine. " 'Tis our babe . . . our son . . . got taken with the strangling . . ." He turned away from us, but our ears heard what he tried to hide from our eyes.

Father placed an arm about his shoulders and directed him out-of-doors. Perhaps the Angel of Death had passed us by, but it had stopped at another's house instead.

It was several days before I could leave the child's side. Fear of death had left us, but the child had been broken and we did not yet know if he would strengthen or simply linger in weakness until another sickness took him from us. But as soon as I could, I took some of our best preserves and paired them with a basket of biscuits.

"Mary, watch the child. See that he stays warm. Set the day-girl to sweeping the floor. I am going to Abigail's."

I nearly ran to her house. When she opened the door, I wanted to throw my arms about her neck and weep with her. What I did instead was offer her the preserves and the basket.

She only looked at them.

I held them out toward her once more.

When she failed to take them, I walked past her into the house and set them on her board, which was already laden with food.

Goody Baxter and Goody Ellys were sitting on the bench. They had been conversing as they knit, but now they abandoned their labors and turned toward us.

I ignored them and did what I had longed to do. I comforted my friend, enfolding her within my arms.

But her own did not rise around me.

"I am so sorry, Abigail."

"He was never the same. Not after that . . . *witch* . . . brought him up out of the wood."

I did not need to guess of whom she spoke. I had only heard her speak with such venom of one person: Small-hope. I looked beyond her at Goody Baxter and Goody Ellys. They were both staring at us with rapt attention. I smiled. Tried to choose words that would soothe. "You cannot mean it."

"She cursed him. She must have."

Goody Ellys coughed. "Of whom do you speak?"

I squeezed Abigail's arm and then spoke past her toward the

women. " 'Tis grief that speaks. I know its sound. Our babe was touched with the same illness."

Stiffening, Abigail pushed me away. "Nay. Not the same. Not the same at all."

"Aye. The strangling sickness."

"But yours—" She choked on her words. "Your babe was not strangled."

"He might have been. But let us not argue. I simply wish to be of some comfort."

"Comfort? To me?"

"Aye. As a friend."

"Friend!" She tried to laugh, but her mouth seemed frozen. "Oh, your life has always been so perfect." She spat the words at me.

"Perfect?" Surprise opened my mouth. And a pent-up frustration made me speak. "Let me tell you—"

"Nay. Let me tell you, who are soon to be wed to the finest man in town . . . and who dangled John Prescotte from the crook of your little finger just the same. The one will take you to live in his great house. The other would have built a home for you. I did not have a row of men standing in line, waiting to ask for my hand. And I did not have a house. When I got married, we lived with Henry's parents, he and I, sleeping in the loft between the barrels of grain and drying oak leaves."

"But—"

"Nay. I do not wish to hear of your *tribulations*."

I latched on to her forearm and pulled her close. "But you have Henry. I would give anything to be marrying a man that . . . well . . . should there not be love at least—"

"Love! Love is not for such as you and me. Love only serves to bludgeon the heart and drive one to weep. How can you speak to me of love when my poor sweet babe lies dead? When he has been torn from my breast? While he rests forever in the cold, dark ground? You will be wearing black every day of the week and having your every request granted by servants. Everything will change for you, and nothing will change for me except that I will have to learn to live without a child that I yearn to hold every moment of the day. Get you gone from here!"

I looked over her shoulder at Goody Baxter and Goody Ellys. They had risen, coming to stand beside Abigail.

"Leave me!"

Goody Baxter grabbed my friend's arm.

Abigail threw her arms around her mother's neck, weeping.

Goody Ellys took my arm. "You had best do as she says."

"But I only wished to . . . how can she not remember that God's victory is best accomplished in the grave? Why does she wallow in despondency when she ought to place her faith in the eternal resurrection?"

Abigail responded to my words of comfort with a wail of grief.

"She will want your words of consolation later, but now . . . 'tis only a mother who can know a mother's grief."

❧

Wolves were on the prowl. They rarely went near the smithery but confined their skulking to the area of the house. I saw their tracks when I worked outside to make soap or to accomplish the wash. I felt a kinship with the creatures. Though they left their signs about, they were seldom seen. And when they were seen they were hunted, driven off, and despised.

I woke one night with a start. I lay still, though my heart thudded within my chest and my eyes searched for something amiss in the darkness. My ears told me that Thomas still slept. My nose told me the fire still burned within the hearth. But as I lay there listening, I began to discern a howling.

The keening wavered, gathered strength, wavered once more, and reached a high echoing pitch before tumbling off into silence. It was the lonely that howled so. They ranged far, wolves did, and I had been told it was only a howling and an answering reply that could lead them back to their pack. And so I listened for the answer, trying to guess the direction from which it would come.

There was naught but silence for quite a long while. I had almost given up on the poor wolf and determined instead upon sleep, but then the strange wavering howl began again. And it came from the very same direction.

It was only then I understood it was no wolf at all but my neighbor, Abigail Clarke. Her howl was not one of seeking but one of grief. And so I pulled the blanket over my head and set my thoughts on sleep, knowing that she would never find what she sought, that there would be no answering howl come echoing for her through the night.

❧

I meant to return to Abigail's several days after I had first visited her, but there were candles to be dipped and washing to be done. Ironing to be seen to and biscuits to be made. Shirts to be mended and warm caps to be knitted. Kisses to be stolen of a night. Of a sudden it seemed November was long past and December nearly over.

I placed a tray of biscuits upon the table one morning, adding a cup of ale and a wedge of cheese.

Father prayed a blessing over our bounty and then all bent to eat. All but Daniel. "Merry Christmas to all!"

Father's biscuit tumbled from his hand. Mary gasped.

"What?" Daniel looked round. "Have I erred? 'Tis not this day?"

" 'Tis not any day! Not in Massachusetts Bay Colony." Father retrieved his biscuit, a frown etched upon his face.

"Not here? But for what reason? Was not our Lord born to die for all?"

I leaned toward him. "Aye. But we are not meant to *celebrate* it."

"Then what *are* we meant to do? Mourn and weep?"

Father sighed. "We are meant, Captain, to honor His birth by treating this day as any other."

"What, no goose? No pies?"

"Nay."

Daniel looked round at the rest of us with narrowed eyes as if he suspected we were making sport of him. "Then what is there?"

"For dinner? This day? Porridge and perhaps a sauce of beans."

"On Christmas Day?" His eyebrows shot up in exclamation. "Give me one hour and I will come back with at least a hare."

"There will be no celebrating here. 'Tis the end of it."

Mary and the day-girl and I went about our business while Nathaniel and Father worked in the shop. I had no time for idle thoughts of Christmas and its revelries until after supper had been served and the Bible had been read. And then, when I stepped outside, it was only to go to the necessary.

It did not much surprise me to see Daniel smoking by the house upon my return. 'Twas only then we were able to partake in sweet communion.

"You people truly do not celebrate Christmas?"

"Nay."

"I knew you did not celebrate Christmastide, but Christmas . . . ?" His voice had risen even as his words trailed off. He seemed deeply offended at our custom.

" 'Tis written nowhere that we are to celebrate our savior's birth."

" 'Tis written nowhere that we are to eat three times a day either. And still we do."

I put a hand up to touch his face, to try to ease the reproach of my words. "God has given us His Word. If we cannot find a thing within it, then that thing is something we must not do."

"I would rather do as it says than to infer those things it does not say."

" 'Tis no inference, Daniel. 'Tis written . . . or not written . . . as plain as can be."

"Hmm. Then I suppose I could not interest you in this?" He

pulled a scarf from someplace inside his doublet and placed it into my hands.

It nearly slipped from my fingers, so delicate and fluttery it was. I held it up to the moon to better see it, and that wan light spilled through the fabric, obliterating the pattern from view. " 'Tis lovely."

"And since it was meant as a Christmas gift, 'tis also completely inappropriate, or so I have just been told. I should reclaim it." He closed a fist around one end of it and began tucking it back into its hiding place.

"Do not be so hasty about it!" I pulled at the other end to wrest it from his grasp.

He pulled back. Harder. And he pulled me right into his chest. "Nay?"

"I want it."

"And in spite of all my best intentions, I want you . . . but we do not always get the things we wish for."

I stood on the tips of my toes to better reach his lips.

He bent down and obliged me.

Once.

Twice.

Finally, and with some regret, I broke away. "Thank you."

" 'Tis I who should thank you . . . for kisses such as those." He leaned away from me, pulled the tail of the scarf from his doublet and then looped it around my neck and fashioned the ends into a knot.

I had never felt anything so exquisite against my skin.

" 'Tis silk."

I sighed and moved to undo the knot. "Then I cannot keep it."

"And whyever not?"

"I am not fit to. Father does not make the money owning such a thing requires." Of course, Simeon Wright probably did, but as soon as I thought of him, I pushed him from my mind. "I cannot wear it."

"Not even when 'tis a gift, freely given?"

"Beneath the nose of Simeon Wright? Especially not then."

He frowned. Then he sighed as well and unwound it from my neck. "I will keep it for you, then. Just here inside my doublet." He patted at a place near his heart. "That way you will always know where to find it."

And what would he do with it once I married Simeon Wright? If only I could choose! If I could choose whom I wanted to marry, then I would have that man be Daniel. What could it hurt, then, to imagine? What could it hurt to pretend? Once I married . . . once I married Simeon Wright . . . there could be no more pretending. And I feared it might hurt quite a bit to imagine anything at all. But for now, for this moment and the next, Simeon Wright was not here and I was not yet bound to him for all time and eternity. And what should stop me from storing up memories?

I had become a very hedonist! A seeker of happiness, a grasper of pleasures. But with Daniel . . . with Daniel . . . I lived for nightfall, for the few sweet moments when we could be together. Why could my life not be lived thus always? With Daniel?

He kissed me once more and then let me walk past him and into the house.

After a while, after I had joined Nathaniel and Mary and the babe in bed, he followed.

I felt my lips curl as sleep hovered over me. What a lovely thing, to celebrate Christmas. But immediately I was overcome with guilt. What a vain creature I had become. Christmas was not about me. And not about Daniel. 'Twas about Christ and the reason for His birth. It was then I decided that it was no good having a Christmas to celebrate. It inspired too much in the way of confusion.

29

THE NEW YEAR HAD seen life change for some in Stoney-brooke Towne. Without access to the common for cutting wood, some were forced to throw a portion of their fall harvest onto their fires for heat. Others sacrificed their remaining corn cobs and still others the flax intended for spinning and weaving. But God had chosen to bless the Phillips. Little had changed for us.

I rose each morning, determined the tasks for the day, and went about the doing of them without giving much thought to my approaching marriage, nor to the approaching change of the seasons, nor to Mother's return. But though I wasted no thoughts upon them, the burden of those unspoken, unwanted events weighed heavy upon my heart.

One forenoon, thinking on supper, I decided on serving a simple pottage and a pudding of Indian bread. With some dried blueberries mixed into it for a bit of cheer. It would be not unlike the previous day's offering or the day before that, but no one would leave the table wanting.

Once decided on my course, I turned my attentions to other things. Though I had meant to start the pudding to steam, my fore-noon seemed taken with other tasks. And soon the door opened and Goody Hillbrook pushed through. She was laden with baskets and bundles and jars.

I left my work upon the table and moved to ease her of her burdens.

She smiled around her snaggled front teeth. " 'Tis a taste of our dinner that I have brought you."

A taste of her dinner? It was known throughout the town that not even her own hound cared to taste of her dinner. And, indeed, as she pulled a kettle from beneath her worn cloak, the greasy thin liquid sloshed over the edge and turned my stomach at its smell.

"Have you a kettle?"

I took her kettle from her and turned its contents into one of our own, reminding myself that it was not the food but the intention which mattered most. I forced my lips into a smile. "I thank you, Goody Hillbrook, for your food and your benevolence. I have scarce had time to think of our own meal and now you have shared yours with us."

Her lips turned up at the corners, but the smile slid from her face as her eyes settled on the fires. "Have you put nothing by for your supper, then? At this late hour?"

I looked at the fires and realized there was no sign of what I meant to lay out for supper. But there was no reason for her to know what I had planned. And why should she? Why not let her think her good will had saved us?

"With your poor mother away, I wonder how you girls have been getting on?"

"We miss her. And 'tis not easy to manage in her stead. But between Mary and myself and the day-girl, we get on."

Goody Hillbrook nodded. Looked around once more. And then she gathered her basket and her kettle and I showed her out the door.

After the door had shut behind her, Mary came to life. She had kept herself hidden in the parlor, where she had been tightening the ropes of the bed.

"A fine help you were!"

"And would you rather have had me laugh in her face?"

I sighed. Shook my head as I looked at the feast Goody Hillbrook had brought for us.

"What is this?" Mary had picked up something which looked like a biscuit. She put it into my hand.

I nearly dropped it, its weight unexpected in a food usually so light.

"Do you think Goodman Hillbrook truly eats her food?"

I looked from the biscuit up into her eyes and considered her question. "He is painfully thin. . . ."

Mary smiled, then began to laugh in earnest. "But do not throw it away. Perhaps Father can carve a trencher from it!"

I could not help but join her in laughter. Poorer folk often used a slab of bread as a trencher, but Mary was right. Goody Hillbrook's could probably be carved as if it were wood.

"And what shall we do with this slop?" She eyed the kettle sitting on the table.

I bent close and soon wished that I had not! "I cannot . . ." It was difficult to think when the odor had so penetrated my nostrils.

Mary bent her head to do the same and came away from it swift. " 'Tisn't fit for consumption!"

And it wasn't. At least not by us.

We waited until after supper had been served, the supper I had intended, and then took out the kettle, carrying it between us, and gave it to the pigs as slops. They grunted, hobbled over, and bent their snouts to it. But then, instead of eating of it, they blew out great breaths of steamy air, turned their backs on it, and ran away.

We doubled over, the both of us, screaming in laughter. And the mass stayed there, unmolested, in a squat gelatinous lump.

The next day I decided to go myself to fetch the water. It felt as if I had lived an eternity within the walls of the house, and with my thoughts pushing at me from the inside, and a want of change pushing at me from the outside, I forgave myself the indulgence.

Snow had begun to fall once more and I meant to go direct from the house to the brook, but the snow-shrouded wood caught my eye. And the stillness and solitude of the place enticed me into it.

As I stood there, glorying in its perfect white sanctity, a voice disturbed the silence.

"You have kept yourself from me."

I jumped at Simeon's voice, as startled as if I had encountered a real savage. "I had not meant to." For certain I had meant to, but I would not have him know it.

He had propped his shoulder against a tree as if he had been standing there for some time, watching me.

The hairs at the nape of my neck went prickly.

"With the snow this deep, no one will question if you do not return with speed. Come here and kiss me."

I shook my head, more vigorously perhaps than I should have. " 'Tis not seemly."

"Seemly!" He laughed as if I had made some great jest. Then he pushed off the tree and began walking in my direction. "Come now—you do not have to pretend with me."

"I make no pretense."

"We are to be wed. You do not have to preserve your virtue. Not for me. Not any longer."

I stepped away from him.

He stepped toward me.

"The way you look at me, the way you want me, haunts my dreams." He caught me, clenched my chin in his hand and wrenched my face up toward his. His mouth descended upon mine, lips greedy, grasping.

I tried to turn my head from his, but his palm was like a vise. I pushed at him.

He captured my wrists and cuffed them within his hand.

Confined as his prisoner, he no longer needed a grasp on my

face. That freed his other hand to roam my body as he willed. It deprived me of my hat and coif and seized at my hairs. Grabbed at my waist, squeezed at my breast.

I twisted to try to escape him, but with a jerk on my wrists, that movement became impossible. I gasped.

It was the wrong thing to do. He took advantage of that opening in my lips to force his own further upon me.

"Do you not think there will be time for such as that after the wedding?"

We both stilled at the sound of Daniel's voice.

Simeon debased me with one last torturous, bruising kiss and then turned toward Daniel. "We could be married in three weeks if she would just say so."

"Ah, but you made a promise to her father calibrated upon the return of her mother."

Simeon threw my wrists away from him, causing me to stumble at the motion. I found my balance and moved quickly toward Daniel, wrists sheltered beneath the stuff of my cloak. Simeon's grip had left the skin raw and burning.

Daniel stepped in front of me. Held an arm out to his side as if to shield me. "Have you no business to see to?"

Simeon's fists clenched as if he would challenge Daniel's authority, but he did not. He collected his hat from the ground and left without a backward glance.

Daniel shook his head and spat in the direction of Simeon's disappearing back. And then he turned around to face me. Gently he pulled out the pins that clung to my hairs and handed them to me. Then he raked his fingers through my locks, smoothing them and pinning them into place. He found my coif, placed it on my head. Collected my hat from the ground and gave it to me. "You tremble."

I did. When I set my hat upon my head it was with quaking hands.

"You must not place yourself alone with him."

"Can you even think that I wish to?" I drew my cloak around me, trying to rid myself of the memory of Simeon's hands.

"I did not mean . . . 'tis just that . . . he is not safe."

I could not meet his eyes. "I know it." And that knowledge terrified me.

"You must not—"

"What can I do? I am betrothed to him. He is . . . monstrous . . . and I have no recourse. I have no choice. And who would believe me? Girls throw themselves at his feet. Men gather at his call. No one knows what he is." Why would my cloak not be drawn shut? Why could I not hide myself within it?

Daniel touched my arm and turned me round. Then he gathered me close.

I threw my arms about him and gave way to tears that threatened to engulf us both. "What am I to do?"

"You will not marry him."

"What other choice do I have?"

"Marry me."

I laughed. "At least a dozen persons would give just cause why I should not. You are a stranger, you are the king's man, you are as good as a heathen, you—"

"Marry me."

Words fled as his hand reached out to stroke my neck. His gentle touch was a balm to the wounds Simeon had left behind. Our breath mingled, heavy in the air, wrapping like a veil around us.

He reached out into my cloak and drew forth my hands. Turning them over, he placed kisses on my wrists over the marks that Simeon had made. His lips were so very warm, so tender in the chill, cruel air. And suddenly I wanted nothing so much as to be wrapped in his warmth. To be secured within his arms.

I reached up, took his head in my hands, and brought his lips to mine.

That kiss, his kiss, was nothing like Simeon's. The touch of Daniel's lips on mine only created within me a desire for more. A desire to feel more, to share more. To have more, to taste more. Instead of recoiling from him, I was driven toward him. I wanted to be held against his chest—nay, to crawl inside his chest. To burrow there, safe and protected, where no one would ever find me.

Each kiss between us birthed another and still another. They were hot, deep, impassioned kisses that spoke of the desperation shared between us.

Finally, he pulled away from me, clutched me to himself for one fierce moment and then held me back from him so he could press his forehead against mine.

"Careful, lass."

"Daniel." The sound of his name whispered through my thoughts, entwined itself about my heart. I reached out to him, reached up to him to bring him back to me and then we were violently wrenched apart.

I fell to the ground from the force of it and watched, astonished, as Simeon leaped at Daniel.

Daniel staggered under the impact. Attempted to fend off Simeon's blows.

But Simeon was enraged. He punched and kicked and pounded. And soon Daniel was knocked to the ground.

Simeon kicked at his side. Bent down to pound his fist into Daniel's ear. Took a step back.

For one giddy moment, I thought he was done. But he crouched down and drew back his elbows in preparation for a jump.

"Cease!"

Simeon did not react to my words, but they seemed to strengthen Daniel. He rolled away from Simeon's feet and then kicked out at them, causing Simeon to crash to the ground on his knees.

Daniel scrambled away from Simeon's reach and then stood, panting, on unsteady feet. Reaching up a hand to his face, he wiped at a trail of blood that had trickled from his mouth. "You will have to do better than that to keep me down."

Simeon, too, was pushing to his feet.

Daniel tensed.

But Simeon no longer wanted to fight. He spit into the snow. Wiped his mouth on the sleeve of his doublet. And then he turned his attentions to me. " 'Come hither; I will shew unto thee the judgment of the great whore that sitteth upon many waters: With whom the kings of the earth have committed fornication—' "

"Shut up your mouth." Daniel's tone was even but deadly.

" ' . . . and the inhabitants of the earth have been made drunk with the wine of her fornication.' "

"Shut it up or I will shut it for you."

Simeon sneered and continued on, " 'Her fornication—' "

"Shut—"

Simeon only spoke louder. " 'And upon her forehead was a name written . . .' " He paused in his speech but began walking in my direction. " 'Mystery, Babylon the Great, the Mother of Harlots and Abominations of the Earth.' "

I shrunk from each of his accusations. They were true. All of them. Once again, my cape proved too small to cloak me. I was an abomination. I was a harlot. And I might have become a fornicator had he not torn us apart. I was all of the things that he said. And many things I did not wish to think of. Had I not recoiled from Simeon's advances only to throw myself, in desperation, at another? I was exactly the kind of woman of which he spoke. I deserved his words, his condemnation.

I do not know what he would have done to me had Daniel not been there. His skin had purpled with rage. His eyes had gone malicious with disgust. His voice sounded odd, as if it had been consumed by that of another. And his words, though from the Holy Scriptures, had the cadence of another's speech.

Daniel took hold of him by the shoulder and spun him from me. "Do you not—"

Simeon knocked his hand away. Stepped close to him in belligerence. "Do *you* not defend her. I intend to go before the meeting

233

and tell everyone what I have seen here. And when I speak of her debaucheries and her virtue, I will also speak of yours."

"If you even begin to mention her name, I will tell them all of your little secret. I will make known how you used the threat of savages to—"

"Silence!"

They stood there facing each other, panting.

'Twas Daniel who broke the quiet. "Be very careful what you do and what you say."

" 'Tis you who have need of care. Be certain of this: If you dare to touch her again, I will kill you. I will see your blood poured out upon the ground, your body eaten by worms, and then we will see who is strong. And who is dead." Done with Daniel, he turned once more to me.

My cheeks flamed in shame.

"As required, I will have our banns published the next three Sundays in succession. The very day your mother returns is the day we will wed."

He left us then, striding through the wood, fallen limbs snapping beneath his feet.

Daniel moved toward me. I turned from him.

"Susannah, you must go. Just as soon as you can."

"Where?"

"Anywhere. Far from here." He placed a hand on my arm.

I shrugged it off.

"Come away with me. Leave with me."

I pretended I did not hear him.

"You will never be safe. Not while you live here."

"And neither will you." Fear overcame my shame. I looked up into his eyes. "Hear me: He was not lying. Or threatening or boasting. He means to do as he says."

"He is an overgrown boy who takes cowardly pleasure in hurting others who do not have the strength to stop him. Now that he knows I see him as he is, he will not harm me."

I was not at all certain of that. "I fear him."

"He will not conquer me. His words mean nothing. They are hollow threats spoken by some boy playacting as a man."

"I beg you. Please. Go. Save yourself."

"Not unless I can save you as well." He caressed my cheek with a gentle hand. Kissed at the place where a snowflake had fallen upon it. "Besides, how would I leave? The snows have left me no choice but to stay."

30

THAT SABBATH, AS THE minister stood, I wanted to push to my feet and stop him. I wanted to protest my betrothal, to cry out my objections. But I could not tell any what Simeon Wright had done to me. Were I to give voice to his offenses, I would not be able to live with the shame.

"I publish the banns of marriage between Simeon Robert Wright, son of Robert Wright and Arabella Howard Wright, resident of Stoneybrooke Towne, Somershire County, Massachusetts Bay Colony, aged thirty and two years, single, to Susannah Elizabeth Phillips, daughter of John Phillips and Susannah Phillips, resident of Stoneybrooke Towne, Somershire County, Massachusetts Bay Colony, aged twenty years, single. If any of you know cause of just impediment why these persons should not be joined together, ye are to declare it."

I looked round, hoping to catch someone's eye, hoping that someone would stand and give cause. Surely someone must know of some cause. Surely someone must speak.

31

THE NEXT SABBATH WAS the same. "I publish the banns of marriage between Simeon Robert Wright, son of Robert Wright and Arabella Howard Wright, resident of Stoneybrooke Towne, Somershire County, Massachusetts Bay Colony, aged thirty and two years, single . . ."

I closed my eyes as I heard the words . . . and as I felt them. They pierced me, body and soul, as if driven through my flesh with a hammer.

If only he would stop speaking. If only he would fail to finish the banns.

Perhaps, perhaps . . .

" . . . to Susannah Elizabeth Phillips, daughter of John Phillips and Susannah Phillips, resident of Stoneybrooke Towne, Somershire County, Massachusetts Bay Colony, aged twenty years, single. If any of you know cause of just impediment why these persons should not be joined together, ye are to declare it."

Would no one give cause?

Would no one speak?

32

MY HANDS WERE FOLDED on my lap, my eyes downcast, head bowed, as the minister stood. There was no use protesting, no use pretending my marriage would not happen.

"I publish the banns of marriage between Simeon Robert Wright, son of Robert Wright and Arabella Howard Wright, resident of Stoneybrooke Towne, Somershire County, Massachusetts Bay Colony, aged thirty and two years, single, to Susannah Elizabeth Phillips, daughter of John Phillips and Susannah Phillips, resident of Stoneybrooke Towne, Somershire County, Massachusetts Bay Colony, aged twenty years, single. If any of you know cause of just impediment why these persons should not be joined together, ye are to declare it."

It was finished.

When my mother returned, we would be wed.

33

THE TRAP WAS SPRUNG. Susannah Phillips was caught.

A reading of banns three weeks in succession meant the marriage was as good as accomplished.

She did not appear to like the man, but I wonder if she truly knew? Perhaps in part, for she had begun to wear a cloak of shame, which fit so well about my own shoulders. It was not a heavy burden to bear. Not at first. It slipped about the body so lightly. It covered one with such ease. It seemed, at first, to offer a sort of protection. It was only in the wearing that it became unbearable.

It wrapped itself tighter and tighter until you could scarce breathe from the constraint, and then, finally, it sewed itself shut. Once the cloak was fastened, it could not be cast off, for by then, it had joined itself to the flesh, to one's very soul. It was only then that one realized just how stifling the cloak had become; only then that one began to wonder why it was that no one else wore such a thing. But by then it was too late.

Beneath the binding of the cloak, the secrets of the heart festered. And what had once been shame turned into a shield, a safeguard. For it was certain by then that the secret one had tried so hard to protect, no one—not one—would ever wish to see.

I knew exactly what would happen to Susannah Phillips.

The cloak she took on to preserve her life would soon become a guarantee of death. A slow, daily death that rotted the soul and gutted the mind. And once wrapped around her shame, it would absorb her, putrefy her. And soon, without it, she would be nothing. Aye, once the cloak joined to flesh and heart, it could not be cast off.

～

I could no longer think. Not about any one thing for any particular length of time. If I did, then my thoughts would spin toward Simeon Wright and my impending marriage. And so, I determined not to. I did not think. Instead, I acted. And it was easy enough to act when there was so much to be done. The first task of which was the washing.

The day-girl fetched the water, Nathaniel fetched the wood, Father built frames above the snow to hold the kettles, and I lit the fires. Mary gathered the clothes, giving a pair of stockings to the babe to carry as they stepped out of the house.

It was brutally cold. A northern wind blew around our ankles and up our skirts, tried to wrench our hats from our heads, and dove down the necks of our waistcoats. Worst of all, it limited the fire's reach, dispersing the flames' heat as soon as it had gathered.

As we waited for the water to boil, I went inside to mix the dough for the day's biscuits. Tipped the crock of mother dough to take a measure from it, but the crock slipped from my hands and tipped too far. The whole of it plopped out into my bowl. And then I heard the babe's cry.

Leaving my work, I rushed out the door to find the child wailing, intent upon pulling his arm from Mary's grasp.

"Goodness and mercy, let him go!"

"If I do, then he will only launch himself toward the fires as he has already done these three times."

"Let me have him." I grabbed hold of his other hand and coaxed him away from Mary and the fires. Then I promptly put him into the day-girl's care. "Do you not let him wander from your sight!"

I returned to the house, added flour and water to the dough, kneaded it smooth and set it aside.

In my absence, the water had begun to boil. We added the clothes to the kettle, pushing them toward the bottom with the beating staffs. After adding soap, we worked the clothes with the staffs, trying to loose the dirt from them. The chill air sapped the heat from the clothes the moment we pulled them from the washing water to transfer them to the rinse water.

Again, we worked them over with staffs to get them to release the soap. As I beat Daniel's shirt against the side of the kettle, the fabric began to disintegrate beneath my hand.

With growing dismay, I plucked it from the water, and spread it out to see the length of it. It was done for. I left off washing it since it was fit only for rags. Sighing, I turned my attention to Nathaniel's, and then to Father's. After I had hung the wash on a rope inside the house to dry, I bundled the remnants of Daniel's shirt upon the table. But next to it, I placed the shirt I had made so long ago for John.

As he came into the house for dinner, he saw it sitting there. "What's this?"

" 'Tis your own shirt. And a new one."

"A new one?"

"Your old one is . . . become . . . old."

He held up the old one and shook it out. Light poured through its holes. "I would offer it up to you for some use, but I confess, I cannot think of any."

I took it from his hands and placed the new shirt into them.

"You cannot have made this for me."

There was no use in prevaricating. "I made it for John, but as he will never wear it, 'tis yours."

The captain unbuttoned his doublet and took it off, pulled the shirt off that he was wearing and put the new one on. "If he had any kind of sense in his head, he might change his opinion." The look in his eyes as he gazed at me let me know he hoped that would never happen. He crossed his arms in front of him, pulling the shirt taut in back. Then he stretched out his arms in front of him.

He had broader shoulders than John had. And longer arms. " 'Tis a bit short in the arms . . . but then, beggars cannot be choosers."

"Nay." I gestured for him to take it off. "But I can take off the cuffs and add some length."

"You do not have to clothe me."

"You do not have to . . . protect me." I said the words beneath my breath so none would hear them. Though I took refuge in his presence, I knew I would not have that luxury for long. He had proposed marriage, 'twas true, but how could I run away with him from my family? From the town? My name would be tarnished forever. My reputation ruined beyond all redemption. Somehow, I would have to learn to live without his constant intervention.

His smile turned grim. "I will do it as long as I have breath. And if, for any reason I cannot, then have no doubt: God will."

God would? He said it as if he believed it. And if he did, he had more faith than I.

When I woke the next morning, it was to find the clothes frozen upon the rope. I pried them from their perch and stacked them in front of the fires to thaw. Then I turned my attentions to the making of the day's biscuits. I retrieved a bowl from the cupboard. Got the crock of mother dough. Opened it up to take a measure from it. But there was none.

I looked again.

Tipped the crock over and shook it.

Nothing. Not one sticky glob. Not one clinging residue. There was nothing left inside.

Where had it gone?

And how could . . . I thought back to when I had mixed the dough the day before. Realized that I had been distracted in the making of it. The child had shrieked. I had gone outside. But of course I had kept a bit back. I was certain of it. I closed my eyes, set my thoughts to the previous day.

I had taken a bowl from the cupboard. Taken down the crock. Tipped it over to take a measure and . . . it had slipped. All of it had come out into the bowl. 'Twas then that I had gone outside. And when I had returned to my task, I had added water and flour and kneaded it smooth . . . my ears grew thick and warm with the realization of what I had done.

Where had the mother dough gone?

Into my stomach and Mary's. Into Father's and Daniel's and Nathaniel's. I had baked it all up in our last batch of biscuits.

A cold sweat broke out upon my brow.

Using up the mother dough was not like using up the last bit of corn or the last grain of salt. That dough had a heritage. It had been passed down to my mother from her mother. And to my grandmother by her mother . . . and who knew from how many generations in the past that dough had descended?

All of the women in my mother's family had touched it. All of the women had left a bit of their touch, a drop of their sweat in that mixture. All of them had made biscuits from it which, more than flour and salt, had been composed of their hopes and dreams. A portion of it was to have been passed on to me upon my marriage. And now my legacy, my inheritance, had vanished. The connection with the past had been severed. And it was entirely my fault.

I might have wept over my transgression, but there were still biscuits to make and I would have to beg a bit of someone else's dough in order to do it. I could not ask just anyone or it would soon be common knowledge that I was worthless. That I could be no man's good wife. I might have returned to Goody Baxter's, but I decided to go to Abigail's instead. Surely she would understand.

"You want a bit of what?" Abigail had leaned forward as if she could not hear me.

"A bit of your mother dough. Just a small amount. Not very

much. Enough to make a batch of biscuits. And then I can expand it." My tone made it sound as if I were pleading, but that was foolish. Abigail was a friend, even if the eyes beneath her raised brows had just narrowed.

"What happened to yours?"

"I . . . used it all up." Feeling quite suddenly rebuked, the words issued from my mouth in a whisper.

"All of it?"

I nodded.

"But how did—"

"Please, Abigail. I would not ask if I did not need it."

"How could you use it all up?" She railed at me as if I were daft. "Is that not the first thing we were taught? Always set aside a portion of dough. And do not forget to feed it."

"Well, I forgot!" I took a breath in. Slowly, slowly let it out. "It has been dreadful since Mother left. The child was sick. And all the work. I cannot sleep. I just . . . and Simeon Wright."

Her face closed up. "Why can you not ask his mother?"

"I—but—please. Do not send me there!"

"Why not? The largest house in town? With servants aplenty? And everything you could ever need? Find what you are looking for there." The door swung shut in my face. She had denied me.

I stood there at her door, not knowing what to do, not knowing where to go. I could not go to Simeon Wright's house. Would not. Not one second earlier than I had to.

Nay.

But where was I to get what I needed? If I chose to ask the wrong person, my failing would soon be known by all.

I turned away from Goody Clarke's and in doing so, Thomas Smyth's house came into view. Small-hope. Perhaps I could ask Small-hope. The worst she might do was send me away. The best she might do was fulfill my request.

The door cracked open at my knock.

"Small-hope?"

"Susannah?" She opened it wide, something like pleasure cross-ing her face as she did.

"I need to . . ." When I looked into her eyes, my words left me. It seemed to me that she understood everything. That she knew. That she saw.

She gripped me by the hand and drew me into her house. Bid me sit on her bench. And there, in that clean, ordered, tidy space, I felt peace for the first time in many months.

❧

Susannah sat on the bench, staring at the house around us. When I had answered her knock, she had looked so care-worn, so agitated, so harried. But as she sat there, in Thomas's house, some of those worries seemed to fall from her.

" 'Tis so . . . tidy."

"We are only two."

An odd look crossed Susannah's face. Guilt? Shame? She did not seem to want to speak and I did not know what to say, so I picked up my knitting and moved to sit beside her.

"I am to be married."

I nodded.

"To Simeon Wright."

She said the name as if she summoned her own death. And, indeed, perhaps she had.

"My own sister, Mary . . . ?"

I nodded. I knew very well of whom she spoke.

"She thinks I stole Simeon from her."

"You did not. He always had eyes for you."

She looked up at me, sharply.

I looked away. "He has been watching you for these last three years . . . at least. I could not say for how long before I came."

"Half the girls in town want to marry him . . ." She let the thought linger for a moment and then abandoned it.

We sat together, side by side, the fires snapping, my needles clicking.

"Perhaps . . . it is just me. He cannot possibly be so—"

He could be. He was. I stilled my needles, stretched out a hand, and put it atop one of her own.

She looked over into my eyes.

"It is not just you, and aye, he can be. He is."

"Our banns have been published. Thrice. To withdraw now . . ." She looked up at me, eyes wide with desperation. "It would be an embarrassment. A humiliation."

I knew it. And like me, she now knew enough of Simeon to be careful. Very careful indeed. I knit first one row, then two. A third and a fourth.

Susannah sat there beside me.

We were not friends. She could not have called just to . . . sit . . . and talk. "Did you come to . . . ?"

She started. Seemed to work at gathering her thoughts. "I have come to beg a bit of your mother dough."

"For biscuits?"

"Aye."

I put down my knitting, moved to take a crock from a shelf. Measured some starter out onto a trencher. "Is this enough?"

She looked at it, a flush spreading over her cheeks. "You should not be so generous. I used up all of mine."

I gave no pause but felt my eyebrows rise just the same. The perfect Susannah Phillips had used up all her dough?

"I was . . . I did not . . . It was not . . ." She stuttered for a moment, and then she dropped her head. "I used it all up. All of it."

We are none of us what we seem. None of us what we would like to be. "I have enough for you and myself both. Will it keep until you get home?"

She drew it into the warmth of her cloak, clasping it to her chest. "It will. Thank you."

"It is not, perhaps, so good as your own."

With a smile something like the one she used to bestow, Susannah laughed. " 'Tis far better. My own is gone."

I felt my cheeks warm with the idea that Susannah Phillips was sharing a jest. With me. It was an unfamiliar sensation, but not unpleasant.

She clasped my hand in hers then. "I came for a bit of mother dough and I found a friend. You are the only—" Her words seemed stuck to her throat for a moment. She flashed a smile. Tried again. "You are the only one here who truly sees. Who understands."

" 'Tis because I am the only one here who knows . . . I know what it is like to live with a man like that. Not with such as his mother, but . . ."

"She is not quite right."

"Nay. It has changed her."

She clutched at my arm. Suddenly. Fiercely. "Will it change me as well?"

"It already has." And it would get worse. She would become an animal, shrinking from human touch, keeping to the shadows; seeking not to be seen, not to be known.

# 34

I WALKED HOME IN despair, carrying a burden of affliction. Like a yoke newly acquired, it chafed. Was Small-hope right? Had I changed so much?

Ahead of me a door creaked open. I shrunk into a shadow at the corner of a house before I even realized where my feet were taking me.

From what was I hiding?

I did not have to create the answer. It was there, in my thoughts, at the ready: I was hiding from the truth. From the truth of Simeon Wright. For if I told what I knew, then I would be shamed. And if I did not want to be shamed, then no one must know. No one must even suspect. I had to pretend, I had to make certain all was as it seemed. And because I could not do that, I had to hide.

When I returned home, Mary was teaching the day-girl the catechism. I went straight to the other end of the table, but I blocked the dough crock from sight as I scraped Small-hope's gift into it. Then I took off my cloak, hung it on its peg, and went to work making biscuits.

As much as Abigail's rebuke had stung me, my time at Small-hope's had more than covered over that offense.

I worked through the morning, dreading the coming dinner. 'Twas then I would have to admit to what I had done. It came all too soon and long before I had decided what to say. I set the tray of biscuits before Father. Took my place on the bench. Waited for what I had no doubt would come.

Father picked up a biscuit. Put it to his mouth. Chewed. Swallowed. " 'Tis . . ."

My mouth went dry. I could not swallow, nor could I speak.

" 'Tis good! Your mother would be proud."

The next Sabbath at meeting, a fog of hoary breath rose from us, ebbing and flowing from our mouths and noses, as regular as a tide. I wriggled my toes within my shoes, trying to persuade warmth back into them. A surreptitious lifting of my thighs allowed me to slide my hands beneath to warm them.

After the service the captain came round the side of the building where he had stood watch and joined us on our walk home. " 'Tis cold enough to freeze the teats off a cow."

I frowned. 'Twas true, but not all truths were worth mentioning. "If God had wanted us to have warmth in February, then He would have done it."

"He has. Have you never heard of the Indies?"

Nathaniel heard Daniel's words and came to his side. "Is it true what they say?"

"That there is gold to be had for the taking, savages walking about unclothed, and mosquitoes big as birds?"

"Nay. Is it true that sugar grows from the ground like grass and that all one has to do is pluck it in order to eat it?"

"Aye. 'Tis true."

"It must be . . . paradise."

" 'Tis very much like it."

"You have been there?"

Daniel looked over Nathaniel's head at me. Winked. "Nay. But I have desired to. 'Twas my plan to head to Virginia, and then from there to catch a ship bound for the Indies. Go along, lad."

Nathaniel obliged and sped his pace to join Father and Mary.

At his leaving, Daniel glanced over at me and smiled. " 'Twas in the Indies I had hoped to settle and bask my miserable self in the hot sun."

"I have never thought you miserable. A heathen, perhaps, but—"

He lifted a finger and brandished it like a sword. "Ah ha! I have caught you out."

I continued walking, endeavoring to ignore his foolishness. "*But*, I confess I cannot think of you in that way any longer. You speak of a God who saves and protects and . . . loves. You have a knowledge that even the godliest among our men do not."

" 'Tis because I put my faith in what is found inside God's book instead of what is not. On the words of God himself, instead of what those sanctimonious, knobbly roundheads say about him."

" 'Tis as simple as that?"

He smiled. " 'Tis no harder."

"But—"

"There are no buts in faith. There is only grace."

"And work."

"*God's* work. God's saving grace." He spoke the words with quiet confidence.

"And our own to go along with it."

"Nay. That is something I do not believe. 'Tis all on God's side, the work. We have nothing to add to it that He has not accomplished."

He seemed to be fully informed about matters on God's side of things but remarkably lacking in knowledge of our own. "But we must labor to show ourselves approved by Him."

"You mean you must labor to save yourself?"

"Aye." That was exactly what I meant.

"You leave no saving work for Him to do at all!" His protest was evident in his volume.

"Then . . . what must I do to be saved?"

"Throw yourself at God's feet."

"And . . . ?"

"And trust that He will go about the keeping of His promises."

'Twas curious strange in the way of gospels. It sounded much too . . . simple.

❧

Thomas had gone to the smithery for his morning's work. He returned for dinner, carrying a sack between his hands. Before I could lay the board with a board cloth and the trencher, he touched my hand for a moment.

"I . . . have something . . . brought something . . . for you. I bought it. Last time I was to market."

Last time he was to market? That had to have been at least two months ago. Before the snows had come. And stayed. "For me?" Had I ever asked him for something? I did not have need of anything.

He drew a red bundle out of the sack and then he laid it on the board and pushed it toward me.

I took it. Unrolled it. Held it up. It was a cape. A cape of some of the softest, finest wool I had ever seen. But it was scarlet. A bright, blinding red that could never hope to be hidden. He had brought me a new cape. But why could it not have been green like Susannah Phillips's, or blue like Abigail Clarke's? All I wanted was to live my life unnoticed. But how could I do that in a red cape?

I could have wept. From Thomas's simple kindness and for my inability to welcome it. Must I be forever marked? Would I forever be soiled?

"I thought . . . yours has holes."

Holes aplenty. I took the stuff between my two hands, though what I wanted most to do was to rub it against my cheek. It had the feel of a chick's downy feathers, it was that soft.

"Do you . . . like it?"

Though I could not look at him, I nodded. "Aye."

Did not one say 'twas the thought that counted? In the whole of my life, no one had ever thought of me before.

Not like Thomas had.

He moved toward the pegs where my old cloak was hung. "Shall I put this somewhere else?"

Aye. "Nay."

He paused in his movements, hand still reaching out for it. "I shall put it elsewhere so that you can put up the new one in its place."

"Nay. Do not move it. I thank you for the gift, but 'tis far too . . . fine. I shall soil it. I will put it away, keep it—" I did not finish my thought because by then he had left, pulling the door shut behind him.

I stood there for some time, holding the scarlet cloak to my face, letting it absorb my tears. I wept silently. I wept in wonder. Who would have thought that I would ever be given something so fine? And because I would never have thought it, never expected it, I settled the cloak about my shoulders and went to find my husband.

I heard Thomas at work before I saw him. But it was only after I stepped into the smithery that I fully understood the violence of his mood. He had stripped to the waist, flinging his shirt over the handle of his bellows. As I watched, he bent again and again, striking his hammer against a piece of iron with such ferocity that it birthed sparks.

"What do you do?" Whatever it was that he worked at, the iron had long since cooled, rendering his work utterly useless.

He threw one more savage blow at the iron before setting his hammer atop the anvil. Pausing, he stood, cheeks reddened, panting, steam rising from his body into the chill air. "I am beating your father."

I did not know what to say.

"If I could kill him I would, and I am more than half convinced that God would forgive me. But, alas, he is not here. So . . ." He picked up the hammer and continued his pounding. "I am beating that despicable, vile, loathsome coward for beating you. For tormenting you. For torturing you. For condemning his only daughter, his only child, the woman that I love to a life of fear." *Clang.* "And terror." *Clang.* "And shame." *Clang.* "That is what I am doing."

35

SMALL-HOPE. THOSE WERE THE first words my father spoke to me. "Small hope of ever amounting to anything now." He said them as my mother lay dying, as her life blood poured out of her, wrenched from her womb by my birth.

Least that is what I was told.

I was not a boy child. I had killed my mother. I was despised by my father.

At first his anger was manifested only in neglect. He left me to the care of a day-girl until he threw her into the board one day at dinner. She struck her head and died. 'Tis my first real memory. Not the confrontation that proceeded it, nor the vile curses that came after—though I have no doubt they occurred—but the red, red color of her blood and the way that it glistened upon her temple as it flowed down her face.

Now I wonder at the fact that no one approached my father about taking another wife. He was not a destitute man. There were widows aplenty and young girls ripe for marriage. But unlike other widowers, he never courted any of them.

He had no need because I provided all that he required.

Perhaps they suspected, those goodwives of Newham, for they

convinced my father to offer me to them in service. They told him it was so I could be groomed under the influence of a watchful feminine eye. It was in their homes I learned to read and recite the catechism. To bake biscuits and take up a needle. It was there, I am sure, that those townswomen thought I was safe. But they erred. They always sent me home at night.

And so I became two persons. The Small-hope who worked and laughed and prayed in the midst of those good townspeople and the Small-hope who went home at night. I existed in the middle of a town, in the middle of a people, sitting with them of a service every Sabbath, and they did not know me. Or if they did, they chose not to see me. They did not wish to see me. And there was nothing I could do.

I wonder now about that. I wonder now why I took no action. Why I did not run away. But when one is made to feel so very small, when one has been shamed by the unthinkable, when words cannot be shared, be spoken . . . then there can be no help. When one doubts the merit of one's own existence, when one is nothing to begin with, then why should anyone care? Why should anything be changed?

But then Thomas came.

Of course, he had come before. He was a blacksmith and he came to the market to deal in his wares. But when he came that day three winters ago, he saw my father strike me in the middle of the green. And instead of diverting his eyes, instead of pretending he had seen nothing at all, he spoke.

And he moved.

He moved toward me and then went right on past. He had a gaunt, wormy look to his height, but he gripped my father by the collar of his doublet and hauled his feet from the ground. " 'Tis a puny coward of a man who strikes a woman."

"She's my daughter. 'Tis my own business."

"If she is your daughter, and a daughter grown, well, then 'tis certainly my business. I have seen you exercise unnatural severity toward her, and I will stand as witness to it. She shall have free liberty to complain for redress. The Code of Liberties guarantees it."

" 'Twas but a simple disagreement."

"Aye. And preceded by several weeks—several months—of disagreements, if I do not read the marks on her hands and round her eye incorrectly."

I drew my hands out of sight beneath my apron. The bruising about my eye I could not hide and so I lowered my head. They were not the only marks upon my body, but the less he saw of them, the better.

"I have seen your daughter in town on previous visits. And a girl of her years should not be hobbling about like an old woman." He cast my father to the ground, far from him, like a dirty old rag.

The crowd gathered round us stepped back.

The blacksmith turned to me. "Come. We will make a complaint to the authorities for redress."

At my hesitation, he extended his hand.

I looked at my father, who had picked himself up from the dirt, and I read the look in his eye. It was well and good to have a champion, but what would become of me after the stranger had gone? I was already certain that it would go twice as bad for me now that someone had come to my defense. And if I went with the man and lodged a complaint . . . I had good reason to fear for my life. The sight of that poor day-girl sprawled across the floor, bleeding, dying, had never left my memory.

And so, eyes downcast, I shook my head at his invitation.

He stepped closer. Spoke to me in a tone only I could hear. "You have fear of him."

I did not dare to answer, but I lifted my eyes to his.

"And you have reason for this fear." He did not expect an answer. He had already obtained it. From my hands, from my walk, from the dread in me that even I could smell.

He spoke a bit louder now, to be heard above the murmurs of the gathering crowd. "Will you trust me?"

How could I answer that? And for what cause?

"Marry me."

I remember stealing a glance at my father. And then stealing a glance at the stranger.

He took one step closer. We were toe to toe. My father was approaching, and so he spoke rapidly. "If you marry me, I will take you from here. You would have no need for fear."

Behind him, my father clenched a fist and came at the stranger in order to accost him.

Interpreting my sudden stiffening and intake of breath, the stranger turned, dodged my father's blow, and then dropped him to the ground with a solid fist to his gut.

My father kneeled there before him, gasping for breath.

Surely this man could be no worse than the one I had lived with for all of my life. And if he was, then I would run away. Or kill him.

"Will you marry me?" He asked it loud enough to be heard above my father's groanings. Loud enough to be heard by the crowd.

I nodded.

He stretched out a hand to me. "Then come."

I put my hand in his quickly.

My father called out as he stumbled to his feet. "I have not given my permission."

The stranger placed himself between us. "You lost your right to give permission the moment you started to accost her."

"She's my girl."

"And I wish to marry her."

"You cannot have her." My father put up his fists and lowered his head as if to assure there would be no mistaking his words.

"I will give you five pounds."

A gleam shot from father's eyes at the stranger's words. He dropped his hands. "Agreed."

The stranger placed me in the care of the deputy's wife, who cleaned me up and tended to my wounds. He saw to it that our banns were read each Sabbath at the meetinghouse three Sundays in succession. And after that third reading, the next week when he came to town for market, we were wed.

I rode pillion behind him when he brought me to his house in Stoneybrooke Towne. It was new. And clean. It smelt of freshly planed wood. I breathed deeply and held the scent of it within my nostrils. There was no smell of stale sweat, no scent of rodents hiding in the corners, no fumes of liquor here.

I made him a supper of bread we had brought from the market and a cheese I found in his lean-to. I explored the place while I was at it. There was sugar and salt in abundance. Both of them things that I had seldom had.

I placed the food and drink upon the table and then stood back to let him eat.

"Do you not join me?"

"Do you wish me to?"

"Was it not the custom in your father's house?"

I shook my head. He would not want to know what was done to me in order that I might eat. But I sat down on the bench beside him. There was only one bench in that place.

I ate my food quickly, as was my habit. And then there was nothing left for me to do but sit, since he ate slowly. Once finished, he laid aside his napkin and took up a Bible. After he finished reading, I stored away the bread. Put back the rest of the cheese. Wiped clean the trencher. Stirred the fires.

And then, there was nothing else left to do.

"I will just . . . step outside and . . . while . . ." He shrugged and disappeared out the door while I stood staring after him.

Quick as I could, I stripped to my shift, grabbed a knife, and slipped into the bed. I would not give up my newfound freedom so easily. The sheets were clean and soft. They smelt of him. And if he tried to attack me, then they would be soaked with his blood.

He returned some time later. I had almost fallen asleep.

He came toward the bed and then took off his own clothes, hanging them upon a peg.

I clutched the knife in my hand.

He drew back the covers, saw my knife. "I married you to protect you; to free you. I would never take you unwilling and I will never force myself upon you." He held out a hand for the knife.

Could I trust him?

He waited for a long moment, and then he sighed. He slid between the sheets, turned his back to me, and fell asleep as if he did not care what I might do to him. As if he trusted me.

I stayed pressed to the wall, trembling, knife in my hand, until I knew him well and truly asleep. Then, knife clasped at my chest, I gave myself to sleep as well.

I slept that way, with the knife between my breasts, for three months. And then, when I realized I would not need it, I placed it beneath my pillow.

He wanted me, Thomas did. I could see it in his eyes whenever he looked at me. But . . . I could not do it. How could a good man like him want one such as me? I would soil him, shame him, besmirch him.

Nay.

I would protect him from me at all costs.

36

THOMAS STOPPED HIS HAMMERING eventually. Then he turned toward me, panting and spent, and he asked me one question. "Why do you despise me?"

"I do not despise you."

"You do not love me."

I thought about that. Was it true? Did it even matter? "Do you love me?"

There was agony at work in his eyes when he replied. "I have never done anything other since the day that I first saw you."

"With my eye blacked and my hands covered with burns?"

There was puzzlement at work on his brow. "On the day I took you from your father? Nay. The first time I saw you was several years before, on my very first trip to market. 'Twas from Boston I came then."

He had seen me so long ago? A stranger to our town? Well, he was the only one. I had never been noticed by any I had lived near.

"And why else would I have married you? Why else would I have paid your father for you?"

"If I despise you, then 'tis for that reason."

"Because . . . I paid for you?"

"Like some prized ox."

"How else was I to save you?"

" 'Tis that exactly. I had to be saved. I had to be rescued. I could not do it myself."

He blinked. "And so . . . you punish *me* for it? For saving you?"

"Nay! I punish *me* for not being able to save myself." I left the smithery at a run, going I cared not where. My footprints in the snow would lead me home. My feet kept to what I took for the cart path, punching knee-deep holes in the snow, but then they veered off into the wood of their own accord. The snow was not as deep there, the drifts not so high.

At the start I had been running from the brutal truth of my own words, but now I ran for the joy of it. For the freedom of it. Every foot that crunched down into the snow, every stride I took was a footprint I made, was a mark that I left in a place of my choosing.

And so I walked on. And on. And on.

I did not deserve Thomas, and that was the plain truth.

Why should he love one such as me?

He deserved someone decent. And kind. And good. Someone who did not even know that the things I had seen, the things I had felt, the things that had been done to me, could happen.

And how could I love him? How could I do that to him? How could I curse him with the stain of my affection?

I would not do it.

I could not do it.

He was too good a man for one such as me.

My steps had slowed, and I found myself entering the cave of a snow-covered forest.

But I was not alone.

Somewhere in the trees ahead of me were voices speaking a language that I could not understand. Indians. Must be. And I was standing alone, in a forest bleached by snow, wearing a bright red cape. Even were I to run now before I was seen, a trail of footprints would lead them right back to my front door.

I sunk to my bottom at the base of a tree, putting the trunk between myself and the savages. And then I drew up my knees to my chest. There was nothing to be done about my cape, so I drew it right around me. At least I could keep myself warm until they slit my throat.

I sat there, trembling, listening in terror, until I realized that the voices were coming no closer. And that the words were punctuated by the sounds of an axe and the sighs of a horse. Or two.

What could they be doing with an axe? Besides murdering people?

Even as I asked myself that question, the yawn of a falling tree swept through the wood. It was followed by a muted thud.

I pushed myself forward onto my knees. Peered around my tree.

I could see nothing. Taking refuge behind the trunk once more, I sat, thinking. Trying to make sense of the sounds I heard.

But I couldn't.

The voices were not coming any nearer.

Hitching up my skirts, I crouched beside the tree, eyes probing the woods once more.

Nothing moved.

And so, thrusting my cape behind me, pinning it back with my elbows, I sneaked to the next tree. If I were killed, then at least Thomas could find someone else to marry. Someone kind. And good. And willing.

I slid to another tree. And another.

And so on and so on.

Until at last I could see what those Indians were doing. And once I saw it, I still did not understand . . . not until I saw Simeon Wright.

And once I did, I could not get away fast enough.

Aye, there were savages in these woods, and they were doing evil work, but it was a mischief not of their own making.

I slipped through the trees, walking backward, having no wish to alert them to my presence. And once I had gained the spot where I had sat in terror, I turned around and began to run back the way I had come. At least then I would not be leaving two sets of tracks in the snow.

I slowed as the realization struck me that one track would be quite enough. One set of tracks could still lead them to my door. Stopping, I looked around me. Maybe . . . I could sweep them away. Fill them in. Hide them.

With what? They were as deep as my knee, some of them. What would I use? My cloak? My foot? A decrepit fallen branch?

Nay.

I would just have to hope that it snowed again.

Pray that it snowed again.

And I started to do that very thing as I headed back toward home.

❧

Placing the babe in Mary's care, I stepped out into the forenoon for a breath of air.

Please, God, please make it snow.

As long as it snowed, as long as the drifts did not melt, I was safe.

Please, God, might it snow right through spring . . . and on into summer.

I looked up into a clear sky, knowing, even as I prayed, that my wishes would not be granted. Not this day. Everywhere I looked and everywhere I walked, I saw, I felt, that time was slipping away. The snow drifts had already gone clear at their edges and then crumbled into a mush. If I stood quite still by the garden of a day, I could hear the suggestion of water melting, dripping into the earth beneath the snow.

Time was dissolving, and I could do nothing to stop it.

But still, each evening brought a reprieve. Each night's chill arrested the melting and froze the snow solid once more. But it was only a matter of weeks . . . perhaps days . . . before the post road to Newham toward Boston would be open. And when Mother returned, I would be married.

How to stop time? How to stop spring from coming? Such a cruel irony, that the relief of warming, the beauty of spring, should signal the end of my own life. That the opening of the prison door into which I would soon be stepping would be heralded by butterflies and blossoms.

The next day one of the Wright servants appeared at our door midmorning with a request for me to join Simeon and his mother for dinner the next day. I did not want to go, but I had been summoned and there was no reason to decline. And so, after having been assured thrice by Mary that I had left nothing undone, I put on my cloak and left the safety and warmth of our home for that solitary house on the hill.

The manservant opened the door to me. My cloak was taken, and I was ushered into the kitchen. Simeon and his mother were already seated. Already eating. Neither rose to greet me.

"You are late."

"I—it was—the snow—please—"

Simeon held up a hand.

I stopped up my words.

"Be seated."

And so I joined their dinner. Simeon was seated at the head of the table in his chair, his mother at one side, I at the other. The servants placed a plate upon the table before me and then took themselves away to their corners. I wish I could have joined them, but there was nowhere for me to shrink away to. Nowhere for me to go.

Bread had been set upon the table and butter to go with it. A portion of stewed hare and a pudding had been placed before me.

Mistress Wright did not move to pass me any bread and neither did Simeon. They simply took from the tray what they wanted.

I followed their example. I reached forward and took a slice. The butter had been placed at Simeon's elbow.

"May I have the butter, please?"

"Nay."

I blinked in surprise, and then smiled, realizing he was jesting. But as I waited for him to return to seriousness, as I looked into his bland, indifferent face, I realized that he was not. Feeling foolish, I dropped my eyes to my plate. Concentrated on the food. But it was hard to eat, harder still to swallow without a taste of ale.

As I looked up with that thought, searching for the cup, Simeon picked it up and took a drink. But he made no move to pass it around, setting it down near the top of his plate.

I looked at his mother, to see if there was aught to be done in protest, but she only worked at shoveling food into her mouth. She had not finished the half of it when Simeon signaled a servant.

That girl slunk forward quickly and pulled the plate from his mother while she was still eating. Mistress Wright followed the plate with her hand for a moment, pulling off one more morsel of meat.

"Cease."

At Simeon's voice she withdrew her hand and folded it with the other into her lap.

While I had been watching them with disbelief, another servant had taken my own plate from me.

And so we sat there, his mother and I, for a long time, while Simeon finished his meal. I might have left during that time, but how would I have excused myself? And with an army of servants trained to do their master's bidding, I am not certain that I would have been allowed to leave. There was naught to do but sit and pretend that everything was just as it should be . . . and in that household, it seemed that it was.

When Simeon had finished, he beckoned for a servant. After she had taken his plate, he turned his eyes to me. "You may leave."

I wasted no time in doing as he had commanded. As I walked

home, I determined that I would tell no one what I had seen, what I had experienced. What would I have said? Their custom was odd, perhaps, but it was not contrary to any law.

And beyond that, who would believe my words?

37

I HAD FINISHED SLOPPING the pigs and had come round the corner to find Daniel leaning against the house, smoking his pipe. His form was thrown into shadow by the moon's light. "Goody Ellys told me you had dinner with Simeon Wright."

With Simeon Wright? Nay, not with him. I had dined at his house, 'twas true, but I doubted he would ever let me do anything with him at all.

I tried to walk on past Daniel into the house, but he put an arm to my waist and pulled me toward his chest instead.

I wrapped my arms about him, closed my eyes, and breathed deeply of his tobacco-laced scent.

He pressed a kiss to my temple, underneath the brim of my hat. "I asked you a question over a month ago. You never answered. When the snow melts, when I leave here, will you go with me?"

To default upon a marriage agreement was a grave offense. Fathers arranged marriages and girls entered into them. That was the way of it. But when Simeon Wright had published our banns, I had not known there was Daniel. I had known of him, of course, but I had not yet come to know him.

I did know him now.

And I loved him.

Perhaps Simeon Wright only treated me as I deserved, and perhaps, absent my knowledge of Daniel, I might have gone to him meekly. But something pliant and submissive within me had dissolved in the radiance of Daniel's love. I knew now that there were other better ways to live. I had drunk of the sweetness of love and it had ruined me for anything else. I understood now what I could not have known six months before. I did not have to marry Simeon Wright. I could not marry Simeon Wright.

I could make a different choice.

Once, long weeks ago, Daniel had asked me to marry him, but he had never repeated that offer. I had assumed it was because of what had followed, because of the kind of woman I had shown myself to be. Had I not been willing to give myself to him without any attachment at all? I had known myself to be aberrant, but I had not known just how wicked I had become. Though my heart soared from joy, I knew I did not deserve him.

"Susannah?"

I shook my head. "I am not the kind of woman that . . ."

"That?"

My secret came out like the rush of a wind. "I am not good, Daniel."

His teeth flashed in the darkness. "Only God is good."

"But I could be better."

"So could we all. Hear me now. 'Tis important: Only God is good. But more than that, God is only good. Do you believe it?"

"Aye, but—"

"Do you believe it?"

"Aye." I had to. To think otherwise would be . . . unthinkable.

"Then there is nothing that can happen which God cannot overcome." He held me close for a moment in an embrace and then let go a heavy sigh. "We can only cast ourselves upon God's goodness, trusting that in the end, He is only good. And that His purposes, whatever they might be, shall stand. And so, I must ask you, one final time: Will you marry me?"

It took me a moment to gain control of my emotions. Would I go with him? He asked it as if there were some sort of risk, some kind of danger involved. But there was none. "Aye."

Marriage. To Daniel! There was no risk. I could envision exactly how it would be. It would be filled with respect and gentleness and . . . and laughter. It would be filled with love. There was no need to consider how to respond. "How will we do it?"

"When your father goes to fetch your mother, we simply ride from town."

"But . . . I am known."

"Here. But surely not in Newham. Not in Boston. Not anymore."

I shook my head. It would not work. "I am known by my dress. By my hat. By my mien. No minister would marry a Puritan girl without the consent of her father. Perhaps if we could reach Virginia . . . I could change my ways. My fashion."

He glanced at the door beside us, then took my hand in his and led me to the woodpile. From some place deep within it, he drew out a sack, opened it, and pulled a bundle of cloth from it with a flourish.

I gasped.

Held before me was a gown. It was made of some sort of shimmery fabric with trims that glittered even in the moon's muted light. There were ribbons and bows by the dozens and lace frothed from its low-cut neck and high-cut sleeves.

I was scandalized.

But I was also entranced.

Before I knew they had done it, my fingers reached out to stroke the skirt. "It is too immodest! And too fine. I cannot wear it."

"A captain's wife can wear almost anything she wants."

"But . . . how did you . . . ?"

" 'Twas intended for a cousin. But what she does not know, she will not miss."

" 'Tis . . . beautiful."

"Believe me, 'tis nothing compared to your own beauty."

And so we made a plan. Daniel hid the bundle back beneath the woodpile. On the day Father left, I would retrieve it as I went out for the purpose of fetching water. Once dressed, I would join Daniel in the wood. And together we would make our escape.

I lay in bed that night dreaming of the gown. It was too wonderful to behold and much too grand for me. That woman, the selectman's wife in Newham, rose to my thoughts. It was a gown made for such as her . . . not for such as me. How could any modest woman, any moral woman, think to don a gown like that one? Surely it was a lure meant to entrap me. To tempt me. But tempt me from what? From marriage to a monster? From a life of misery and certain abuse? The gown would be no enticement into sin. Nay, it would be my salvation.

I did not have another chance to speak to Daniel until several days had passed. And when I did, the moment was a stolen one. Taken from time that I implied would be used for necessary purposes.

Daniel greeted me at the edge of the wood by the privy house with a kiss.

"Speak to me of Virginia."

"What do you wish to know?"

"How are . . . the people?"

His teeth flashed. "Much the same as you and I. They each have one head. Two arms. Two legs, even. Most of them."

"But what are they like?"

"What are they like? Well, now . . . I seem to recall hearing that they like a good wager as well as the next man."

I felt my eyebrows rise. A wager? They were gambling men?

"And they raise a cup to each other now and then too. But not so often as to be taken for drunken sods."

They toasted each other and drank? To excess? And it was there I was to go with Daniel?

"But more than anything, they like to dance."

"They dance? But we dance here."

"Aye. A group of meek maids sashaying to and fro. Nay. In Virginia they dance what is called a gavotte, men and women together."

"Together!"

"Aye. In a dance that goes like this." He took my hand into his and began to slide back and forth, crossing his feet and then hopping. He pulled me into the dance beside him, moving first this way and then that, singing a sprightly tune all the while. And then he sped from quick to quicker, wrenching me about the wood, spinning and twirling with abandon.

"Cease!"

"Oh, never! The people in Virginia never stop dancing." But he did finally, with a suddenness that left me gasping. And he did not loose me. He kissed me instead. " 'Tis how it ends."

It took me a moment to collect my breath. "How what ends?"

"The gavotte."

"It cannot."

"But it does! It ends by kissing one's partner."

"Those people in Virginia . . ."

"Aye?" He was looking at my lips as if he wished to kiss them again.

"Those people in Virginia . . . I wish very much to join them."

"And so you shall! If your Father does not first separate us. I have done my best, thus far, to shield you from my basest improprieties, but I fear I will soon lose my will . . . and most of my convictions. Go. Quickly now."

I left him alone in the wood, humming a tune and dancing with shadows. I had to take care to leave the smile from my face before I entered the house.

It was difficult to conceal my joy. I was to marry Daniel! I wished to shout my happiness from the town green.

SIRI MITCHELL

But I did not. Instead I went about my work quietly, humbly, and kept my thoughts to my tasks. Most of them. But as I warmed our sheets for bed one night, I could not resist peering into the future, dreaming about that gown. Perhaps it was because I had never seen Virginia and could not imagine it. Or its people. But I did know what it felt like to be in Daniel's arms. And I knew what it was—precisely what it was—that I would wear.

How could it be wicked to wear something so lovely?

I checked my thoughts as soon as I knew them. Surely my soul was mired in vanity!

But, as Daniel had said, it was entirely within the rights of a captain's wife to wear such a gown. A captain's wife in Virginia. Or the Indies. Or wherever else the winds might take us.

It seemed the next week that I had summoned those winds with my thoughts. A strong breeze rose up from the south and began to melt our prison of snow. There was a restlessness, an expectancy, that worked through our home. Mary found herself tasks that could be done outdoors, and she took the day-girl with her. The babe toddled often to the door. Father took Nathaniel with him to the fields to begin mending fences, and then they started an inventory of the shop. But still the nights came early and cold. And still we sat, as was our custom, together on the settle. Mary and I had tasks to keep our hands busy. Nathaniel had mallets to shape and handles to carve. The captain his gun to clean.

I am sure I looked the perfect daughter. The perfect good wife in training, but my thoughts were far from God and His words to men. As typical of late, my mind had gone on ahead of me to Virginia, that land of hope and promise. And my thoughts were of escape and freedom, rather than submission and piety.

In a few short weeks time I would draw on the gown gladly and I would leave this town. Of course, I would also forfeit the chance to say farewell to my mother. Though I pondered that loss with sorrow, it seemed to me a worthy trade.

But before I left, I determined there was one last thing that I must do.

I did it on the day Father left. On a day that saw snowbanks collapse, bleeding meltwater. A day lit by spring's pallid dawn. I watched Father ride from the house, lifting a hand in Godspeed, knowing I would never see him again. I stayed my tears as I lifted my cloak from its peg and started out upon my errand. I was going to Abigail's to bid her farewell. In spite of all that had passed between us, I could not leave her behind without a word.

I slipped through the growing light, from house to house, unwilling that any should see me on my way. I waited until Abigail's Henry had gone inside the barn before I stepped into her house.

"Abigail."

She started and turned from her fires toward me. "Susannah?"

"I have come to say farewell."

"But . . . why?"

"I leave town. This day."

"Where do you go?"

I shrugged. Smiled. My joy was boundless, and I could not contain it. I laughed. "I do not know!"

"Have you gone mad?"

"Nay!"

"Where does Simeon take you?"

At the mention of that name, my happiness was quenched. "I go nowhere with him."

"But—"

"I cannot marry Simeon Wright. I will not. I am leaving with the captain. You must tell no one."

"The captain! But you cannot—you are pledged!"

I shook my head. "You do not know him."

"I know enough. He is the king's man!"

"Not Daniel. Simeon! He is . . . he is not what he seems."

"I do not know how he seems. I have never known him." Her voice had gone stiff and cold.

I moved to embrace her. To summon the warmth that I had once felt between us. "I could not leave without seeing you. And now that I have seen you, I must go."

"When do you leave?"

"Soon. This day. Now."

She evaded my arms. "Then it seems I must let you go."

"Do not . . . I wish . . ." Her face had grown as hard as her eyes. "Farewell." I left then, and she made no move to stop me.

I had no other wish than to be gone from town as fast as Daniel's horse could take us, but I could not leave without paying one last visit. To Small-hope.

"Small-hope."

The words were so soft, I hardly believed I had heard my own name.

"Small-hope!"

I left off stirring my wash and looked round.

Susannah Phillips was gesturing from the corner to me.

I withdrew the beating staff from the kettle and sent a quick glance around the place before I went to her. No good would come from our being seen together. It would heap trouble upon her shoulders. And possibly upon my own as well. "What is it?"

"I am leaving."

"Leaving?"

"Going."

"Where?"

"Away from here. With Daniel."

"The captain?"

"Aye."

"You can't." But even as I said it, I knew she could. Knew it was best if she did. "When?"

"This morn."

"Then God be with you."

She clutched at my hands and then let them go to clasp me about the neck. "And with you also."

I felt my cheeks redden above her embrace. "Do you need anything?"

"Nay."

"Will you tell your father?"

"Nay. But I could not leave without bidding my friends farewell."

38

HEART BEATING IN MY throat, I walked past the house toward the privy. As I passed the woodpile, I slowed, thrust my hand into its depths and grasped at the sack. Shoving it beneath my cloak, I walked into the privy house and shut the door quick behind me. I took a deep breath in the safety of that shelter . . . and then almost choked on the stench.

Laughing at myself, I hung my cloak on a peg and then stripped off my clothes and threw them down into the hole along with my hat and my coif. Long ago, picking blueberries in the barren, I would have given anything to go hatless through the day. Now I had been freed!

I drew the gown from the sack, shook it out, and stepped into it. Pulled the slippery fabric up around my shoulders and drew the laces tight beneath my chest. I draped my cloak once more across my shoulders, gathering it tight beneath my chin. With another deep breath and a wordless prayer, I opened the door and stepped out into my freedom.

Slipping away behind the privy, I ran into the wood to the place where Daniel waited.

When he saw me, he opened up his arms to me.

I ran into them.

He pressed a kiss to my hairs. And then, still holding on to my hands, he took a step back from me. "The gown becomes you."

I felt my cheeks flush.

"It does. It does not make you any prettier—nothing on God's earth could to that—but it . . ." His eyes found mine as he searched for words. "It . . ."

I closed the distance between us with a step forward and placed a kiss upon his lips.

He held me fast when I would have bestowed upon him another. But as we drew apart, he was smiling.

And so was I.

He boosted me up onto his horse with a strong hand. "The sooner we are gone, the sooner we may wed."

We rode through the wood for a while and then out through the meadow and down the road to Newham, me perched behind him with an arm about his waist. He held the reins in one hand and held my arm to him with the other.

❧

I had stepped from the house to see to the chickens when I saw Simeon Wright. It had to be Simeon Wright. He was the only one who rode his horse when he might have walked instead. If he were this far from the mill, this far up the road, it must be Thomas he was wanting. I shrank against the side of the house. I did not want him to see me. Not on this day, not when I knew something he did not.

As he passed by, he turned his head in my direction. Drew up on the reins.

I closed my eyes, hoping, praying, that he would not see me, doubting for once the shield of my invisibility.

Finally, I heard a soft cluck, and then the slop of hooves through melting snow as he rounded the corner toward the smithery.

I stayed there against the wall for some long moments, trembling. So shaken was I by his presence that I failed to note the coming of

Goody Clarke. Not until she passed me by and came to a halt not two paces from me, at the shadowed corner of the house.

As the sound of hooves approached once more, Abigail stepped away from the corner. "Simeon Wright!"

The splash of hooves stopped. "Goody Clarke."

"I have news."

"And so have I. The smith is to make a pair of gates for my marriage. To place at the entrance to Wright's hill."

"Then you must tell him to be hasty about it."

Simeon Wright glanced round, his eyes coming to rest on the shadowed remnants of the winter's snow still clinging to the side of the house. "Aye. With the snow melting, Goody Phillips will return."

"Nay." The word rang with the peculiar triumph possessed by those who know something that others do not. "With the snow melting, Susannah Phillips will leave."

"Leave?"

"She leaves with Captain Holbrooke."

"Leaves?" He spoke the word as if he did not know its meaning. "With Holbrooke?"

"This day. Now."

"She leaves with Holbrooke!"

I closed my eyes against the fury in his voice. Cowered as he spurred his horse forward, thrusting Abigail aside.

She was flung into a puddle of mud. And as she pushed herself up from it, she saw me. But she did not shrink in surprise. She did not cower in guilt. She smiled up at me. With malice.

Why had she told him? What had she hoped to accomplish? Did she not know Simeon Wright? Did she not know that he would destroy something? Or someone?

And then I knew.

I knew without any doubt what would happen. I could see it plain as a vision before me. I took to Newham Road at a run, hoping that I would not be too late.

278

After several minutes' ride, my anxieties began to settle. I began once more to hope. Began to believe. I lay my cheek against the broad plane of Daniel's back. How wonderful to love and be loved.

He raised one of my hands to his lips and kissed it.

"How now, Captain Holcombe!"

Daniel stopped the horse so abruptly it began to rear. Though he fed it some rein, it danced about in a circle for a moment before coming to rest. But as it danced, as Simeon Wright spun in and out of our vision, I saw the grip he had on his musket. And the look in his eye.

"Daniel?"

He answered with a squeeze to my arm.

Simeon gestured toward me with his musket. "Come down."

I clutched at Daniel.

He pried my fingers from his waist. "All will be well." He held out his arm to aid me in dismounting.

The moment my feet touched the ground, Simeon grabbed at my arm and threw me behind him. I landed on my back in the mud-stained snow, cloak flying out around me.

Simeon's eyes turned from satisfaction to rage as he traced the neckline of my gown with his gaze. He reached down, seized my hand, and wrenched me to my feet. Throwing my cloak behind me, he grabbed at an arm so that he could look at my sleeve. "I always knew you were a whore. Now you dress like one!"

I tried to twist my arm away from his grip so that I could wrap my cloak around me, but he turned his hand in the opposite direction. The pain dropped me to my knees and I cried out.

"Do not—" Daniel leapt from his horse and moved to help me.

Simeon motioned him away from me with his gun. "Do not what? Do not paw at your whore? I'll do better than that. Watch!"

He reached out with his other hand and ripped the stomacher of the gown from my chest.

Daniel reached for his musket.

Simeon drew back the hammer on his own.

I threw myself at his legs, but he shook me off like a dog.

"Cease!" Done with me, he turned his attentions to Daniel. "I would let you have her, but she was promised to me and I keep what's mine. Even if it's not fit to wipe the dirt from my feet."

I scrambled to my knees. As I did so, a flash of red in the wood caught my eye.

Daniel spoke again. "She is not yours."

"She will be."

"She will not have you. She is—"

"She is mine."

Standing as I was behind Simeon Wright, I could not understand for a moment what had happened. Why had Daniel fallen upon the ground? Why did blood bloom forth from his chest? And why was it that my ears would not stop ringing?

I pushed past Simeon Wright and dropped to the ground beside Daniel. The snow beside him had already gone pink from blood. If I could just stop the bleeding. If I could find something to bind his wound, then I could help him to his feet and get him back on his horse. I lifted my head to see if I would have to help him far, but the horse, feckless creature, was nowhere to be found.

No matter. I would stop the bleeding first.

Putting a hand to his chest, I plunged it into the gaping hole, trying to staunch the blood. With my other hand, I tore at the buttons of his doublet searching for the silk scarf, my silk scarf, which he always kept close to his heart. I wrested it free and meant to stuff it into the wound, but Daniel pushed up on an elbow and lifted a hand to grasp at mine.

I tried to loose it. "Nay. Nay, Daniel. 'Tis a wound. A great one to be sure, but I can bind it."

"So little time . . ." He clutched at my hand with a grip so fierce it kept me from my work.

I felt tears course down my cheeks as I tried to free myself. He did not understand. I could stop the bleeding. I *would* stop the bleeding . . . if only he would let me.

"Hush you now." He groaned, face contorted, and then he dropped my hand and collapsed into the snow. " 'Tis finished. I am . . . finished."

"Nay! Just let me—"

"Cease."

I did then, I ceased my efforts, but only because he seemed so adamant, and I knew there would be time enough to help him later.

"Let me . . . look upon you . . . once more . . ." His skin had turned a ghastly shade of pale and the look in his eyes was at once pleading and resigned.

He did not think . . . he could not mean . . . "Do not—" My voice had gone tremulous with sudden fear. "Do not leave me!"

"Never." He coughed. A froth of red burbled from his lips. "Never. You will always find me just . . . here . . ." He lifted a hand out toward me, and I leaned forward to receive it.

He placed it over my heart.

I covered it with my own, and he stepped into eternity as I held on to his hand.

As I moved to kiss him, Simeon Wright grabbed me by the cloak and tried to pull me up by its hood.

I would have none of it. Though I knew my efforts were useless, still I clung to Daniel as if I might save him.

But Simeon Wright jabbed the muzzle of his musket into my chest right above my heart. Right where Daniel's hand had been. I only wished that he would pull the trigger and let me die.

"Listen well. 'Tis murder that happened here, but still you might save yourself. Marry me and I will tell them that I was stopping him from dragging you away. That he forced himself upon you."

I could not make sense of his words. Daniel forcing himself upon me? I could only shake my head.

Simeon threw the musket to the ground, wrapped the hood of my cloak about his fist, and forced me to look at him, to plead with him for air. For life. "Then I will tell them all that you made a harlot of yourself with that . . . that . . . *cavalier*. And that in seeing you and the gown you wore, you incited me to lust. I could not control myself. It was you who drove me to murder him. 'Twas you who forced me to do it."

Still I could not reply. But I let go of Daniel and placed my hands around Simeon's fists, begging for air.

He released me then and did it so quickly that I fell back onto Daniel. And that is where the townsmen saw me when they found us, my tears mixing with his blood, my hands smoothing back his hairs. My lips seeking one last kiss from a man who would never embrace me again.

39

I RAN TO FIND them just as quickly as I could, but I had not been fast enough. I burst from the forest onto the road as Simeon was shouting at the captain. I called out, hoping that a witness might stop him from what I knew was coming, but my cry had been drowned by the musket's report. Then I slipped back into the wood from which I had come.

Thomas found me, some time later, sitting in the snow, shivering.

"Small-hope?"

I turned my face toward him. I tried to speak, tried to open my mouth, but I could say nothing.

He picked me up, an arm beneath my knees and another around my back, as if I were a child. He carried me home and put me into our bed and piled me with covers, but still I could not stop shivering. And so, as I watched, he took a bucket and went outside. When he came back, it was filled with snow. He poured it into a kettle and swung it over the fires. After a time, he wrapped a blanket around me and carried me to the bench. And then he set the kettle in front of me and placed my feet into it.

It only made me shiver the more. And his kindness brought tears to my eyes. When my teeth stopped clattering against each other, I finally said what I had been trying to say since I saw it happen. "He did it."

"What?"

"He did it."

Thomas took my chin into his hand and turned my face toward his.

"He did it."

"Who?"

"Simeon Wright. He did it."

His brows knit themselves together. "I know it. 'Tis he himself who admitted as much."

"But he did it willingly. With intent." It seemed no warmth could reach me. I sat there and shuddered as the water grew tepid.

Thomas realized it and pulled my feet from the kettle. Then he took a long look at me. A look so long and so tender that I could not look away. He banked the fires and undressed, and then he carried us both to bed.

I slept that night, all of it, nestled within his arms, my head tucked beneath his chin. I dreamt of nothing at all. And when I woke the next morning, he was still with me.

❧

I awakened slowly, dragged toward wakefulness from a sleep that was both heavy and hollow. It had been a dreamless sleep. But the sentiment that there was something left undone kept tugging at me from the edge of that great chasm of nothingness.

I yawned. Opened my eyes. Squinted against the brightness of the fire's glow. I was in bed. But . . . that did not seem right. And how had I arrived there?

Sitting, I saw that I was not clothed. Not in the gown that Daniel had given me to wear. His gown. My gown. It had been so soft, so smooth, so fine against my skin.

I saw my mother's feet shuffle into view. "Child?"

I lifted my head. My mother was home! But how could she have . . . had not Father just rode out to get her that morning? How had she arrived so quickly? At the sight of her, at the scent of her, tears stung at my eyes.

She put a hand to my cheek. "You have been sleeping these past days."

"My gown." I plucked at the shift I wore. "My gown." I did not want this one. I wanted the other.

"Hush you, now. 'Tis gone."

"But . . . but . . . 'tis mine! He gave it to me. To wear."

"He gave it to you." She said it with such immense sadness, as if it was the worst, the most terrible thing she had ever heard.

"To wear. Aye. I was to wear it. For Daniel. Where is Daniel?" Where could he be and why was I here?

She placed her hands on my own and pried my fingers from my shift. "Hush you, now."

I did not want to be hushed. I wanted my gown. The one I was to wear. The one I was to have put on to ride away from Simeon Wright. The one I was to be married in. "I want my gown."

"Be a good girl, Susannah." Mother clasped my arm and tried to help me back into bed.

"Where is my gown?" If I was not in my gown and Mother had already come home, then . . . then I must leave at once with Daniel before Simeon Wright could catch me. Could trap me. Could marry me.

"You cannot have it."

"Where is it? And where is Daniel?"

"It is not here. The deputy has taken it."

Mother's hands were pulling the covers up over my lap. "Where?"

"To his house."

I let myself be bundled back into bed. But I clutched at Mother when she would have left.

285

She turned back toward me. Put a chill hand to my forehead to smooth my hairs back from my face.

"Why? Why did he take it?"

"For use in the trial."

"What trial?"

Her hand stilled. "Of Simeon Wright. For taking the life of Captain Holcombe."

"Daniel." My eyes were open. I know they were, because I blinked. But I saw nothing of my house. Everywhere I looked, all was drenched in blood. Buckets and buckets of it. My mother was speaking, but I heard nothing. I could hear nothing because of the great boom of Simeon Wright's musket. I turned my eyes toward the fires, toward the kitchen. I ought to have smelled biscuits baking and a pottage simmering, but the only scent that filled my nostrils was the smell of gunpowder.

And burnt flesh.

I no longer wanted to see. Or hear. Or smell. And so I let Mother place me back into bed and pull the covers up to my chin as if I were a child. And then, carefully, slowly, quietly, so that Simeon Wright would not turn his musket upon me again, I pulled my knees up to my chest and snuck my arms up round my head, curling into the tightest, smallest ball that I could.

I must have fallen asleep, for I woke some hours later after all had gone to bed, screaming and thrashing, pressing a hand to my chest trying to stem the blood. All that blood that kept flowing from my heart.

"I've been shot. I have been shot!" And it felt exactly as I had imagined that it would.

"Hush you, now." Mother was bent over me, trying to wrest my hands away from my heart.

"I have been shot."

"You are fine. You are safe. All is well."

"I have not been shot?"

"Nay, child. Be at peace."

"But . . ."

She tugged at my hands.

I looked down at them to find that what she said was true. There was no blood. None. But how could that be? I could feel it all over my fingers. Daniel's blood. If I could just keep it from coming out, then maybe he would live.

She brushed stray hairs away from my head and slipped my braid back behind my shoulder. " 'Twas just a log in the fires that snapped. 'Tis nothing at all. Sleep now."

I let her settle me back into the bed.

I glimpsed the faces of Mary and Nathaniel before I closed my eyes. They were pressed against the wall, the child held between them, looking at me with terror.

I closed my eyes. If I could just figure out some way to keep all that blood from coming out of his chest. I woke some time later, hands pressed to my own chest, held so hard, so fast, I could scarcely breathe.

Mother kept me in bed for two days in succession, as if I were a babe. She came every now and then to press a cool hand to my forehead, to feed me, to aid me to stand and use the chamber pot. And every so often, she repeated a single question. "Can you speak of it, Susannah?"

I would simply shake my head. And then slip back into sleep. Sweet sleep. It was the only thing I wanted to do. My dreams, the only place I wanted to be. When I slept I could see Daniel. I could hear him and smell him and taste him. But no matter how hard I tried, I could not touch him. Nor could I keep him alive. When I reached out to place my lips upon his, to put a hand to his hairs, that curly mane grown long and proud once more, all would crumble around me. And more often than not, I would wake screaming his name.

The third morning, early, I perceived Nathaniel waking from

sleep. I was filled with my own wakefulness, though I had no desire to move about or leave the bed. I was imagining myself in Virginia with Daniel. I was envisioning the house that would be ours. And it was so comfortable there. So safe. I kept my eyes closed. It seemed vastly easier.

But then he spoke. "Susannah? 'Tis I, Nathaniel."

I sighed. Opened my eyes and turned toward him. "Aye?"

"I have been thinking, Susannah."

"About what?"

"About Simeon Wright and how it was that God saw fit to send him to rescue you."

Simeon Wright? "Rescue me?"

"Aye. By taking you away from the captain. The captain seemed noble and he appeared to be . . . good . . . but . . . well, they say all was not as it seemed."

I could not bring myself to speak.

"Though none of the rest of us could see that, God could. And He rescued you. Is that not grace?"

Grace?

"Remember how the great prophet Isaiah said, 'Therefore will I give men for thee, and people for thy life.' He did it. He sent Simeon Wright to rescue you from that heathen! Could this not be my experience of grace?"

A heathen? But Daniel was no heathen. He had known more of God than any man in Stoneybrooke. So like my grandfather he had been . . . in so many ways. God said He would give men for me? He had: one. But he had taken the wrong man!

I was not worthy of his life. I was not even good.

Only God is good; God is only good.

How could God be good? He had torn life away from the only man who had ever convinced me to proclaim His goodness. I could not keep myself from weeping. Nay, Nathaniel's message was not one of grace. It was a hoax. A torture. The ultimate of cruelties. It was a hope turned in upon itself if my tormentor was now being lauded by all as my rescuer.

Later that morning there came a rapping at the door.

Mother left her work at the fires to answer it.

'Twas the deputy, Goodman Blake. He swept a quick glance around the place. "I have come for Susannah Phillips."

"Why?"

"She is to be placed in confinement. In Newham."

"In Newham! But the child is not well."

The deputy lifted his chin against Mother's protest. " 'Tis been ordered."

"By whom?" Her tone held a promise of woe for that authority.

"The selectmen."

"She has not spoken, not truly. Not since . . . that day."

" 'Tis not for questioning. 'Tis to be . . . well . . ." The man dropped his gaze, shifting about on his feet. "She's to be sequestered. Just for some few weeks until . . . well . . ."

"Then you will have to speak to her father." Mother put a finger to his chest, pushed him back from the door, and shut it in his face. Then she turned toward me. "The time for grieving is done. Be up. And get dressed."

I just lay there and blinked.

"Now! Unless you want him to drag you off in your nightclothes! Mary, help your sister."

I threw off the bedclothes and swung my feet out to the floor.

Mary moved to find my stockings and skirts. My waistcoat and shoes.

My legs protested my weight and were slow to lend support to my standing.

Mary grabbed at my elbow to pull me upright. "Here." She held out the shift to me, then sighed and pulled it down over my head when I was too slow to do it myself. "You are worse than the child!"

She pulled the strings tight and tied them off. Then she aided my arms into the sleeves of my waistcoat. "Do not pretend that you need help with your stockings. I have helped you enough these past days! 'Twas me who tended you when Father was gone, when the captain was dead, and the day-girl abandoned me. 'Twas me who took care of the child. And you! Me who changed the clothes, changed the sheets while you were yet sleeping. When you would not wake, not even to use a chamber pot." She shoved stockings toward me and then waited with growing impatience as I tied them with ribbons beneath my knees.

Mother came while I was stepping into my skirt. She stood there until I had fastened it about the waist, then she led me by the hand to a bench, combed out my hair, gathered it into a twist and set my coif upon it.

As she finished her work, the door banged open. Father strode through it, followed by the deputy.

"They wish to sequester her."

"Why?"

Father turned to Goodman Blake, clearly waiting for an explanation.

The deputy spread his hands, as if groping for the reason.

Mother lowered her chin with a glower. "You burst in here of a morning and tell me you're to take from me my eldest daughter and have not the decency to tell me why?"

"She's to be placed on trial."

"For what?"

"The murder of Captain Holcombe."

40

THE INQUIRY INTO DANIEL'S death had fastened upon Simeon Wright as the defendant. There was no surprise about that, for he justly admitted he had done the killing. But what was unexpected was his defense. He claimed that it was my fault that he had done it. That he had come upon me with Daniel and that he had been driven beyond reason by the immodesty of my gown. Because he could not be held responsible for his actions, I would be. And so the case would be tried at the quarterly court in Newham when it met in two weeks' time. It was there that I would plead for my life.

I was taken to Newham that day by oxcart. It was Goodman Blake, the deputy, who took me. I wish I could say that the ride to Newham was the luxury of which I had dreamt that fall day I had accompanied my father to market, but in truth, I very much wished I were walking. And that my destination was not a cell but the victualler's or the milliner's.

Once in Newham, I was removed from the cart and placed into confinement at the house of Selectman Miller. His wife, the woman I had met at the milliner's shop, recognized me at first sight. I could see it by the flare of recognition in her eyes. I knew it in her sudden intake of breath when she looked upon me. But she said nothing. Not one word until the selectman had dismissed Goodman Blake and seen me secured into his own cell at the side of his house. Not one word until he had bid his wife adieu and left on other business.

It was then Mistress Miller sent her servants on some errand and dragged a chair over to the door that separated us.

"I place myself here with my mending so that we can speak. But be warned, if any shall ask, I never spoke to you."

"Nor I to you."

I could almost imagine her nod. "Were you not betrothed to Simeon Wright?"

I knelt before the door and put my mouth to the keyhole so that no one passing the lean-to would overhear us. "Aye."

"And now you are being tried for the death of Captain Holcombe?"

"Aye."

"I must tell you that I knew Captain Holcombe. We journeyed across the sea together. And if his life was lost at your hand, then I bid you good riddance straight to hell."

"I did not do it." How could I have done it?

There was silence for a time. And then she spoke again. "Nay. I thought not. You do not have the look of a murderess about you. But Mister Wright's defense is your guilt in the incident. Or is it not true what I have heard?"

" 'Tis true."

"So what have you to do with it?"

"I was wearing . . . a gown."

"Don't we all? So 'tis a gown you were wearing . . ."

"Aye, when Simeon Wright tried to stop us on our way from town."

"And where were you going?"

"Away. Anywhere. To Virginia. I could not marry Simeon Wright. Even though I was pledged. He is not a man . . . he is a monster."

"Aye. 'Tis that which I had heard. So you were off to Virginia?

'Tis where we had all hoped to land at the first. And you were wearing this gown."

"A lovely gown. A gown of satin. Of ribbons and bows, with lace in abundance."

"It sounds beautiful in the way of gowns."

"It was. But not very . . . modest."

"So it was no gown for a Puritan to be caught wearing."

"Nay. It is said I incited Simeon Wright to lust."

"I do not understand you people! Clothes are weapon and armor both. I have seen more corruption and more vice hidden beneath a sober, sad-colored frock in this colony than I ever saw in England. Modest dress covers a multitude of sin here. And the laws to do with them! One must not wear this sort of ribbon or that kind of lace. And beware the boot too great or the collar too long!"

"But you wear one . . . a gown very much like the one I wore. And none molest you."

"None but my husband. But I am used to it. He takes me half in greed, half in shame at his own want and need. Nay, do not think that all is well for me. 'Tis only because I am the selectman's wife none will accuse me to him. And he will hear no complaint. He parades me for all to see, but be sure that I answer for it. In private, where none can see."

"Then there is no hope for me."

"Who can say there is hope? Or no hope? You must pray. 'Tis what they have taught me."

"I have little to say to God."

" 'Tis what I thought as well . . . at first."

"But . . . I *was* at fault. In a fashion. 'Tis me, the reason for Daniel's death. If I had not loved him . . . if he had not loved me."

She *tsk*ed. And when she spoke once more, her voice sounded hollow. "I cannot believe that he still does not exist somewhere on this earth."

Then she had not seen the body and all the blood that had ushered forth from his mortal wound.

"He was such a man for amusement. And for laughter. I always felt safe when he was near. Believe me, you do not want to discover yourself alone with sailors." She stitched on in silence for a while. I heard the prick of her needle and the pull of yarn through canvas. "He made you feel safe as well."

"Aye. He did."

"He must have loved you to have run away with you. He was always one for a gallant gesture, but very rarely did it ever come at risk of reputation. I suppose you all thought he was some sort of heathen cavalier with those great boots and curling hair and drooping hat."

A tear slipped down my cheek and dangled from my nose before dropping to my chest. It was joined by dozens of others, which wet my neck with their number. "We did. I did. At first."

"His looks were deceptive. I tried to turn his head a time or two, and though I could open his mouth in laughter, I could never convince him to open his arms. Not to me." She sighed. "You won him honestly, then . . . and it does my vanity no good to realize that he preferred you to me."

"We were to marry. Just as soon as we could leave the colony. 'Twas the reason for the gown."

"To leave this Puritan life behind."

"Aye."

"In a respectable sort of way."

"Aye."

"It was a good plan. It would have worked."

" 'Tis what he thought." But then, he had not reckoned on Simeon Wright.

All they that take the sword shall perish by the sword.

It happened just as Daniel had said it would.

But where is your sword, God, when it comes to Simeon Wright?

❧

294

"You must speak. We will go to Newham for the trial and you must speak." Thomas had put down his spoon and his knife and trained his gaze upon me.

I quailed under the weight of it and could not look at him. "Do not make me go back there. I cannot."

"But your father has long been gone from that town. And you were there. You were there when the captain was killed."

"Aye. But what did I really see?"

"What did you see?"

My eyes faltered when I tried to meet his gaze. "The whole thing."

"Then you must speak of it."

"Why? It will not matter. He will win just the same."

"Not if you speak."

I lifted my eyes to him. "But if I speak, then he might hurt you. And that would be even worse."

"If you do not speak, then Susannah Phillips will surely be convicted. And how could that be just?"

Just? Nothing was just. Not one thing in this world. Only blessed, favored people ever looked for justice. The rest of us knew how cruel this world could be. How could it be just for a child to be born to a father like mine? How could it be just for Captain Holcombe to be felled by a monster like Simeon Wright? And how could it be just for Susannah Phillips to be faulted for it? I no longer looked for justice. I wished only to survive. And if survival required silence, then that is the price I would pay.

41

MISTRESS MILLER KEPT ME warm and she kept me fed, but I had nothing to do and time aplenty to spare. I had grievances and they were many, and so I began once more to talk to God. My prayers were halting at first. Supplications whispered through tears. And then, as the days passed, they became treatises on the injuries that had been done to me and the offenses I had suffered. At the hand of God himself.

If He were going to take Daniel from me, the least He could have done is left me something to remember him by. I no longer had the scarf, I no longer had the gown. I had nothing at all. And so I hoped against all hope, I prayed and pleaded for the impossible, for one small miracle. I hoped and prayed for Daniel's child. God had done it once for his blessed mother; why could He not do it again?

He owed me so much. And I had asked for so little.

Did I not have faith, though it be small as a mustard seed? Did not my back ache? Were not my breasts growing more tender with every passing day? I was alone, kept in the darkness of the lean-to, and so I began to talk to the child I decided was growing inside me. I spoke to him of his father. I told him the story of when we first met. Of how Daniel had walked into Stoneybrooke from the wood, as wild as any bear. I told him of savages and silk scarves. Of conversations. Of kisses in the moonlight, underneath the stars.

I lived each day for a week in that illusion, and then my dreams were shattered once more. I went to the corner to make water, and after I did, I knew utter desolation. My monthly courses had come and dissolved all of my hopes. I gathered my skirts to my face and keened like some mad she-wolf at my misfortunes.

Later, after Mistress Miller had tried and failed to comfort me, after the neighbor's shrieks for silence had stopped, my voice grew hoarse and my tears dried up. I spent the night in wakefulness, mired in the thought that Daniel was gone.

Forever.

And I could not escape the knowledge that I was soon to die. How could the trial have any other outcome than my conviction? I was not the woman the gown proclaimed me to be, but I might as well have been.

I had feared that people would discover what I was truly like beneath my pretense of goodness, but they might as well have. Which were worse? The sins I had committed or those I might have, given the chance? I no longer cared what anyone thought. They assumed the worst, and there was no reason not to let them. Not anymore.

I did not fear death. I might have, had I still believed that God loved me, that He took any sort of notice of my life. And I did not fear judgment, for I had just as many things of which to accuse God as He had to accuse me. Neither did I fear my reputation. I had not done the things of which I was accused, but given the opportunity, I might have. Nay, my anxieties were not for myself; there was little to live for with Daniel gone.

I worried most about my family. I worried they might be driven from town. I worried that no one would buy Father's wares. That Mother would be dropped from her whang. That no one would take Mary to wife . . . and no one give their daughter to Nathaniel in marriage.

Two weeks I spent in worry and restlessness, and then I was placed on trial at the meetinghouse. The building was filled to over-flowing with people from Newham and around the edges, stopping up the gaps, were people from Stoneybrooke. Simeon Wright acted as his own lawyer.

"The death of Captain Daniel Holcombe was unnatural and unexpected. 'Twas done at the hand of Simeon Wright, and yet he claims it was no willful slaughter. But a man is dead. What say you, Simeon Wright?"

" 'Tis not what I say. 'Twas what was done to me. I came upon my betrothed fornicating with the captain. And look you to that gown Susannah Phillips was wearing! What man would not be driven to lust by it? When I avenged myself upon him, how could I be expected to control my actions? 'Tis not me to blame. 'Tis her." Simeon snatched the gown from the clerk and held it up in front of him so that all could see it. The stomacher yawned from the bodice where he had ripped it. Blood had stained the front. But still it shimmered. Still the ribbons and bows fluttered at his movements. Still the lace cascaded from the collar, delicate as a spider's web.

A murmur rose up around me as he stood there with it, in front of the pulpit. And then, quite suddenly, he flung it at me.

It landed in my lap. As he continued to speak, my hands reached out to stroke the fine material. They played with the ribbons. And my thoughts went to remembering that dance I had danced with Daniel. I lost myself in that memory, that thought, until I felt my mother's hand upon my arm.

I realized then that my eyes had closed, that I was swaying on the bench. Rocking first forward and then back.

And all eyes were fixed upon me.

Until Simeon snapped them all back to himself. "How can a death be willful when a man is driven to madness? How can it be willful when a man is tempted by a harlot beyond what is reasonable? How can he be held accountable for his actions when one such as this parades herself in front of him? Was she not pledged to be my wife? And is not the penalty for adultery, death?"

He spoke for over an hour, laying out his defense, all the while accusing me. As he spoke, his words grew louder, his gestures more animated. Spittle flew from his lips; his hair grew damp with sweat. He looked like a man who had lost control. But I knew differently. I was looking at something else. I was looking at his eyes. And they were not the eyes of a man who had taken leave of his senses. They were cold. Dispassionate. Calculating.

After he took his seat, a break was called. And after the break, the selectman called for witnesses to my character. Someone thrust our day-girl from the seated crowd to the front of the meetinghouse.

"Aye, girl. You have something to say?"

Her gaze crept back toward the crowd.

"If you have nothing to say, then remove yourself."

"I had been working at the Phillips's this winter."

"Aye?"

Again, her eyes were drawn toward the benches that crowded the room. Whatever she sought there must have given her courage, for her words came out in a blurt. "Susannah spoiled the family's small beer and we had naught to drink for a whole week but melted snow and then one week she forgot to make it altogether."

Aye, but that had been the week of the child's illness! How could I be expected to keep up with matters of daily life, when there was a question of death?

Around me, there were rumblings and mutterings.

The selectman dismissed the girl. She fled back toward her place as if chased by demons, without a glance at me.

"Is there anyone else who wishes to speak to the defendant's character?"

Goody Baxter appeared at the edge of those gathered.

"Step forward."

She took a visible breath, straightened, and walked toward the front of the pulpit.

"I am Goody Baxter, a neighbor. From Stoneybrooke Towne. One forenoon, long about several months ago, Susannah Phillips came to my door."

"And what of it?"

"She asked me for a coal, since she had let her fires go out."

There was a great murmuring at work behind me.

But had not she put my fears, my humiliation, to rest? Had she not said that all of them, all of the women, had done such things in their youth? Why would she speak now of the blunder she had so readily excused? I closed my eyes against the slight. Bowed my head.

Goody Hillbrook pushed to the front. She took Goody Baxter's place.

"I am Goody Hillbrook. Also from Stoneybrooke Towne. I went to visit the Phillips to check on their welfare and take them a taste of my dinner, since their mother had gone—"

"Their mother had gone?"

"To Boston, to wean the babe."

"Continue."

"The girl received me with some gladness, since she said she had not had time to even think of what to offer, let alone prepare for supper. *And there was nothing put to the fires for the meal.* At four o'clock in the day!"

We'd had pottage and a pudding at the ready. With blueberries! And nothing to do to prepare it but steam the pudding. I was simply being polite.

At Goody Hillbrook's retreat, my father stepped up to the front. Cleared his throat.

All went silent.

"I am her father. This is not right. Her mother was gone, kept from us by the snows. How can a girl be expected to keep up? With all that must be done to manage a house?"

I was grateful for his support, but anyone who looked at me did not see what he did. They saw a woman grown. A woman who should be able to manage a household. A woman who should be ready to become a goodwife. But the truth of it was that I had failed. I was not good. Neither was I fit to be anybody's wife.

Father's place was taken by another. And still another.

Slattern, sloth, and whore.

They were right. That is who I had become. Nay, that is who I was. Who I must have always been. As the witnesses kept coming forward, I felt smaller and smaller. And soon I did not feel at all.

It was with some surprise that I saw Abigail step forward. Tears blurred my vision as my friend moved toward the pulpit. She did not have to speak for me. Nothing she could say would turn the tide of words that had preceded her. But it was kind of her to wish to try.

"I am Goody Clarke. From Stoneybrooke Towne. One morning last month, Susannah Phillips came to my door. She begged me for a bit of my mother dough . . . because she had spent all of hers on bread the day before and had forgotten to keep any aside. *She had used it all up.*"

There were audible gasps from the crowd behind me.

Beside me, my mother recoiled.

Surely I was doomed. Not only had I been derelict in my duties, but I had also failed to protect the legacy that had been passed down to me. For want of forethought, I had consumed my inheritance without knowledge and without remorse. I had devoured that which gave life.

I had not been wrong. Abigail's witness had not turned the tide of words from me. But I had not expected that hers, when added to the others, would threaten to overwhelm me.

"Do you wish to speak on your behalf, Susannah Phillips?"

I stared at the selectman for a moment, wondering what he thought I might possibly say. And then I shook my head. There were no words to combat those testimonies. They were right, all of them.

Perhaps not about the details or the why of what I had done, but their intent in speaking was plain. And I agreed with them.

I deserved to die.

As I was led out of the meetinghouse that day, Goody Baxter stepped in front of me. "You must know, Susannah Phillips, that I am bound to tell the truth. Even if I do not like it or wish to do it."

I could not bear to look at her. To know that she had felt some secret scorn for me that wanted only opportunity to be told. Certainly she had to tell the truth. But she needn't have been so hasty in the doing of it.

The deputy held one of my forearms while another man held the other. They marched me down the street. Along the way a woman gathered her children to her and stood aside as we passed. Far aside. Against the wall of a building.

Another woman, the Millers' neighbor, cried out as we passed by. "Can she not be kept somewhere else?"

" 'Tis the selectman who holds her. Where else should she be kept?"

"I just . . . 'tis all my children and all my servants living right here beside her. What if . . . she does . . . something to them?"

"What might she do?"

"A girl who wore a gown like that? She could do anything!" If the goodwife had meant the words to be whispered, she had not succeeded.

"And if she does, then let the constable know of it."

She addressed herself to me then. "Susannah Phillips? If you work any mischief in this place, know that you will only be the sorrier for it!" She glared at me as I entered the Miller house.

Mischief? What kind of mischief did she think I might work? My mischief had been done. I had enticed a good man to come to my aid and now he was dead. Because of me.

Only God is good; God is only good.

God was not good! God had taken the good man and spared the evil man. How could that be good?

Tell me, Daniel, what to think! You were wrong. God is not good. God does not love me. God does not want me. And what have you to say about it?

Nothing.

He had nothing to say because he had been wrong. Entirely and completely wrong about the God he thought he knew. And had I not always suspected? Had his God not always sounded too accepting, too understanding, too loving to be true?

I stood in the center of my small cell for a long while, cloak wrapped around me, hugging my arms to my sides. And then I sat. And when I tired of looking at the dirt on the floor and boards comprising the walls, I lay down on my pallet and went to sleep.

∽

It took some two hours to gain Stoneybrooke Towne, but we had walked it with the rest of those returning for the night. Though I was glad to be gone from Newham, my return was not so difficult as I had expected. Not with my father having gone. Aye, I had crept around corners and searched through the crowds for him at first, but by midday, I had been assured of my deliverance.

I was working to place supper upon the table while Thomas paced the length of the kitchen, muttering. "If Susannah will not speak, then Simeon Wright must be made to perjure himself."

"You would do as well to pray for snow in June."

"We know that he lies—"

"Aye. But 'tis a lie couched in truth. He did kill the captain. But he admits to it. What more is there to say? It must be proven willful in order that he be convicted. And how can that be done if 'tis just his word against mine?"

He stopped. Glanced over at me. Continued his pacing. " 'Tis true. If Susannah does not speak, then 'tis your word against his.

If we could just prove something other than willful murder . . . something else for which he might be accused."

"He should be judged, then, for his own accusation."

"To which he is witness."

"A false witness."

"False witness . . . aye! If he could be proved to be a false witness, then . . ."

"He shall be put to death."

"According to the laws God gave Moses. And there can be no higher law. If he cannot be accused of willful murder, then perhaps he can be accused of bearing false witness."

I placed biscuits upon the table and went to the lean-to for cheese and some butter. Put a trencher of hot pot between us. We ate in silence, Thomas working at his food as if he hoped to discover something of importance within it. But there was nothing there. Nothing but corn and meat and beans.

"Does she wish to die?" Thomas asked the question of me as if he truly wanted to know.

I shrugged. "I suppose it might not matter to her one way or another."

"How could it not matter?"

"The man she loved is dead. The town she lived in has turned against her. The admiration once shown her is gone. She is a woman alone with none to rescue her. Why would she wish to live?"

"But . . . how could one wish to die?"

"Perhaps the question is why would one wish to live when there is nothing to live for? Perhaps, if God truly does see, if justice truly is done, then she will be acquitted. But what sort of life would she have? Who would marry her? Who would speak to her? She might hope to teach at a dame's school, but who would send their children to her for teaching? Hers would a fate worse than a leper's."

"So you argue for her death?"

"Would it not be kinder than to argue for her life?"

"How could you even say such a thing?"

"I say it because I used to think it. Every day. Every day, Thomas, before the day you spoke to me. Every day I woke hoping that it might be my last. That perhaps that day might be the day my father would hit me hard enough to kill me. I had nothing else to hope for."

His eyes searched mine, tears trembling at the edges. "You wished for death? Truly?"

"Every day."

He placed his hands over his face and wept. "What kind of world, what kind of place do we live in when the best our women can hope for is death? What sort of Zion have we created? We are no City on a Hill, we are only a place of horror. What have we become?"

I did not know what to do. And so I put my hand upon his shoulder.

He reached out and pulled me to himself.

"Do not grieve yourself, Thomas. 'Twas not your fault. I am the least of women . . ."

"Which makes it worse. 'Tis the least among us who should receive the most compassion, the most protection. And they do not. If we had hoped to build some sort of earthly paradise, then we have failed."

42

THE SECOND DAY WAS the same as the first, taken over by a parade of witnesses vouching for some heinous act that I had done. But when the testimony stretched back to the time I had been a babe, when I had toddled about without knowledge, I knew then that there was no hope. If I could be convicted on the basis of being a child, then there was no doubt I would be convicted for killing the captain too.

It was interminable, all the talking. All the words. All the truths. Truths that might never have been assembled were it not for the existence of Daniel's gown. And the fact that I had been caught wearing it. But it was so . . . beautiful. So lovely. If I closed my eyes, I could remember how Daniel looked at me when he had seen me in it. And what was the wrong in that? What was the sin in loving and being loved?

A gown? They would convict me on the basis of a gown when I could state a dozen, nay, a hundred offenses more grave? Had I not been harboring rebellious thoughts for years? Had I not been pretending to be the good Susannah Phillips even as I knew that inside I was as wretched as the thieves that hung upon the cross beside our Lord? Aye, I was as wretched as they thought me to be, but it had nothing to do with a gown.

And what about Simeon Wright? What about his offenses, what about his abominations? They would try to convict me on spurious charges and not even for one second pause to turn their eyes upon him?

They were blinded, these people, by the persons they believed us to be!

Tears of rage, of impotence, welled up beneath my eyelids, and I let them spill out upon my cheeks into the day. It did not matter. I was responsible for Daniel's death. If I had not loved him so much. If I had let him leave alone. If I had been able to stop the bleeding.

If it were not for me, then Daniel might have lived.

And that was Simeon Wright's point entirely.

Simeon Wright. He had taken to staring at whoever was speaking in a grave but impatient manner. As if Daniel's death were a mere inconvenience that would soon be set aside. I watched him frown. I watched him nod his head. I watched him preen. I watched him fondle the gown with his eyes as he sat there. That such a man should live when Daniel had died!

And then he smirked one time too many, held up a finger and spoke. "But the gown—"

"A pox upon the gown!" The words leapt from my mouth before I could stop them.

The crowd gasped.

The selectman tried to restore order. "Susannah Phillips, you wish to speak?"

I took to my feet, indignant. "This has nothing to do with the gown!"

The arm of the selectman went up to stay any words Simeon Wright might say.

"The taking of a man's life requires an accounting, and yet you quibble over a gown? 'Tis true. I wore it. And what of it? Perhaps I wore the gown, but he killed a man . . . and yet you hold me responsible? That man"—I pointed toward Simeon with a shaking finger—"says that he cannot be held responsible for his actions because of my gown. You, all of you, assume that because I was wearing the gown, I must have been fornicating with Daniel Holcombe. How does a gown give you permission to judge me? How can a gown give you the right to convict me? And how could it possibly matter what I was wearing when Daniel was killed?"

The selectman cleared his throat.

"Aye, I wore it. Do you know why? I wore it because it was the only way out. That gown was my only escape. Simeon Wright is a tyrant and an extortionist and a murderer. He published our banns without my father's permission. And because none in Stoneybrooke Town knew, it was left to a stranger, to Daniel, to save me."

I had taken the gown from the clerk and clutched it to my chest. It was soaked with blood and ripped at the seams, but still, it was the most beautiful thing I had ever seen. "I will confess to the sin of vanity. But who among us has not desired to look beautiful for their beloved? Who among us has not desired to be called lovely? For this, for all of this, I am to be hanged? I am to be hanged because one man could not look on me without lust in his heart? How is that my fault? How is it that the gown made him pull the trigger of his musket?"

I let go of the gown and it dropped to the floor. I returned to my seat.

Around me rose up a murmur that reverberated through the meetinghouse.

I suffered from no delusions. They would still convict me, for it was my statement against his, but at least they would do it with my words on their conscience.

As I sat on my bench, however, there rose up another to take my place.

"I saw him." Small-hope could barely be heard over the noise of the crowd.

"Silence!"

Small-hope barely waited for the meetinghouse to quiet before she continued. "I saw him. Of late I am Goody Smyth from Stoneybrooke Towne. But I was raised here in Newham among you. I was in the wood the day that Simeon Wright shot Daniel Holcombe. He shot the captain willfully."

The place erupted once more.

"Quiet!" The selectman looked round with a frown. And then he beckoned Small-hope closer.

She would not go. But neither would she remain silent. "Daniel Holcombe was speaking to Simeon Wright, face-to-face."

"And where was Susannah Phillips?"

"On the ground. Simeon Wright had thrown her down."

Simeon leapt to his feet. "That is a lie!"

The selectman ignored him. "Did you see him push her?"

Small-hope frowned. "Nay. But she was lying on her back behind Simeon."

"Was there no sign of fornication?"

"She was clothed and she was protesting . . . something. She took to her feet, but Simeon Wright threw her to the ground again."

Now the selectman was frowning. "So . . . he and the captain were arguing?"

"They were speaking."

"And 'twas then the captain moved to take Susannah Phillips?" The words were spoken with the satisfaction of a man who has finally divined the answer to a riddle.

"Nay. He never moved toward Susannah. He was talking to Simeon Wright, and in the middle of their conversation, Simeon Wright killed him."

"I did not—"

"Enough, Mr. Wright!" The selectman once more turned his attentions to Small-hope. "Susannah Phillips was not ravaged?"

"She was not."

"But surely Simeon Wright was inflamed by passion."

Small-hope stepped forward toward the men's side of the

meetinghouse. She stopped three paces from the selectman. She looked him square in the eye. "They were speaking as I am speaking to you, and then Simeon Wright shot the captain dead."

"But . . . he was not overcome by . . . surely . . . the gown . . . he said he was . . . ?"

"It was never about the gown. I was raised by a man like Simeon Wright, and I never knew when he would beat me. It was about burning bread, or stirring the pottage too quickly or the wash too slowly, but it was never about a gown. It was never about me; it was about him. And this was never about Susannah Phillips. It is about Simeon Wright and his own pride and wrath."

"What do you mean by that?"

"I mean to say that lust never figured into what my father did or what Simeon Wright did. Their own vanity, their desire to conquer, is what governs them. How can you stand and accuse Susannah Phillips of Simeon Wright's lust when his own pride and wrath overtake him? By my count, 'tis three of the seven deadly sins that are evidenced in his own actions . . . and none of them in hers."

"You say the gown did not enflame him to lust, overcoming his actions?"

"Nay. In truth, it probably did enflame him to wrath. But it might as well have been a burnt biscuit. Or the way his horse trotted through the wood."

"Her father's behavior has no bearing on mine!"

"Silence, Mister Wright!" The selectman nodded at Small-hope, dismissing her.

But then Thomas raised a hand and stepped up to take her place.

"I have had dealings with Simeon Wright."

"Speak, then."

"I am Thomas Smyth, the blacksmith in Stoneybrooke. 'Tis no secret that a blacksmith has need of a nearly endless supply of

310

wood to make his charcoal." He looked at the men in the jury as he spoke.

They nodded.

"And the town has been generous in offering me what I need, for no charge, from the common."

Again, they nodded. It was general knowledge and an accepted practice.

"However, access to our common has been denied me, denied us all, due to the threat of savages, and so I approached Simeon Wright about the possibility of providing that need instead. I reckoned that buying it from him would save me time in laying up wood that would be better spent on my work."

Again, the jury nodded.

"He agreed quite happily to my proposal . . . at the price of four shillings a tree."

Now the jurymen were frowning. One of them stood. "Four shillings a tree? When the price of a tree from the common is two shillings? But why were we not told of this before?"

"In the interest of Small-hope and her fears of Simeon Wright, I decided that cutting my own wood was a small price to pay to keep the peace." As I watched Thomas speak, as I saw him stand in the multitude, shoulders squared, I wondered that I had ever thought his eyes were in danger of popping from his head, his cheekbones sharp enough to skin a rabbit. I was shamed to think that I had ever referred to him as "poor." And it occurred to me then that out of all of the men in Stoneybrooke Towne, he was the only man among them.

"Is that all?"

"Excuse me." One of the members of the jury was waving his hand in the air. "I would question Thomas Smyth further."

The selectman nodded.

"You had experience with your wife's father?"

"Aye."

"And how is it that Simeon Wright has anything to do with him. And her?"

Thomas turned and looked straight at Small-hope. After a long moment, she gave a slight nod. And then she cast her gaze toward the floor.

"When I first met my wife, her eye was blackened and her hands burnt. It was not uncommon for her to walk among you here in Newham evidencing such signs of abuse. That abuse was meted out by the hand of her father, and it was I, a stranger, who was the first to say or do anything about it."

The room had gone silent. But still the selectman pressed his question. "But how has this anything to do with Simeon Wright?"

"When I see her cringe in that man's presence the same way she cringed in her father's, to my way of thinking, it has everything to do with it."

"Are there any more questions for this man?"

None replied.

Thomas nodded at the selectman, but as he removed himself from the floor, Goody Metcalf stood to take his place.

"I was up to Wright's hill once and I heard Simeon Wright yelling. At his mother."

Goody Hillbrook replaced her. "Their girl servant came to my house once asking for a poultice. For her arm. Said it was an accident, but how does the whole mark of an iron get burned into your arm unless 'tis pressed there?"

Another woman stood to take her place, but the selectman waved his arms for silence. "Goody Metcalf, how do you know 'tis his mother Simeon Wright was addressing?"

"I . . . well . . . who else could it have been?"

"Goody Hillbrook, did the girl tell you Simeon Wright had accosted her?"

"She did not say exactly, but—"

"I cannot see how this has anything to do with the trial of Susannah Phillips!" Simeon had come to his feet and was now glowering at the women.

"I have something to say about the character of Simeon Wright."

Simeon Wright turned to identify the voice. A look overcame his face that I could not understand. Not until I realized 'twas my own sister who had spoken.

43

"I AM MARY PHILLIPS, Susannah's sister, and Simeon Wright promised himself to me before he published banns with my sister."

The room grew quiet so suddenly that it brought pain to my ears.

Our minister blinked his eyes open and looked around the room, drawing a finger beneath the collar of his shirt as if it had grown too tight.

"Did he say aught to anyone about it?"

"None but me. But he did say it."

Half the girls from Stoneybrooke were now looking at Simeon Wright as they might look upon a serpent.

Simeon stood. " 'Tis not exactly . . . I mean to say . . ."

"He promised himself to me and then he went and pledged himself to my sister."

"Fanciful dreams from a fanciful girl." Simeon dismissed her with words as well as with his actions. He refused to even look at her.

"He told me that we would be married before the new year."

"I said nothing of the sort."

"He said everything of the sort. All those things and many more."

"I promised nothing." His appeal was made to the jury. "I cannot be held accountable for the imaginings of a foolish young girl."

Mary's face went flush. Her foot stamped at the ground. "I am not foolish, Simeon Wright. The only things I knew were the things that you told me. I hated Susannah for stealing you from me. But now I only pity her."

He had not broken any law, but he had certainly broken every woman's faith. It was not right to dangle one girl from a finger while you were intent upon winning the hand of another. Especially if it were her sister.

"Do you have anything further? To add?"

Mary shook her head and walked back to her place, head held high.

I did not know how she could do it. Her admission had cost her. And had she even once turned in my direction, I might have thanked her.

As it was, John Prescotte stood and took her place.

"I spoke to Simeon Wright back in October about buying boards enough to build a house." As he paused, his eyes came near to meeting mine. "I had asked Goodman Phillips for his daughter Susannah's hand in marriage and I meant to build the house this winter. Simeon Wright told me he would be happy to sell the boards to me . . . for . . . much more than I could afford."

The clerk looked up from his transcript. "How much more?"

"Three times more than they should have cost. It was enough that I did not have the money. Nor did my father. I decided I would wait until spring, after the threat of savages had disappeared, when I could forest the lumber myself. But before I could do it, banns were read at church for Simeon Wright and . . . Susannah."

Simeon Wright protested. "He makes it sound as if I stole the girl from him. I asked her father—"

Father pushed to his feet. "But you did not wait for an answer.

315

The banns were read, 'tis true, but not with my blessing. And not with Susannah's."

"But—"

"Order!"

The selectman waited for the three of them to cease their speaking. " 'Tis not our custom to force our daughters to marry."

It was an implied accusation. And it was one best answered by me. "Father did not force me. He asked me. He asked me whether I had any reason for him to refuse Simeon Wright. What reason could I give? The man I wanted to marry no longer wanted me. So what excuse did I have? That I did not like the way he looked at me? That he frightened me? And how is it that I would want to damage the relationship between my father, a carpenter, and the man who supplied his wood? If you, Thomas Smyth, had spoken. Or if you, John Prescotte, had said something, then perhaps . . ."

The selectman turned the full force of his glare on Simeon Wright. "You have several offenses to explain."

"I? *I* have accusations to answer? I am a man of business. Do you know how hard it is to gain timber from the wood? The trees are huge, their trunks almost too enormous to fell. There are some several miles over which the logs must be transported, over the bridge and then down the hill to the mill. There are biting flies in the spring. There are bears about in summer, and wolves that prowl in the winter. And just when all the beasts have bedded down for the winter, there is snow."

Of all the long list of his complaints, there was one thing he had forgotten. One thing that he might have placed before the others. And so, I reminded him of it. "And the savages."

"The what?"

"The savages."

For the first time, he looked at me not with confidence but with uneasiness. And it was then that I knew. "There were never any savages, were there?"

"Of course there—"

"Daniel doubted there had ever been any at all. After all his time standing watch, he never saw any signs . . . none but the savage killed in the attack and the footsteps left at Goodman Blake's." I turned my eyes toward those from my own town. "Did any of the rest of you ever see them?"

There was silence.

The selectman repeated the question. "Did any of the rest of you ever see a savage in those parts?"

From the quiet there came one small voice. "I did."

All eyes turned toward Small-hope.

"I saw savages."

It was not the response for which I had been hoping. "You . . . you did?"

"Aye. I saw them in the wood cutting trees and I saw Simeon Wright speaking to them."

"Where?"

"Well, I . . . it was in the snows. I ran across the cart bridge. I kept to the path for a while, but then I left it. . . ."

Across the aisle from me, Father stood to question her. "And which way did you leave it? To the west or the east?"

"To the west."

To the west of the cart path was where the common was located . . . and the trees in the common were for the use of all men as determined by the town constitution. They were only to be cut and paid for with the town's approval. Simeon Wright had his own lands for cutting timber. They were located in the pines, east of his mill, which was located east even of the river.

The outrage amongst the townspeople could not be contained. And then one of the jurors from Stoneybrooke addressed himself to Simeon Wright. "You stole trees from the common?"

Another stood beside the first. Both were reddened with rage. "You cut the town's trees when you had your own to do with as you wanted?"

And then a third stood. "I threw nearly all of fall's harvest into the fires this winter! I sacrificed my family's food for warmth, and all the while you were taking from the common what you pleased?"

Simeon held up his hands in protection, as if the words were blows. "This is not about me! 'Tis about Susannah Phillips and her gown. Look at her! She is a harlot! A whore! And that captain would never have come if I had not told you there were savages about. Savages!" He snorted with derision. "They were only there because I was paying them. You never would have known it. Never would have suspected it. My father would have said . . . my father would have said . . ."

" 'Ye have troubled me to make me to stink among the inhabitants of the land . . . and . . . being few in number, they shall gather themselves together against me, and slay me; and I shall be destroyed, I and my house.' " At the sound of Goody Wright's voice, the room stilled.

The selectman silenced Mistress Wright and turned his attentions to her son. "For what then did you kill the captain, Simeon Wright? For absconding with your betrothed or for working out the treachery you were about in the common?"

"Susannah is mine!"

The selectman dismissed the jury so they could make their decision. They returned scant minutes later.

"President of the jurymen? How do you find?"

"We hereby determine that the plaintiff, Simeon Wright, has willingly and wittingly done wrong to the defendant, Susannah Phillips, in commencing and prosecuting an action against her. We thereby impose upon the plaintiff a fine for this false clamor. The promise made by Susannah Phillips to marry Simeon Wright is declared not valid, since it was made by threatening compulsion. The plaintiff, Simeon Wright, is ordered to stand trial as defendant for the willful murder of Captain Daniel Holcombe. We suggest that Simeon Wright be tried also for bearing false witness against Susannah Phillips."

"This is an outrage!"

The president of the jury cleared his throat. "We also wish to question the young girl who is servant to the Wright household. If she is determined to have been disfigured by Simeon Wright, she shall obtain her freedom with the possibility of recompense—"

"This is beyond the scope of—"

"As these crimes are capital offenses, we suggest also that Simeon Wright be held here in Newham at Selectman Miller's house."

"I shall appeal to the General Court!"

At that threat, the demeanor of the president of the jurymen cracked. "And do not forget to tell them, Mister Wright, that you murdered the governor's own cousin!"

They led Simeon Wright away in manacles. His mother followed behind him, wringing her hands, muttering. So faint was her speech that I could only hear phrases. " 'Simeon and Levi . . . instruments of cruelty are in their habitations.' "

After Simeon's departure, the people of Stoneybrooke moved to gather about me. John Prescotte reached me first. And at his approach, all the others fell back.

"I am sorry. I feel as if . . . if I had only . . . when you asked . . . I would like, if you are still willing—"

I shook my head. "There is no debt here, John."

He looked at me then. There was little left of the boy I used to know. But in his eyes, I could see the beginnings of the man he would become. He nodded once. And then he turned and walked away.

Goody Baxter came up and shook my hand. " 'O Lord, thou hast pleaded the causes of my soul; thou hast redeemed my life.' "

Goody Hillbrook patted my arm. " 'And we know that all things work together for good to them that love God . . .' "

People offered felicitations and platitudes as thanks, as if I had been responsible for freeing them from Simeon Wright's oppression. I had not been the author of their freedom. But I knew who had been. Quietly, I disengaged myself from them and I stopped Small-hope and Thomas before they left Newham for home.

"Thank you, both of you, for what you did for me."

"You did not deserve such treatment, Susannah Phillips. Not from such a man."

"Thank you, Thomas . . . even if you were the only one to think it."

"I was not the only one."

"But you were the first. If you had not spoken . . ." There was no need to say what might have happened.

Small-hope would not look me in the eye. But I needed her to know something. "Small-hope?"

Finally, she raised her head. But the look she gave me was filled with guilt, and soon her eyes slid from my gaze. "I could have saved you. I could have stopped him."

"You tried to warn me, you tried to stop him, and you did save me. You did everything that you could."

"But . . . at first . . . I did not . . . I felt . . . I knew what kind of man he was from the time I first met him. And I said nothing."

"And neither did any of the others."

"But you see, I wanted—"

"You wanted to be safe."

"Aye." It came out as a sort of sob.

"I have reason to believe, Small-hope, that your name has been mispronounced. In my experience, no hope is small."

At that, finally, she looked straight at me.

At that, finally, the strain of the trial began to tell its tale through my tears. "I owe my life to you, Hope, and I will never be able to repay you."

She stepped forward with some hesitancy, but then embraced me. "You already have."

☙

We walked back from the trial, Thomas and I, in silence. And in that space, something worked its way up from inside me. Something of which I wanted to speak, but for which I had no words.

When eventually we reached home, Thomas, ever a gentleman,

stood aside to let me enter first. But he did not come in after me. He stood, in the doorframe, eyes busy. Finally, they fastened upon his axe and then he strode over to it and lifted it from its place. "There has been too much neglected in these past days."

It was then I finally knew the words to say. "Aye, Thomas. And you the first among them." I approached him slowly so that I would not startle him. I went to him, placed my hands round the handle of the axe, and took it. I set it in the corner and walked back to him. "I owe you something, Thomas."

He was already shaking his head before I had finished speaking. "You owe me nothing."

I smiled. "Perhaps not. But there is something I wish to give you." I went to the door and shut it. And then I pulled in the latch string. "But only if you want . . . only if . . . you want . . . me . . . ?" The most difficult thing I have ever done was to look into his eyes right then. But I did it.

And in his eyes, I saw me.

I saw hope.

44

AFTER MY TRIAL, THERE was another trial, of course, at which Simeon Wright was convicted of willful murder and of bearing false witness against me. They were both capital crimes. He was sentenced to die by hanging.

Having killed the governor's cousin, we all knew there could be no appeal to the governor's mercy. After the conviction, a four-day period was required by law before he could be hanged. But at some point during those four days, Simeon disappeared. He and his mother both. It was expected that he might sneak back into Stoneybrooke intent upon harming me. And so, as Daniel had done so many months ago, a double watch was instituted.

April turned into May and then into June.

It was during harvest, some weeks later, that we heard Simeon Wright was found up in Connecticut Colony with his throat slit. They said it was savages that did it, but his mother was never found.

All they that take the sword shall perish by the sword.

God is my judge.

The men tried, through that summer and into fall, to convince a millwright from Boston to take up Simeon's place, but none would have it. And the road to Newham had been enlarged and cleared. Truly, it was not so far a trip to go to buy lumber. And so finally the town put the house on Wright's hill to the torch.

I watched it burn, along with everyone else. At times, a spark would leap from the pyre, searching for something to ignite, but the men stood ready with buckets and blankets and nothing else was threatened by that place. I saw everyone I had ever loved on that ridge, silhouetted by flames, as they stood watching.

Mother and Father stood shoulder to shoulder, with the look of one body and two heads about them. Mary stood beside John Prescotte, the child's hand in her own. I doubt any had noticed yet, but Mary and John seemed to have eyes only for each other. Nathaniel stood away from the group with his friends, bounding this way and that, taunting the flames. Over at one end was Abigail, her newborn babe nestled in her arms. Hope Smyth stood at the other end, a babe ripening inside her womb. Since the trial she seemed to be in all places at once in that quiet way she had.

Aye. Everyone I had ever loved was there.

Everyone save one.

By evening, the house had been reduced to a pile of bricks and a few scattered embers. They were raked free from the ashes and then doused. The next morning, again everyone gathered at the Wrights', but this day, there was no idleness. It was a day for work. A day to sift the ashes, to recover the nails from the ruins. To retrieve from the destruction that which could be salvaged.

There were other things recovered from Daniel's death. Nathaniel found his conversion experience in all of it and became a member of the church. And Nathaniel was not the only one. I had experienced my own conversion as well.

I had been interviewed by the minister about my profession of faith. I knew exactly what it was I wanted to say. But somehow, it all got lost in the telling. And I realized, as I spoke that day in meeting, that Nathaniel had been right.

I had pondered the verse in Isaiah that he had quoted to me

as we lay in bed that morn. I had learnt it forward and backward, but never before had I put the two parts of it together. Not as I did that day.

Since thou wast precious in my sight, thou hast been honourable, and I have loved thee: therefore will I give men for thee, and people for thy life.

God *had* seen. God *had* understood. God *had* loved.

God loved me.

He had sent a man to rescue me.

He had sent a man to die for me.

A man had died *for me.*

I had never been worthy of such sacrifice, and I knew that I never would be. I was not good and could never hope to be, but still God loved me. Still He had pursued me. And so, as I stood from my bench and walked to the front of the pulpit, it was with tears streaming down my face.

"I am not good. I merit no favor, deserve no grace from God. There is nothing I can do to coax God to save me. Nothing I can do to deserve to whisper in God's ear, to feel His eye upon me. There is no work that I could accomplish that would place God in my debt or coerce Him to act on my behalf. But still, He does it. Still . . . He did it."

I had to pause then, for tears threatened to overcome my words.

"Daniel once told me that faith like mine was a gift. The irony of his words was that I had none. My poor faith was based on my own goodness. It was based on what I could do, all the things that I had done which merited God's favor. But now I know that faith is the last thing in which I should place my trust. Far better to rely on God's mercy and His grace. I can never hope to earn those. I will never deserve them. But . . . I have *no doubt* that God loves me."

The gasp of those seated before me drowned my words. But I reminded myself of what I had just been taught. "God saved me. I am certain of God's saving grace. I stand convinced of His love. And it has nothing to do with my faithfulness, for I have none. I am faithless. But He pursued me because He loved me. He wanted me."

I looked around the room, but no one would meet my eyes. And I knew why. I had spoken a blasphemy. Truly, God wanted none of us. Surely, He would toss us, all of us, into hell, without a qualm. None could be convinced of His love; it was not for us to truly know of His grace. It was only for us to hope. And pray for His goodness.

But I did not hope, not anymore, because I knew with a growing conviction. God was only good. Oh, that He should even want one such as me. But despite all reason, despite all teaching, I knew that He did. He had shown it. He had shown that He loved me by reaching down and rescuing me and exchanging the life of a good man for my own.

I covered my face with my hands and wept from that knowledge. Wept from God's vast love, which had been wasted on such as me. Though I had done nothing, would never do anything to merit it, I was grateful for it. Beyond grateful for it. I was jealous of it. I would let no one pry it from my hands. Not ever.

The minister coughed into his hand and then brushed it against his beard. "It is commendable, Susannah Phillips, that you are so certain of grace."

"I have no doubt." And oh, how it shamed me.

All eyes were fixed on me once more. And there was present in them a judgment. I knew they thought me a heretic, but I was no longer bound by their opinion. Grace had freed me.

"However, has your . . . experience . . . not changed you, somehow, on the inside?"

"Aside from recognizing the depth of God's love? Nay . . ." I fairly sobbed that word. "I am the same wretched soul I always was." Amen and amen.

"If there has been no change in your heart . . . if you can state no internal evidence of this . . . this . . . experience of God's grace . . ."

I knew then that I would never be accepted as a member of that church. As I moved down the aisle to take my seat, people pulled their skirts from me for fear of contamination. Mothers shielded their children from me for fear of contagion. From this point onward, I knew I would take Hope's place. I was the outsider now, the stranger. But there can be no stranger thing than the saving work of God's grace. Or the goodness of His mercy.

Autumn chilled as it whirled toward winter and the month of blood was soon upon us. We turned our attentions to making sausage and soap and candles. But there is no pleasure in the labor when one labors alone. Two are better than one, because they have a good reward for their labor. For if they fall, the one will lift up his fellow: but woe to him that is alone when he falleth. . . . And one alone always does eventually fall.

They were little things, those first mistakes of mine. A shirt sewn too short. A kettle of pottage spoilt for want of concentration. I saw the reproach each time in my mother's eye. But how could I explain that my ear was tuned to sounds not heard? My eye calibrated to things not seen? For the turning of autumn to winter was the season of Daniel. And my heart longed for all the things that I could no longer have.

I would turn in the silence to listen to an imagined word. Take pause at my work to share a thought. And in that space, my heart would continue its conversation with its beloved. Why do we think a conversation between souls stops when one of the people has gone? It continues on just the same, though only one remains to keep the vigil.

We suffer such ideas from the mothers of lost babes. Why cannot such grace be allowed others of us who grieve? Because the knot of matrimony was never tied? Because the two bodies were never united?

My responsibilities were soon relegated to tasks given the simple. But when they were done, none objected if I wandered the ridge alone. And so I did. I wandered. And as I walked, I pondered the coming days of darkness. Of the season to be spent in chill solitude. And I did not know, not for certain, if I could survive. It was on one morning following just such a wander that a stranger rode up to our door. I would not yet have returned from my walk but for the snow, which had begun falling in earnest.

Hearing the clatter of hooves on the path, Mary threw open the door to see who it was. Snowflakes swirled into the opening and through them came a man who filled the doorway with his frame and then stooped as he came through it.

"I, Joshua Eton, come from Boston."

Mother's hand flew to her chest. "My mother?"

" 'Tis you, then, who are Goody Phillips?"

"Aye. Have you news for me?"

" 'Tis indeed your mother. She has sunk into a decline. Your father, the minister, fears that it must signal the end. He asked me to come for help."

"But—'tis November. The snows!"

"Aye. The snows might keep one gone until spring."

Not again. I did not know if I could face the coming months without her. But then I did not know if I could face the coming months with her, either. Not in Stoneybrooke, where so many could not comprehend the astonishing bounty of the grace of God. And so, I made a decision. "I could do it. I could go."

"Nay!" Mother sprang at me, as if I might take flight at any moment, and held fast to my arm. Then she turned toward the stranger. "Nay. Susannah has not been well. If my father wants a hand for aid, then he'll want my Mary."

"But . . ." Mary's voice sounded of ten thousand injustices.

I freed myself from Mother's grip and took a step toward him. "I could go."

The stranger fixed his eyes upon me, doubt shading his eyes. "But are you well? Are you willing?"

"Am I . . . what?"

"Are you willing?"

My glance met my mother's. How many times had I heard the tale of the courtship of my father? And how many times had I longed for my grandfather's presence since our move from Boston? In offering up myself in Mother's place, I had discovered that more than being able to go, I wanted to go. Very much. "Aye. I am willing." And I formed my lips into a smile as I said the words.

"If we leave now, we can surely make Newham by nightfall. I know I have no right to ask this and 'tis likely it means keeping you away until the roads thaw in spring, but the minister . . ."

"Just let me gather my things."

The tension left his stance then, and a smile flickered across his face, throwing a shadow across the cleft in his chin.

I collected my night shift and my night cap. My other skirt and waistcoat. An extra pair of stockings and a petticoat.

Mother took them from me and tucked them into a sack. Mary added a scarf.

I wrapped my arms about my sister and gave her a swift embrace. Then, after kissing the child, I took my cloak from its peg and fastened it tight beneath my chin.

My mother stepped forward and pressed a palm to my cheek. I leaned my face into that warmth.

"I will tell your father. He will come for you in the spring."

I nodded. "And bid good-bye to Nathaniel."

"We will."

And then, because she was so close, I hugged her too.

The snowflakes that had been sifting softly to the ground since morning had gained in both size and number. When we left the house it was to enter a world slowly turning white. Joshua's horse was a large one, a dappled gray, and eager for the journey. He stamped at the ground when he saw me and turned his head in the direction of the road, straining against the reins that secured him to the fence.

Joshua clicked at him. Murmured something. Took a piece of biscuit from his pocket and gave it to the horse. Then he untied the reins and mounted. He reached down a hand for me and I was soon settled, riding pillion behind him.

We were not far down the road before we came to the place where Daniel had died.

It looked the same, from the snow that covered the ground to the trees that stood watch along the meadow, but somehow it all seemed different. A shiver crept down my spine for a moment, and then we passed by that place and kept going.

Slipping my hood down I turned back just once, like Lot's wife, to catch a glimpse of what I had left behind. But there was nothing there. Only a road disappearing into a wood that was rapidly becoming covered with snow. Soon there would be no mark of our going. No trace of our ever having been to Stoneybrooke. But I knew that it would wait. They would wait. And perhaps one day I would return.

I was rescued. Spared. I did not know why. But I did know who had done the sparing. Was I worth it? Nay. But there must have been some reason. And in spite of everything, I felt myself absurdly free. I was loved with a love much greater, much vaster, than I knew, by a love so impassioned that it had pursued me. Me! As if I was worth that effort. Nay, I was not good. I never had been. But I was loved.

As Daniel had once said, God is only good. And life was a gift. Of that I was certain. I did not know yet what to do with it, or what was wanted from me. But I would. I had hope. For I knew that there remained love enough. And that all eternity could be held for the space of a lifetime within the heart. What I once had would be mine again. Only infinitely brighter, infinitely purer, infinitely sweeter. And all would be righted at the conclusion of love's pursuit.

ACKNOWLEDGMENTS

This book was created through collaboration. I may have begun the process in solitude as I sat down to type, but I leaned heavily on those who lent their expertise and guidance to craft the book from my tattered manuscript. As always, I owe a deep debt of gratitude to those who helped shape these pages. My agent, Beth Jusino, knew the end from the beginning and still she cheered me on. My editors Dave and Sarah Long served as guides as I took the road less traveled. Maureen Lang is a true friend; I benefited from her honest opinions and spot-on advice. I've also long been sustained on this perilous path called publishing by the friendship of Ginger Garrett and the encouragement of Lissa Halls Johnson. It was she who graciously answered a question that proved critical to the development of this story. And my readers Linda Derrick, Trudy Mitchell, and ReAnn Johnson all contributed comments and insights that helped to shape consecutive drafts.

This book, as all the others which precede it, would never have found a place on anyone's bookshelf had it not been for the support of my husband, Tony Mitchell. It is only because I am encouraged and loved at home that I can journey to the far reaches and distant outposts of my imagination.

LOVE'S PURSUIT
DISCUSSION QUESTIONS

1. Have you ever been wrong in your first impression of someone? What were the consequences for you? For your family or friends?

2. Have you ever stumbled upon love in an unlikely place?

3. Small-hope felt invisible to most of the people of Stoneybrooke. Did she render herself invisible or did the townspeople render her invisible? Have you ever felt invisible?

4. Both Small-hope and Susannah felt great shame during the course of the story. Why is shame so binding?

5. Has anyone ever turned on you because of a mistake you made? Why would someone do that? Why did the people of Stoneybrooke do that to Susannah?

6. The treatment of women by Puritans was progressive for its time. In what ways do you see that demonstrated in *Love's Pursuit*? Though 350 years have passed, what similarities do you see between the characters in this novel and women today?

7. What do you find admirable about the Puritan faith? What similar ideas do people of faith have today?

8. There are different concepts of beauty illustrated in this book. Susannah is entranced by the beauty of Daniel's gown. Daniel is captivated by a sunset. Thomas believes Small-hope's hands to be beautiful. Discuss these different concepts. What kinds of things do you believe to be beautiful?

9. Isaiah 43:4 was an important Bible verse for Susannah. How do you feel about this verse? Does it make you uncomfortable? If so, why?

10. The concept of God's grace can be difficult for some people to understand and even more difficult for some people to believe in. Why do you think this is? Do you believe in God's grace? How has this made a difference in the way you live your life?

11. How has God pursued you? Patiently? Relentlessly? Passionately?

12. Would you call this book a romance or a tragedy?

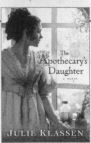

Looking for More Good Books to Read?

You can find out what is new and exciting with previews, descriptions, and reviews by signing up for Bethany House newsletters at

www.bethanynewsletters.com

We will send you updates for as many authors or categories as you desire so you get only the information you really want.

Sign up today!